MW01243293

Sandy!

Enjoy —
Elizabeth G. Jung
" Betty".
July 8, 2014

But God,
I'm Only Eighteen

John

Elizabeth Grace Jung

Also by Elizabeth G. Jung
<u>College: In Sickness and Health</u>.....*<u>Kaitlynn</u>*

WestBow
PRESS
A DIVISION OF THOMAS NELSON

Copyright © 2012 Elizabeth Grace Jung

All rights reserved. No part of this book may be used or reproduced by any means, graphic, electronic, or mechanical, including photocopying, recording, taping or by any information storage retrieval system without the written permission of the publisher except in the case of brief quotations embodied in critical articles and reviews.

WestBow Press books may be ordered through booksellers or by contacting:

WestBow Press
A Division of Thomas Nelson
1663 Liberty Drive
Bloomington, IN 47403
www.westbowpress.com
1-(866) 928-1240

Because of the dynamic nature of the Internet, any web addresses or links contained in this book may have changed since publication and may no longer be valid. The views expressed in this work are solely those of the author and do not necessarily reflect the views of the publisher, and the publisher hereby disclaims any responsibility for them.

Any people depicted in stock imagery provided by Thinkstock are models, and such images are being used for illustrative purposes only.

Certain stock imagery © Thinkstock.

ISBN: 978-1-4497-5388-7 (sc)
ISBN: 978-1-4497-6389-3 (e)

Library of Congress Control Number: 2012911159

Printed in the United States of America

WestBow Press rev. date: 08/29/2012

To all the teenagers who spent time in my home, this book is dedicated to you and to our grandchildren passing through their teen years.

Introduction

John Moore lost his father in a fatal farm accident. His grandfather came to live with the family and became John's mentor. After the death of his Grandfather, John assumes the responsibility for his family and the farm. The stress of farm chores, the death of his grandfather, the health of his mother and feeling as though he is responsible for his three younger brothers, too, makes John feel inadequate for so many concerns.

The decision John faces, is what he should do with his life after high school, and what God wants him to do with his life.

John begins to have flashbacks of his Dad's death and he doesn't want his mother to know. The story begins with a flashback of his Dad's death.

Chapter 1

"MOM! M-O-M! STEVE! WHERE'S MOM? M-O-M! Call 911! Dennis is running from the wheat field with blood all over him."

I shook my head as though it would erase that memory from my mind. Being eighteen and the oldest boy in the family, my life changed forever the day Dad died. I need to get busy because the memory of that day is so real in my mind.

Steve had almost knocked me over to look out the kitchen door, when I yelled for Mom to call 911. Steve ran to meet Dennis, and I went for the phone as Kaitlynn grabbed Mom. I didn't know what to tell the 911 operator.

Dennis came in and said, "Its Dad! He's hurt! He's bleeding. His arm is caught in the old combine."

The 911 operator heard what Dennis said, "We're on our way. Get a clean towel and see if you can stop the bleeding."

I said, "Okay" and hung up the phone.

Kaitlynn wiped Mom's ghostly white face with a wet cloth. She had fainted and fallen to the floor. My littlest brother, Paul, was whimpering as I grabbed a clean dish towel and went out the door to run to where Dad was in the field. Dennis ran past me with a stack of clean towels from the laundry. My legs felt like rubber and wouldn't run as fast as my brain was telling them to do. Dennis slowed down and handed his stack of towels to me. He was as white as a sheet, so I told him, "Dennis, wait right here for the ambulance."

I heard the siren off in a distance, but Dennis was doubled over, "Go—I'll wait!" he said.

When I reached Dad, he was already slumped over the rollers on the old combine with his arm almost severed in two. He had lost so much blood his body was limp, and he had passed out. I reached up and hit the stop button. Dad fell to the ground. I picked up his arm and wrapped a towel around it, not knowing what else I should do. I felt like I was going to faint. I tried to get Dad to answer me. The paramedics arrived with Dennis. One of them pushed me gently, "Son, move aside," he said.

I moved and he felt Dad's neck. He said to the other paramedic. "There's still a pulse."

They put a tight tourniquet around Dad's upper arm, and took another towel and put it around the stump of his arm. Dad's eyes opened, "John, tell Mom and everyone, I love them. Tell Dennis, --n-not his fault."

Dennis said, "Dad, I hear you. We love you, too. The paramedics had Dad on a stretcher and were putting him in the ambulance, when Dennis passed out. I started yelling at Dennis and saying dumb things. "Dennis, Mom's in the house passed out. Dad doesn't need us to pass out, too. Dennis, Listen to me. Wake up you aren't hurt. It's Dad."

A paramedic jumped back out of the ambulance and did a quick check of Dennis and then put something in front of his nose. Dennis coughed and sat up quickly.

He said, "Take him to your house and get him a drink. Have him take a shower to make sure there aren't any cuts on him. Did you say your mother is in the house passed out?"

I helped Dennis to his feet, "Yeah, when she saw Dennis, she passed out."

He slammed the back door to the ambulance and took off for the front door, but he looked back at us, "I'm calling for another ambulance. Go check on your mother and get the boy cleaned up an' all."

By the time we ran back to the house. The ambulance was out of the field and going down the lane. Grandpa and Grandma were there and Mom was still very pale. I sent Dennis to get a quick shower and the rest of us got ready to go to Cape Girardeau and to the hospital.

Grandpa asked, "Which hospital are they going to?"

It suddenly dawned on me that I didn't think to ask, and they were in such a hurry they didn't say. I guess when Dennis fainted, it made them forget.

I don't know why I suddenly took charge and reached for the phone and dialed 911 again. When the operator answered, I told her who I was, and I needed to know where the ambulance was taking my Dad. She said, "Hold-on."

It seemed like a long time before she came back and said, "They are taking your Dad to St. Francis Hospital Emergency Room. They are half-way there now."

I said, "Thanks," and hung up, but redialed 911. When they answered, I'm sure they wondered *what now?* But, I said, "Don't send the second ambulance. We are all leaving for the hospital. Mom and Dennis are okay."

The lady said, "Thanks. We'll cancel."

Grandpa and Grandma took Mom, Kaitlynn, and Paul with them, and I took Mom's car with Dennis and Steve. I don't even remember shutting the doors and locking up the house. I usually did that for Dad if he was working a late shift on the railroad.

It took us twenty minutes to get to Cape Girardeau. I was afraid we were going to get a ticket for speeding, but God was with us. We parked the cars and hurried to the emergency room.

With my long legs, I got to the lady working behind the desk first and asked. "Where's my Dad?"

She must not have had a good day because she frowned and said, "I don't know. Who is your Dad?"

One of the paramedics had come out of some double doors from the emergency room area, with a clip board in his hand, and said, "It's Mister Moore, Ma'am."

A Doctor walked out right after him, "Where is the family of Mr. Moore?"

By then Mom and the rest of the family had joined me. The Doctor said, "Come in here, please."

He ushered us back to where Dad was behind a bunch of curtains. Dad was whiter than Mom was when she fainted. He looked awful. The Doctor said, "Mr. Moore… Mr. Moore, your family is here."

Dad turned his head toward us and seemed to move his eyes and look at each one of us. He said, "I love all of you."

I looked at Mom and then the doctor. Then I heard Dad say, "I'll see you in heaven."

He reached for Mom's hand and said, "Take care of my children." When he said that, his head turned to the side.

The Doctor grabbed his stethoscope and listened to Dad's chest. He said, "Family, I was afraid, he wasn't going to make it until you got here. We shocked him once already."

He pushed a button and two nurses rushed in with a man and prepared to shock Dad again. A nurse said to us, "Would you mind stepping out into the hall for a moment?"

Grandpa took Mom's arm and ushered her out and the rest of us followed. We went back to the waiting room. It was just around the corner. We no sooner got seated, when the Doctor and another man who was introduced as the hospital Chaplain came to the waiting room. He sat down in front of us and said, "We were able to get your Dad's heart beating again, but when he woke up he said, 'Don't do that again. I love my family and they love me. Let me go. They will join me later.' Then his heart stopped again. We didn't shock him a third time. He lost more than half his body's blood. He shook his head negatively and said, "We couldn't replace it fast enough. I am so sorry."

Mom had tears rolling down her face, but she reached over and took the Doctor's hand, and said, "I don't know why or what God is doing, but we will know one day."

Her voice was trembling, but she swallowed and went on. "And yes, the years will roll by and we will see him again in heaven. How about you, Doctor? Did you know Jesus is in heaven preparing a place for all the people who believe in Him and love Him?"

She pulled Paul over onto her lap and buried her head in the hair on his head. I didn't know what to do or say. I felt like I should be doing something for her, but Steve and Grandma were crying, too. Grandpa was trying to comfort Mom, and Grandma had reached for Steve's hand. Dennis and I must have been in a state of shock. We were just looking at each other and the doctor and chaplain.

When I think back on that scene, it is hard for me to believe Mom had that much strength left in her to tell the doctor what she said. Less than an hour before, she had fainted on the kitchen floor. I guess God had taken over the family to comfort and encourage us.

My nine year-old brother, Paul, had tried to move Mom's grip on him and he said, "Mom, can we go in and tell him good-bye?"

The Doctor said, "Sure, come follow me."

A nurse had already pulled a sheet over Dad's face, and the Doctor pulled it back. A man was unhooking all the things Dad had attached to him. Mom leaned down and kissed Dad and said, "Honey, I love you. I'll take good care of your children." Mom had her handkerchief or tissue wiping her eyes and holding it against her mouth.

I lifted Paul up to see Dad, and he leaned down and kissed Dad. Kaitlynn, Steve, and then Dennis and I did the same. Grandpa and Grandma Ross patted his chest and said, "We'll see you soon, son."

Last week, it was a full two years since Dad's funeral, but since Grandpa's funeral three months ago, I keep having flashbacks. I relive the whole scene from seeing Dennis running to the house, to pushing the reverse button on the old combine, then the hospital scene. I know Dad loved us and I try to stay busy with all the farm work and not think about that day. I've tried to be the Dad and Grandpa that my brothers need, but I'm only eighteen. It's sometimes more than I can handle. I know God will see me through this. I think I should focus on something good every time I see Dennis running toward the house with blood all over him. I should know that the flashback is coming as soon as I picture that scene in my mind. I don't want Mom knowing that I'm having such bad disturbing thoughts. *God you are going to have to help me. I need your help.*

I miss Dad and Grandpa. I miss Dad's wisdom, and now Grandpa is gone, too. I miss his wisdom too. He was a humorous person and had a funny way of teaching me some practical truths about farming, about girls, about life, and becoming responsible for my family. Grandpa was eighty years old, but sometimes I feel like I'm twice that age. I guess when you learn responsibility and reliability at an early age, a boy just naturally becomes mature. That's what Grandpa use to tell me when I would talk about some of my friends at my high school not having any responsibility at home, except maybe to take the trash out before school in the morning. Sometimes I envied them, but Grandpa would always tell me, *you, my dear son, have more good things coming your way than most young men, because you are a reliable and responsible young man.* Then he would pat me on the back. I hope I can remember all those good thoughts about Grandpa.

After Dad died, Grandpa and I became like father and son. He would point out to me, when I would work, how good the field looked just plowed and ready to plant, how good it feels to have all the seed in the ground, and how good it looked when the little corn seedlings would start to make a field look green. He would tell me how proud it made him to see how my work was paying off. He did the same for my brothers and their projects. When harvest time came and we watched the market prices go up and down, Grandpa would say, *Son, we did our part, now we leave the rest to God. He knows our needs and will honor our work.*

Somehow, we always made enough off the crops to meet the farm and family needs and to have money left over to carry us through until seed and harvest time the next year. I used to wonder what kind of pleasure my classmates got from just hanging out somewhere with their buddies.

My sister, Kaitlynn, isn't much older than me. She's almost twenty-one and is married to Matthew Davis. They got married two days before Grandpa's funeral. It was before her freshman year at Missouri Baptist University was over. Kaitlynn and Matthew fell in love with each other soon after they met. They probably would have waited to get married, but Matthew developed cancer. He needed to move out of the dorm while taking his treatments because his immune system would be low. He needed to have someone care for him, too. They worried about each other, so the families, Matthew's family and our family, got their heads together and planned a wedding for them in three days. Matthew's Dad was in town for a visit with Matthew and he found an apartment and purchased a few pieces of furniture for them to start with. Everyone seemed to enjoy doing for Kaitlynn and Matthew as they both brought so much pleasure to others. They were able to finish the school year at the university even while Matthew was sick.

Mom, Grandpa, and all of us boys, thought Matthew was a perfect fit for our family. It's like he was another brother. We were happy Kaitlynn met him.

My friend, Marianne, came home for the summer. She went to the Missouri Baptist University with Kaitlynn, but she started going to Calvary Church in Chaffee. Calvary is where we go to church. Marianne and I dated in high school a couple of times. She was a year ahead of me in school, but we are both eighteen.

The church asked Marianne to play the piano for the summer and to be in charge of the children's music program. She enjoys children and loves music. I liked that about her. She hopes to have a children's musical done before she goes back to the university in St. Louis the end of August. We call the university Mobap for short.

I have not mentioned anything to Mom or to Marianne, but I would like to go to the same university and take some Bible classes and maybe even take some music lessons. I know the farm keeps me busy, so I will pray about that. I can go to Southeast Missouri University, which is only about 20 miles from where we live. I would be able to work the farm, so I have to think on that, too.

Dennis is one year behind me in high school and he filled in some for Grandpa, so maybe I will just take some farming or agriculture classes at the university in Cape Girardeau. I should talk to Mom about that. She has depended on my help and would miss me if I went *away* to a college out of town. Maybe I should wait a year or two and just farm.

My brothers, Steve and Paul, are the entrepreneurs in our family. Steve is almost fifteen and still wants to have a business of some kind. Right now he is raising calves with his Future Farmers Association group at school. Steve calls the club the F.F.A. Club. They taught Steve to keeps good records of all three of his Hereford Calves. Last year he raised and sold some premium beef. He likes to make money and he occasionally worked at the Café in Chaffee when the owner, our cousin Stacy, needed him. Steve gives God ten percent from his earnings, gives Mom ten percent for the family account, and puts the rest in the bank. He said, "When I get my license to drive, I will have enough money saved to buy my own car or truck."

Mom says Steve has *tenacity*. Paul is ten years old now, but he is the one that has a heart for missions. He has raised chickens and sells the eggs. He doesn't save his money, because he always seems to find someone in need or a mission project at the church and has given his money away. Mom has tried to get Paul to start a savings program now. She told him many times that God would like for him to give ten percent of his earnings and God will bless him for giving more, but *he* needs to give her ten percent, also. She puts the money away for our needs. Mom keeps a record book of all of our deposits into the account. She calls it the "family account." When we needed shoes or something else, Mom would go to her book and check to see how much we deposited.

Our needs and *wants* made us want to deposit more. When there is an emergency, we all contribute something from our deposits. Mom says she gives twelve per cent to the Lord out of her salary, and deposits ten percent into the family savings account. I'm glad she taught us to do that. All of our everyday expenses, Mom has paid—the utilities, groceries, and things like that. Dennis and I pay the taxes on the farm and buy the feed for the animals.

Steve has had to pay Veterinarian expenses for his beef cattle's medical care. He learned to save out of the sale of his cattle for the time he needed to call the Vet.

If there are any repairs around the farm, we all chip in and help with the cost and do what work on the buildings and machinery that we can do ourselves.

The soybean crop that Dennis brings in off of his ten acres has been good. He wants to expand, but we still need acreage for Steve's cattle, and the ten acres is about all he has time for right now, so I will talk to him about that later, too. He may change his mind, but then again, he may save enough to buy five more acres from our neighbor, Mr. Jenkins.

When Mom was so ill with kidney failure, she made me an emancipated young person so I could be considered the bread winner of the family. I was only seventeen, but I was able to get insurance through the Farmer's Co-op for the farm and the family. It paid for my brothers' medical bills each time one of them got sick. Now that Mom is back to work at the Burlington Northern Railroad, she has good insurance on the family.

I love my mother and my brothers. Kaitlynn is my only sister and she's my hero. It's been great to have Matthew as an *older brother,* even though he is a brother-in-law. My friend, Marianne, and Matthew think the Moore family is one of the best. Marianne tells me we are a very "special" family.

Marianne has become very special to me. I took her to the Junior-Senior Prom when I was a junior in high school. She is only five feet three inches tall, and I am six feet three inches. Sometimes when Marianne comes over for a jam session, I feel things for her. It has made me wonder what God is telling me. She plays the piano while Dennis and I play the guitars. Paul plays his trumpet, and Mom and Steve sing. When Kaitlynn and Matthew come home, they add their violins.

Steve says he doesn't have time to practice, so why learn to play an instrument? He needs to take some voice training and practice. Matthew is Steve's hero because *he* sings at the Mobap University and other places. Steve wishes he could sing just like Matthew. Maybe Matthew can give *him* voice lessons.

Chapter 2

It finally rained last night. It was still raining when I got up this morning. We have needed rain for a long time. My corn is about three feet high and the ground has been dry. I've been forced to think about an irrigation system, and I read about different kinds in my farm magazines. To put in an irrigation system would cost more money than I have saved, so I have been praying and relying on God to send us some rain.

I really should be doing something today since I can't be out in the fields. Paul asked me to help him build more laying-hen boxes for his chicken house, but Mom is working today at the Railroad Dispatcher's office, and I need to talk to her first before I purchase anything out of Paul's deposits in the family account. He doesn't have much. I wondered if maybe I should see what Paul was doing and find out if he has anything in mind for the boxes.

Being June, the boys and I aren't in school, but they can create more things to do or they want me to take them somewhere. I have to remind them of the chores that Mom put on her *Things to Do* list. I guess I should check the list to see what needs to be done.

I was like my brothers a few years ago, but Dad died, Mom got sick, and then Kaitlynn left home for college. We all had to help around the farm and house for the family to survive. When Grandpa died three months ago, I suddenly had to be in charge when Mom wasn't home. There have been times when I've felt terrified and wondered what God has planned for me.

Pastor Bishop told me to read in my Bible—Joshua the first chapter. Dennis asked me if I had read it yet. He did. Pastor Bishop told the whole family to read it together and separately because times would come when we would get discouraged and even a little terrified about the future. I guess I'm having my flashbacks because I'm discouraged. I know there is a verse that says, "I will never leave you nor forsake you." *God, I'm countin' on that.*

Most of the time, my younger brothers are cooperative, and they're reliable when it comes to doing chores. I really need to do some planning to keep them busy with some summer projects. I would hate to have them think *hangin' out* on the IGA or Country Mart parking lot with some other guys is a good thing to do.

I thought it might be fun and I did stop once, but only for five minutes. Grandpa sent me to the Farmer's Supply Store with his truck to get some fertilizer and more seed corn. Since I had Grandpa's truck and saw the guys from school just standing around their cars in the parking lot of the grocery store, I pulled up and hopped out of the truck.

This kid named Buzz… I don't know his real name. We always called him Buzz in school. Buzz Brown is the only name I know. I guess because his hair was cut almost down to his scalp. Anyway, I pulled up and got out of the truck, and Buzz yelled as I walked toward the group, "Hey, Johnnie boy, don't you have any work to do today? Come. Join my buddies here."

I walked the few steps from the truck to where the boys were leaning on two cars. One of them offered me a cigarette. It was a little mashed down one. It looked like he made it and used toilet paper to roll it in. It probably had some marijuana in it. He made me feel angry at him for his cocky attitude. He didn't know how opposed I was to smoking of any kind.

I said, "I'm sorry. I don't smoke. I never have and I never will. If God meant for me to smoke he would have given me a body that wouldn't be harmed by smoking."

I can still hear them laughing. Buzz said, "What's the matter, yer grandpappy won't let ya?"

One guy answered for me and said, "He's a religious jerk, don't you know?" They thought that was funny. Another one said, "Nah, he's just too chicken like that chicken lovin' brother of his."

In one minute's time, my greeting from them was a big turn off. I looked at each one of them and said to the whole bunch, "I thought hangin' out with you guys might be a fun thing to do today, but I was mistaken. As far as my ten year-old brother, he has my respect for learning a business, so he can earn money to give to people that have less than he does. If I ever hear any of you guys lookin' down on him for being so kind and decent at age ten, I'll have your nose in his chicken manure that he sells for three dollars a sack. As far as my Grandpappy, as you call him, you can't find a better man. I know he's a better man than a dozen men, especially those who reach manhood by just hangin' out smoking cigarettes."

As I turned to walk away, one guy grabbed my shirt with one hand and made a fist with the other. I don't know what he planned to say, but I whirled around and grabbed him by his shoulders and lifted him a foot off the ground.

I said, "Do you have something else to say?" It was one time I was glad for my six foot three inch body and all the muscle developed from hard farm work. He didn't seem any heavier than a bale of hay.

Just as I put him down, a Chaffee policeman drove into the grocery store parking lot and stopped beside us. The officer said, "What's going on here?"

I said, "Officer, a whole lot of nothing!" I turned my head toward those immature kids and said, "Those guys need to be rounded up and put to work cleaning the streets."

The officer looked at me and said, "What's your name, buddy?"

I leaned down to his window and said, "John Moore, Sir, and I'm out of here. I'm sorry that I stopped. I thought these guys had something, just hangin' out in the parking lot, but they have less sense than my ten year-old brother. You won't find me here anymore. I'm sorry if I caused you some concern"

The policeman said, "I'm Officer Blair. I'm glad to meet you, John. If you have any suggestions on how to eliminate this *hangin'* out, let me know. By the way, how old are *you*?"

"I am eighteen, sir, and you can call me John. I just graduated three weeks ago from Chaffee High." He looked up at me from inside his police car and said, "Oh."

I looked at my watch and said, "I've got to get to the Farmer's Supply for some fertilizer and seed. I don't guess that fertilizer and seed are going to come to me, so I had better go get it. Grandpa will be waiting."

I get mad at myself for even thinking about those guys. I suspect those boys won't make it to graduation. No wonder Marianne thinks our family is "special." We're different—I guess.

I had better go find Paul and see about those boxes for his laying hens. He might like to build them himself. We can sit down and draw them on paper this afternoon while it's raining.

Paul showed me a picture of some nesting boxes in one of his poultry magazines. They were made out of aluminum and, from the picture, it looked like the boxes could be made out of wood. It measured sixty inches long and had five boxes about twelve by fifteen by fifteen inches. We talked about how many Paul needed. He thought two of them would give him ten nesting boxes. I asked him how he would put them in the hen house without very much space left. Paul looked at me with a puzzled look, so I suggested, "Paul since it stopped raining, let's go out and look in the hen house."

I walked to the chicken house, which sat to the left of the barn. Paul calls the chicken house, "the hen house." Some of us call it chicken house and some of us call it the hen house. I don't know why we do that. The barn is just called "the barn." Anyway, as we walked to the hen/chicken house, Paul skipped along beside me. He was still small for a ten year-old boy, and my long legs out paced him. Dad built the hen house four years ago—about two years before he died. Paul was beside Dad, talking with every cinder block laid and every nail hammered in. Dad must have inspired Paul to have an egg ministry. To sell is to give, seems to be Paul's philosophy. Mom encouraged him to do that, also.

I had not been in the hen house for two months. Getting the fields plowed and planted without Grandpa's help took so much time. I left Paul to keep the hen house operational.

I looked down at Paul and said sternly, "Paul, this place needs a thorough cleaning. Why hasn't the straw been changed for a while?"

Paul looked at me like I had just scolded him, and he burst into tears. He does a lot of that lately. He mumbled, "Grandpa isn't here to help me."

I realized Paul had missed Grandpa as much as I did. I looked at three hours of work. Grandpa apparently had been doing most of the cleaning, while Paul just collected the eggs.

I said to him, "Okay, Paul, before we find a place for new nesting boxes, we have to clean the old ones. The floor has to be cleaned, too. Let's go get some boots and gloves on, two shovels, and the wheel barrow."

I put my arm and hand over Paul's shoulders as we walked to the barn. I asked, "Paul, why didn't you tell me you needed help?"

He said, "Because everyone has their own project. The chickens are *my* project."

He sniffed. I reminded him that in our family our motto was *one for all and all for one*. I asked him if he understood what that meant.

He looked up at me and said, "I'm not sure."

I explained, "Paul, whenever there is a problem in the family, like when Mom got sick, the whole family helped that one person. That means *all* of us helped with the chores that were jobs Mom did around the house. On the other side, it means what *one* person in our family does affects the entire family, and it should be for the whole family's good."

"Oh, so that means my work with the hens give us eggs to eat and sometimes money to pay for stuff for the family."

I wished I could have captured the look on his face when he said that. I answered, "Right on, Paul. You are right."

We got our gloves and barn boots on. Paul grabbed a long-handled, squared-off shovel that was as long as he was tall. I made a mental note to get him a shovel more his size, the next time I was in the Farm Supply Store. I took another shovel and the wheel barrow, and we walked back to the hen house. Paul opened the small door to the chicken yard and shooed all the chickens out. The setting hens wouldn't move off the nests and they let us know they weren't moving.

I shoveled chicken manure off the floor of the hen house into the wheelbarrow. Paul tried. I finally said, "Keep up the good work, Paul. I'm going to the shed for something." He gave me a look like… *"You're quitting?"*

"I'll be right back." I said.

He leaned on his shovel handle and watched me walk to the shed. Dad built the shed for Mom, so she would have a place to keep all her garden tools and flower pots. It's only about a ten by twelve foot building, but it keeps everything she needs. She even has a sink to wash her vegetables before taking them in the house. She has a place for baskets and canning jars, too. Dad thought a lot of Mom and tried to make life easy for her on the farm. Sure enough, Mom had a shovel that was lighter weight and had a shorter handle. It was just right for Paul.

I took the shovel back to Paul and said, "Here, try this shovel."

He handed me the bigger shovel and said, "Thanks, John." His eyes twinkled.

The shovel was just the right fit, and Paul really put his heart into cleaning the chicken manure from the floor. I dumped almost a half of a wheel barrow load about twenty feet farther from the hen house. I spread it out with a rake, so it would dry. The smell would be bad, if I didn't do that. It would be bad for 24 hours anyway. Paul mixes the dry manure with peat and sells it for people to use on gardens or flower beds.

As I raked, Paul got the hose and attached a bottle to the end of the hose with a sprayer. He said, "This is what Grandpa always used. It kills germs."

I said, "Hand it here. I want to read the label."

I looked at the bottle, and it was a disinfectant for hen houses and was not harmful to poultry.

I said to Paul, "Spray your boots first. Then shut it down, until we see if we can dismantle some of the laying boxes."

Like all my brothers would do, Paul asked, "What for?"

His questions can sometimes be annoying, but Dad and Grandpa always answered my questions. I wondered if they ever got annoyed with me. So, I said, "Paul, because everything in this hen house needs cleaning. We need to take down the laying boxes and take them outside."

Paul sprayed my boots and ran out to the faucet and shut it off. We checked the boxes. Sure enough, Dad's engineering mind had fixed the boxes so that they could be easily removed. I showed Paul how each section was hung by some "S" hooks on each corner. Each section had three boxes. There were three boxes in three separate units. The units were easy for me to take down, but, Paul's size was too small to remove them by himself.

There were only nine places for the hens to lay eggs. No wonder Paul thought he needed more. When Dad bought the twelve baby chickens, three of them turned out to be roosters. The flock had grown from twelve to around thirty. Dad figured that might happen.

I told Paul we needed to sell off some of the chickens to feed the poor people. He said... "Do you think?"

I started to say, "I wouldn't have said it, if I didn't think it," but that is the kind of answer that I don't want him giving me, so I said, "Your setting hens are setting on probably a dozen more baby chicks. What are you going to do with them?"

Paul looked up at me with that puzzled look again and said, "I don't know."

I started to ask him if he had ever made the connection between fried chicken, chicken strips, and barbeque chicken, but I decided I should talk to Mom first. We never killed any of our hens for meat. Mom preferred to buy them already to cook at the grocery store as she didn't like to kill them and cut them up. Maybe it is time for one of us boys to do it.

Paul always sat down to eat and didn't help with food preparation, nor did he help in the kitchen that much until Kaitlynn left home. I don't believe Paul ever thought about anything except the eggs. Maybe Mom should ask Cousin Stacy to approach Paul about buying chickens for the Café. But then... who would kill them and dress them out. I have seen it done and I guess I could. I also read about it in one of

Dad's poultry magazines. I wonder why Paul hasn't commented on any articles about killing chickens and how to clean and cut them up. Maybe he's missed those issues of the magazines or he wasn't reading well enough yet when they were printed. I knew I needed to talk with Mom later about getting rid of some of the chickens.

Within five minutes, we had two of the boxes taken down and outside. The setting hens weren't about to move and threatened to bite us if we bothered them, so we left them in the third box. I wondered why the three hens had all chosen the same unit of boxes to be in. I walked out of the hen house thinking *that had to be a God thing. God must have told them, we would be cleaning the hen house.*

Paul was really anxious to spray the other two units of boxes with the hose. I told him, "Put the hose down, turn the boxes upside down, and stomp on them with your shovel handle to get all the old straw out, *before* turning the hose on them."

He said, "Oh." I wondered if Grandpa ever taught him anything. Then I felt badly because I knew Grandpa's interest was the land and he had spent more time with Dennis and me. Steve and Paul didn't always get the same kind of attention.

Paul did as I told him and he pounded on the backs of the boxes and then flipped them back over. He said, "Geez, look at that! Now, can I turn the hose on?"

I said, "Yes, but carry them over on the concrete slab, so you won't make mud and a mess." He started to drag the sections. They were heavy, so I picked them up and put them down on the concrete for him.

I don't know why Dad made an eight by eight slab of cement in front of the hen house. It looked like a hen house patio. I suspected he had in mind adding on to the hen house some day, or maybe a shed to keep the chicken feed and other things we use just for the chickens.

We carried the two boxes to the cemented area, and Paul started spraying them down with the hose and insecticide. We left the one box inside with the setting hens in them.

I went inside and surveyed the interior to see what we should do next. Dad sure made the hen house big enough. He even made a roost out of lathe wood nailed on a platform. It was dirty… filthy dirty.

I noticed there were holes at the bottom of the back wall. I guessed they were for the water to run out when the place was washed down, but—something stuck its head in one of the holes. I gasped. It was a weasel. A blood and egg sucking weasel! I stomped my foot and it hurried back out the hole.

I stepped out to Paul and asked, "Paul, are you finding any broken eggs or chickens that look like they have been fighting?"

He said, "Yesterday, but only one. I think a rooster was fighting it."

I shook my head and walked out around the end of the hen house. Dad had made it out of cinder blocks. The hen house could stand any kind of storm and the chickens would be safe, but those weasels were a whole different story. I didn't see the weasels, but I suspected the weasels were watching me.

I walked back around the building to Paul and said, "Paul, we need to talk. You have a major problem."

Paul looked up at me with questioning eyes again and said, "We do? What do we need to talk about?"

"Protecting your hens from rats and weasels—that's what."

I know I frowned when I said it, because Paul looked at me like he had done something wrong, but he asked, "What are weasels?"

"Did your magazines ever have any articles on weasels?"

"Yeah, but…"

I said, "—but what?"

Paul paused, "I didn't know what they were talking about because I didn't have any."

I sighed, "Well you do now, and they will kill off your chickens one by one."

Paul looked around and I just shook my head. He asked, "Where are they?"

I walked back into the building with Paul behind me. I touched his shoulder and said, "Don't make a sound; watch the holes under the roost."

We stood there for what seemed a long time. Paul kept looking up at me like I had to be crazy. Then a head came in one of the holes at the floor level and Paul's eyes were big when he looked up at me. The weasel squeezed in the hole and looked around. I felt Paul leaning closer to me, so I stomped my foot and out it went.

"That, Paul, is what made your chicken look like it had been in a fight. We have to do something about it, so let's get this place hosed down and set some traps."

Paul was in a hurry then. He hosed down everything including the windows. I started to walk back out and spread more of the manure, but stopped and said loudly, "Paul, Protect your setting hens."

He looked at me and said, "Oh."

I took the hose from him and said, "Go find the dog and take him to the back of the hen house. Maybe the dog can catch those weasels."

Our dog was getting old and didn't do too much tracking of rabbits anymore, but it was a chance I had to take at the moment. Paul went toward the house yelling,

"Jack...J-a-c-k!" I wondered why we ever named the dog *Jack*.

Jack was lying in the shade of the back porch close to his food and water bowls. Paul got Jack to follow him and took him to the back of the hen house. There was movement in the weeds and Jack perked up his ears and slowly walked in the direction of the movement. I sighed and said, "Jack has good ears, but his sense of smell must be diminished."

Paul asked, "What's that mean?"

A young boy's questions again. "I mean, Jack doesn't smell as good as he did when he was younger—*diminished... means less.'*

Paul said, "He never did smell good to me. Maybe he needs a bath."

I was getting hungry and let that remark go or else I would have been laughing at Paul and he didn't need to be made to feel dumber. He gets enough teasing from Dennis and Steve, so I reminded Paul it was getting close to lunch time. I thought to myself, *if I explain again, will he ask another question?* Then I thought about how many times he had said, "Oh." It usually meant that he had learned something. So I added..."That's not what I meant about not smelling as good as he used to smell. I meant Jack's nose can't smell things like it did when he was younger."

I could have answered for him as he said, "Oh." He missed that he had said something very humorous.

Today must have been a day of learning for Paul. I really should spend more time with him and with Steve. I prayed… *"God, help me with my brothers. I'm not old enough to be their Dad. They might resent me if I try to be."*

For some reason, God always answers me quickly and He said, *"I made you to be their brother, so just set an example for them."*

We stood behind the hen house and watched Jack. He followed movement and then stood still, listened, and then moved again. I touched Paul's shoulder and motioned to go back to the front of the hen house.

Paul had sorrow in his voice when he asked. "John, what am I going to do?"

I reminded him that it was almost lunch time and "right now we are going to finish the inside of the hen house by hanging the boxes back up and hose down the area where you stomped all the debris out of the boxes—then, Paul, we are going to put fresh straw in the boxes."

"But, John, what are we going to do about the weasels?"

"Paul, it is lunch time. Let's finish and go eat. We'll look through your poultry magazines to find the best way to deal with the weasels."

He said, "Okay."

We hung the boxes, hosed out the bottom of the wheelbarrow, washed the shovels, and then went to the barn for fresh straw. I let Paul finish the job by putting the straw in the boxes and went back to the house.

Chapter 3

Mom usually cooked big meals on the weekends. She purposefully did that so her boys could just haul left-over food out of the freezer at noon time for lunch. When I went in the back door, a good smell hit me. Steve was baking cookies. I asked, "Did Mom leave any suggestions for lunch?"

Steve picked up a sheet of paper and handed me the chore list. Mom had written several things for us to do. She wrote, "#4- Steve, bake cookies…11 a.m. When done, put two pizzas in the oven."

I admitted to Steve that I was hungry and the cookies smelled good. I started to go in the downstairs bathroom to wash my hands, but Steve yelled, "JOHN, your boots!" I looked down and said, "Oh."

I went back out, pulled them off, and grabbed a mop on the way in. Paul was walking toward the house, so I yelled… "Boots, Paul, and bring me my shoes." He laughed and headed back to the barn. I wet the mop in the back-porch-sink and went back in the house, leaving my boots on the back step. Steve was using a broom and dust pan.

I said, "Thanks."

Fortunately, there were only two places on the floor that my boots messed up. I mopped the floor and went back out and rinsed the mop and hung it over Mom's outdoor clothes line to dry. Paul had come in and beat me to Grandpa's bathroom to wash up.

Mom was using Grandpa's room to sort stuff out to keep, to pass on to one of us kids, or to give away, so I still called the room Grandpa's rooms and Grandpa's bathroom. The bedroom was just off the kitchen and convenient for us to use. Steve had the pizzas in the oven, and they were beginning to make me really hungry.

Dennis set the table for lunch. I wondered what Mom and Dad had done, to give us a spirit of cooperation. That's what I thou-g-h-t... I heard someone yell. "I said, NO... now stop!"

My thoughts of cooperation vanished.

I went to the kitchen and asked, "What is going on?"

Steve said, "Dennis has already eaten two cookies and he won't leave them alone."

I informed them that the family has a bigger problem than our stomachs or cookies. Paul was pulling his chair out to sit down and he said, "Yeah, I've got easels."

Steve and Dennis looked at him, and Dennis spoke first, "I don't see any spots, and the word is measles."

I laughed and said, "Neither one of you is right... it's *weasels.*"

Steve said, "Weasels! They're chicken killers and egg eaters."

Paul looked at me with a pathetic expression and said, "—and Jack can't even find them."

Dennis started laughing and said, "That ole dog can't even find his food bowl most of the time."

Dennis's tone of voice irritated me and I knew I had to eat something. I asked, "How long has that been going on? He may be going blind, too."

Dennis informed us that it had been about a week. He said, "A few days ago, I noticed that he wasn't eating or drinking much."

Steve said, "He misses Grandpa and he's grieving."

I hadn't thought about that. "How old is Jack, anyway?"

The boys had to think for a minute. Steve answered, "Mom said he was one year old when we got Jack, and I was seven, so that makes him about eight years old."

"Times seven," I added.

Paul figured in his head and said, "That would be fifty-six years old—wow, that's older than Mom."

We all laughed, but I said, "I think it is time for Jack to go to the vet for a checkup. I'll call the vet after lunch. Bring on the pizza. I am starved."

Paul asked, "—but what about the easels?"

I sighed again, "I'm hungry, Paul. Please, go get your poultry magazines and give each of us one and we'll look through them to see what we can find."

Steve cut the pizza and said, "I'm leaving the pizza on the stove. You can each get up and get what you want."

Paul ran upstairs for his magazines and came back with an arm load. We chowed down on the hamburger pizza while searching for articles about weasels. I relaxed and quietly read some articles in the poultry magazines.

Dennis said, "Here's an article. Hey, they're cute."

I informed him right quick that what they do is *not* cute. Paul said, "Yeah, go out and look at what one did to my chicken."

I reminded Paul that he needed to watch the hen, and if he thought it would not live, we would go ahead and put it out of its misery. I should have known better than to say anything like that to Paul because Steve said, "Good, then we can have fried chicken for supper."

Paul looked at me with pain written all over his face. He said, "No, John, we don't eat chicken like mine— do we?"

Dennis and Steve started laughing. Steve couldn't help himself. He said, "You eat chicken strips, chicken nuggets, and chicken salad sandwiches. Where'd you think the meat came from?"

I had to intervene. "Don't belittle Paul. His chickens have only been a source of eggs, not meat. He's done quite well with them, don't you guys think?"

Dennis said, "Yeah, but—he still hasn't learned to save his egg money."

I reminded him that problem was between Mom and Paul. "Let's leave it there."

Paul was quiet. He finally got up and said, "I'm goin' out and check on that hen."

As he went out the door we heard him say, "I'm never eatin' chicken nuggets again."

Dennis and Steve burst out laughing. I had to smile, but said, "About that article on weasels, Dennis, let me see it. We really have to do something, and do it this afternoon.

Paul came back to the house and stood at the door of the back porch looking in at us. He yelled, "John, its dead!"

Dennis and Steve turned around in their chairs. There was Paul standing at the back door holding his dead chicken in his arms. The ragged looking chicken's head was hanging over his arm. I felt sorry for Paul and the chicken. I was still having problems adjusting to Grandpa's death and looking at Paul face and the dead chicken didn't help me, but Dennis and Steve started laughing again and one of them said, "Oh, boy! We get to have chicken for supper tonight—maybe even chicken nuggets."

Paul started crying. I wanted to cry with him.

I got up and went to Paul. I took the chicken from him and looked back at Steve and Dennis and said, "Okay, guys, you will scald, clean, and prepare this chicken, and do it *now!*"

They both got up from their chairs looking at each other like, *does he mean it*? I followed through with, "Steve, put some water on to boil. Use the large blue granite pan that Mom uses to can her vegetables. It's in the pantry on the floor under the bottom shelf. Then Dennis after the water boils, you carry it outside. You both are going to pluck the hen clean and that means the inside too."

I turned to Paul and said, "Paul, after we cook the hen, you can pick any family you want and we will give the hen to them. Do you know any kids in school that come from poor families?" He was still looking at me heartbroken, so I changed the subject.

I said, "Paul, we need to call the vet for Jack. Please collect your magazines and mark the one on the weasels. We'll get something for a trap while we are out."

I cleaned up the kitchen while Paul searched for the article that Dennis found in a magazine. Dennis went out with the hot water and I sat down at the table with Paul. I no sooner got comfortable on the chair when I remembered I hadn't called the veterinarian and said "Oh, Paul, I forgot to call the vet."

I looked on Mom's list of frequent called numbers and called Dr. Riley. His office girl said to bring Jack in at two-thirty. I said to Paul, "Don't let me forget."

We read the article on weasels. Their fur is used for ermine fur. I told Paul maybe we can catch them and sell them for the fur. Paul folded his arms on the table and laid his head down.

I said, "What is it, Paul?" He didn't answer, so I reached over and touched his arm, "Paul?" I could tell he was crying.

Dennis came back in the house at the wrong time and said, "What's wrong with the kid?"

Paul raised his head up and said, "I hate chickens. I hate weasels and I hate traps. I hate you and Steve …and I hate Jack."

Dennis looked at me and said, "I believe our boy has gotten a taste of life's negatives."

I was surprised at Dennis' discernment and I answered, "—and all in one day."

I told Dennis to sit down. He said, "I can't. Steve needs something to put feathers in."

I was doubly surprised that Dennis had lost his discernment so quickly and had said something in front of Paul to add to his misery. Paul began to wail. Steve came running in. "What's wrong?"

I told him to sit down, also. I had all the fathering and mothering I needed for one day. I was about to lose my temper. I did get loud and firm.

I said to both Steve and Dennis. "This morning Paul learned a valuable lesson. He learned what *all for one and one for all* means. No one has cared enough for the chickens and Paul to help him clean the hen house. Grandpa and Dad always did it. I asked him why he never asked for help and he said, 'because we are *too busy* with *our* projects. When I ask him what *all for one and one for all* meant, he said he wasn't sure. Do you know why? It's because we rallied around one person. It was *Mom* because she needed us, but we forgot what our youngest brother might need. Grandpa always helped him, but we failed to step in and help Paul in Grandpa's absence. God took care of Grandpa because we couldn't. We rallied around Kaitlynn and Matthew… all for one. I told Paul what the other part of the phrase meant—that what one does affects everyone else, and it should be for the *good of all*. He realized that his chickens and the eggs not only helped him earn money, but helped the whole family, and others, too. I told him, 'Right on, Buddy,' because he was right.

"This morning, he learned that when he has a problem the rest of the family should pitch in and help. He also learned that with everything good, there is work to make it that way, and work to *keep* it that way—such as keeping a clean hen house so his hens won't get sick and they would keep on laying their eggs.

"He learned there is always something in life ready and waiting to destroy things that are good. Satan is waiting all the time, even using weasels. Paul learned that Jack is getting old and might need extra care like Grandpa did. But—Paul, also, experienced ridicule for suddenly learning his chickens can also provide meat to eat. He didn't need that from his family. *All for one and one for all* is this family's unwritten code of honor and I expect you, Dennis and Steve, to honor that code. I also expect all three of you to come to me if you have a problem with anything—or any other person in the family. Not only that, but if anything should ever happen to me, one of you guys will have to step up to the plate and go to bat for the whole family's well-being. So, learn life's lessons well. I am only eighteen. A lot of guys my age are out flittin' around doing a whole lot of nothing. Or they are playing ball or riding around in cars with souped up engines, not going anywhere in particular.

"In this family, we work. We produce eggs for a lot of people, and even our wheat, corn, and soybeans benefit other people as well as us. We are responsible, reliable kids, and Mom is proud of us. Grandpa and Dad were also proud of us, and *I am* proud of us."

Steve said, "Me too."

Paul raised his head up with his tear stained dirty cheek and said, "Me too." We looked at each other with a smiling smirk and Paul began to laugh through his tears.

My tension was so great after almost preaching a sermon but Paul broke my tension. I reached over, grabbed Paul's arm, pulled him out of his chair, and gave him a big hug. Dennis got up first and wrapped his arm around my neck and Paul's. Then Steve did next. He said, "All for one and one for all."

Dennis said, "—about those feathers and other stuff?"

I said, "Get a paper grocery sack and a smaller pan. Put the feathers in the sack."

Dennis rummaged around and found an old basin and a sack. Paul said, "Can I help?" We all looked at each other surprised, but Dennis said, "Sure, Buddy." They all left the kitchen for the back yard to clean a dead chicken.

I got up from the table, put my dish on top of the other dirty dishes, and went to Grandpa's bathroom. I sat on the edge of the tub and cried like Paul did. I prayed and told God, *"I'm only eighteen."* I asked God for help and tried to get my emotions together. After all, a six foot three inch guy sitting on the edge of a tub crying isn't exactly a man. I washed up, shaved, and went upstairs for a clean shirt. I felt tired and decided to lie down for a five-minute nap.

Chapter 4

It was three o'clock, when I remembered the appointment at the vet's office for Jack. My five minute nap turned out to be a long nap. The phone was ringing and I jumped up. It was the vet's office wanting to know if we were bringing Jack in for his check-up. I apologized and told the girl that I had gone to sleep. The lady said, "Can you bring him in right now?"

It was already an hour later, and I felt bad about the delay. I told the lady, "I'll be there in five minutes."

I ran out the door and there was no sign of Jack or the boys. I yelled. Steve yelled back to me, from behind the chicken house. They were making a weasel trap out of chicken wire. I told them I was leaving with Jack. They said, "Bye" without even looking up. I took Jack, put him in the truck, and took off for the vet office without asking what they did with the chicken they had worked on.

After the vet's office, I stopped at the dispatcher's office and told Mom about the visit to the vet's office. I told her the veterinarian said the dog was okay for his age and he had some arthritis in his joints. He was getting older and needed a vitamin supplement for older dogs. I also unloaded on mom about the weasel and dead chicken. It just seemed like the day was all negative. Mom reminded me of Matthew and Kaitlynn's special scripture verse that got them through the rough days. Isaiah 41:10… *Do not fear, for I am with you; do not be dismayed, for I am your God. I will strengthen you and help you; I will uphold you with my righteous right hand.* Mom said, "Why don't you go back home and think about what I said, but first stop by the grocery store for some crackers and two loaves of bread."

I left the railroad office thinking, *I need a motto for my life.*

"Joshua 1:9."

"What!"

"Joshua 1:9"

I looked out the truck window to see who said that. No one was there. I thought I surely was going crazy, with my flashbacks and now hearing things.

When I got home, I went to the bedroom off the kitchen and got Grandpa's Bible from the dresser and looked up Joshua 1:9. *"Have I not commanded you? Be strong and courageous. Do not be terrified; do not be discouraged, for the Lord your God will be with you wherever you go."*

I shook my head in disbelief and could think of nothing to say. I closed the Bible and thought about wanting a motto for my life. All I could say was, "Thank you, God," but my mind went straight to what happened at the grocery store. I shook my head and prayed. *God, I don't know how much more I can tolerate. You're going to have to help me with whatever comes next.*

Since Mom had asked me to stop at the store on my way home from the railroad office. I pulled the truck in the parking lot of the grocery store. Officer Blair pulled in beside me. He said, "Hi, John, how are you today?"

I said, "It's been a rough day!"

Officer Blair hesitated, but said, "Rough day, huh?"

"Yes, I just had to go spill my guts to my mom at the dispatcher's office. I've been Mom and Dad to my brothers today, taken my ailing dog to the vet, and now I'm grocery shopping for my mother. I'll be glad when the sun goes down and this day is over."

Officer Blair laughed and said, "Well, son, I'm going to add to your misery. Your right tail light is out on the truck. I'll just warn you today, but you had better fix it before your day is over."

My response was less than cheerful. I hit the steering wheel with my fist. I looked back at Officer Blair, shaking my head, but I said, "I have never changed a tail light. Do you think you can take a minute to show me how to get the red cover off?"

I got out of the truck, walked to the rear, and he took the red glass cover off... actually, it was plastic. I unscrewed the bulb and looked at it. He said, "You may be able to get a bulb in the store here, but if I were you, I would walk across the street to the hardware store or go to the auto parts store. They would have that size."

"Officer Blair, Thank you."

I turned to Jack and said, "Stay, Jack."

He hung his head out the window and watched me walk across the street to the auto parts store. I bought two bulbs for the truck. I didn't want to get caught again with the left one out. I guess I should check Mom's car tail lights, too.

The boys were all in the kitchen when I got home. I found the dead chicken that the boys cleaned in the refrigerator. Dennis was telling Steve how he would design a trap. Steve was drawing and tapped his pencil on the table. He said, "Dennis and I are designing an animal trap. We're going to make lots of money off our design."

I responded with, "Ah, the businessman is at it again. What kind of trap did you build behind the hen house?"

Paul spoke up and said, "They didn't. I suggested putting chicken wire over the holes between the cinder blocks for now."

Dennis, being prone to negative responses, said, "Yeah, the boy has brains after all."

He gave Paul a playful punch on the arm, and Paul lit into him with all fours. Dennis said, "Oh, you want to fight, huh?"

Paul is still pretty small compared to the rest of us and no match for Dennis. He picked Paul up, carried him to the couch in the living room and said, "I hear you are very ticklish around the neck."

He had Paul laughing, but I wanted to just shut down and go rest again. I was tired of bossing the boys around, but I looked at the clock and said, "Okay, boys, Mom will be home in twenty minutes. It is time to get the place straighten up."

Dennis got up to leave Paul. As he did, Paul stood up on the couch and took a flying leap off the couch, on to Dennis' back and said, "Gotcha!'

Dennis backed up to the couch, went down on top of Paul, and said, "No you don't."

He wouldn't let Paul up until he yelled *uncle*. I finally yelled, "Dennis—Paul! Fifteen minutes. Go check your rooms and make your beds. Make sure the bathroom is tidied up. No towels or dirty clothes on the floor."

Dennis said, "Okay."

Paul yelled *uncle* real loud. They both raced upstairs laughing like two girls. I heard Dennis say, "Go get the towels and any dirty clothes from the hamper. I'll check the bedrooms and carry the clothes downstairs."

I went to the laundry to make sure the washer was empty and to see if anything in the dryer needed to be folded. I heard Dennis yelling at Paul and I was about to scold Dennis for being so loud. Paul came down the stairs with the towels and clothes from the hamper. He was dropping things as he came down the stairs. Dennis was coming down the steps behind him picking up the stuff Paul had dropped. Dennis loudly said, "Paul, I said, I would carry them downstairs."

I stepped into the living room, just in time to see Paul step on one of the towels that was hanging low out of his bundle of dirty clothes. He tripped and fell with his load. I grabbed for him, but missed. Dennis was picking up the things that had fallen on the stairs, and he was right behind Paul fussing about carrying... "all that stuff without a basket."

I took a dirty towel and laid it on the floor, put the dirty clothes on it, and then pulled up both ends and said, "Look, guys, this way there is a bundle and for Pete's sake, I'm tired of all of you laughing or yelling at each other."

Paul said, "Thanks John, but my arm hurts."

Dennis looked at his arm and said, "Paul, it looks like it's busted."

Steve came running in from the kitchen, looked at Paul's arm and said, "Yeah, it's busted."

I handed the dirty clothes to Steve, and he ran to the laundry with the bundle and came back. All four of us were standing there looking at each other like, *What do we do now?* when Mom walked in the back door and came to where we were standing in the living room. Our faces must have looked distressed because Mom said, "What's wrong?"

Paul's face had gotten pale like he was going to pass out. He and Dennis looked at me like I was going to tattle on them or say it was their fault, but I just said. "Paul just tripped and apparently fell on his arm wrong."

Mom looked at us with a skeptical look on her face, but said, "Paul, let me see it!"

Mom's face got white. I said, "Mom, don't faint on us."

Dennis grabbed her and helped her sit down. He ran to the kitchen for a wet dish towel and began wiping her face.

I took over again and said, "Dennis, go get me a clean pillowcase. Steve, go look in the junk drawer in the kitchen and see what you can find in the way of pins or clamps to hold the pillow case together. I'm going to make a sling for Paul's arm.

Steve came back with an old blue-tipped diaper pin. Mom said, "Go look on Grandpa's dresser, there are two pins there."

Paul sat down beside Mom, and he was as white as Mom.

Dennis came back with a pillowcase and I tried to fix up a sling for Paul's arm. Mom tried to help, but when Paul screamed in pain she got pale again and fell back on the couch. I told Dennis, "Go call Dr. Miller's office and tell them who you are and that Paul has broken his arm."

"Steve, go get that dish towel wet again with ice water and wash Mom's face."

Mom kept saying, "I'm going to be okay."

Paul was leaning on Mom when Dennis came back and said, "There was a recording on at Dr. Miller's office and it said Dr. Miller will be out of the office until Wednesday."

I said to Paul, "Buddy, this means it's you and me. Let's take a drive in the truck and get that arm fixed."

I told Steve and Dennis to make sure the stove was off and, when Mom regains her strength, bring her up to the St. Francis Hospital emergency room in Cape Girardeau.

Paul looked at me, and I could tell that mentioning the hospital scared him. He still has memories of Dad, Mom, and Grandma and Grandpa being in the hospital.

"Paul, your bone in your arm will be reset. They will put a cast on it and then you will come home— probably within two hours. Okay?"

He meekly said, "Okay."

"Well, let's go," I said.

Dennis said, "I'm sorry, Buddy."

Steve glanced at Mom and then at Paul and said, "Me too."

Paul looked at them with pain in his face, but hesitantly said, "One for all...and all for one. Take care of Mom."

I gave them a thumbs up, which they returned. I turned to the boys as we were walking out the door, "Dennis go get your license. You drive Mom's car and bring her up if she feels better."

Mom had color back in her face and she said, "I'm okay. Just give me 10 minutes to get myself together."

As I walked out the door I heard her say, "I can handle my pain, but not my children's."

I helped Paul into the truck and took off down the lane. I turned toward Cape Girardeau on highway 25, thinking about the stress Mom might be under with us boys and wondered if this might harm her transplanted kidney. I was picking up speed in the truck. I looked at my speedometer and realized I was going sixty and I was still in a forty five mile zone. I slowed down to fifty. Unfortunately, I looked in my rear view mirror and there was Officer Blair with his lights flashing.

I was glad that I had my good cry earlier in the day. I pulled over to the side of the road and said, "Paul, I am having a bad day too."

He said, "John, what's wrong? Why'd you stop? My arm hurts."

I rolled my window down and put my arms and head down on the steering wheel. Officer Blair walked up to the window and said, "John your bad day isn't over yet, is it? You were going way over the speed limit on this road."

I raised my head up and said, "Yes, Sir."

The officer paused and said, "Just, yes sir."

I could feel my face getting red and I gulped and said, "Yes, Sir."

Paul came to my rescue and said, "Yes Sir, I broke my arm and Mom about fainted. John's taking me to the hospital 'cause Dr. Miller is out of town."

Officer Blair was silent for a moment. He reached in the truck window and patted my shoulder and said, "I'm sorry, John. Let me go around and look at that arm."

Officer Blair went around the truck to the passenger side and opened the truck door. He pulled back the pillow case. Paul screamed and started to cry.

"Man you *did* break your arm."

I wanted to say, *leave him alone,* but I couldn't say anything. I think my brain had stopped functioning.

Officer Blair stepped around to the front of my truck and was talking on his shoulder phone or radio. He came back to my side and said, "John, leave your truck here. I'll drive you to Cape Girardeau."

I rolled up my window and said, "Paul, I'll come around and help you out."

Just as I opened Paul's door, Mom's car, with Dennis driving, zipped past us. He was going a bit fast too and had to back up.

Officer Blair was glaring at him and said, "What the..."

Paul said, "There's Mom and Dennis."

Dennis jumped out of the car and came back to us. "Mom keeps passing out. I had to carry her to the car."

Paul started crying again and saying, "Tell Mom, I'm okay—tell Mom, I'm okay."

Officer Blair looked at me and said, "Bad day, huh, call it a terrible day."

He walked back with Dennis to check on Mom. Steve was in the back seat with Mom, still wiping her face. I followed Officer Blair. He reached in and felt Mom's pulse and said, "Son, I am calling for an ambulance. Have Paul get back in the truck out of the sun."

I walked back to Paul and said, "Paul, let me help you back into the truck. I'll turn the air back on." Dennis did the same with Mom's car. The officer was calling for assistance as I helped Paul climb back in the truck.

He whimpered and said, "Why'd I have to trip?"

I had to get myself together, but I felt like my stomach was in knots, but I said, "Paul, Mom could have fainted at work or anywhere. I suspect her problem isn't you or your broken arm. Just pray for her as we're praying for you. And Paul, you could have fallen over anything and anywhere. Satan is just trying to shake our faith or perhaps God is trying to strengthen our trust in Him. Remember, we've been through tough times before, and God has worked things out for us. Just hang in there with all of us and we will all hang with you."

I stood there beside Paul, leaned on his open door, and thought, *that expression is outdated. It must have come from the era when people used to get hanged for their bad deeds.* I leaned on the truck door watching Officer Blair talking to Mom and Dennis. Paul was really in a lot of pain. His expression was about to make me cry. He was whimpering and holding his arm.

Then Paul said something that almost tipped my emotional scale. He said, "I miss Dad." At that moment, this six-foot-three-inch guy had emotions that were larger than me.

"I miss Dad, too," and wiped a tear with the back of my hand. Then Paul said something that almost made me want to really cry. He said, "John, I'm hangin' and I'm gonna be okay."

I said, "Paul, you are being more brave than all of us guys."

He asked, "When's that ambull-ence gonna get here?"

The ambulance took six minutes to get from the North Scott County station to highway 25. Officer Blair kept his lights still blinking on top of his car, so they found us easily. Another car pulled up in front of the ambulance. It was Pastor Bishop from Calvary Church. He had recognized our truck and Mom's car.

I said to Paul, "See? God sent his servant to start the prayer chain for us." He smiled, but I know his arm hurt and he was worried about Mom.

Pastor Bishop came to the truck and said, "I was headed to the hospital to make a visit. Dennis just told me what happened. I'll meet you at St. Francis Hospital."

I turned to Paul and said, "I'll help you out."

When I reached in to lift Paul out of the truck, Paul said, "Pastor Bishop is the one for all of us, iddn't he?"

I set Paul down, so he could walk to the ambulance but his knees buckled and his face went white. I picked him up and carried him to the ambulance. A paramedic was working on Mom.

I said to Paul, "Hang in there. Help is on the way."

Mom was awake. She looked at me and said, "I'm sorry, John. I didn't eat lunch today and was starved when I got home."

A paramedic was getting a reading on Mom's blood sugar. It was very low. The man asked, "Are you diabetic?"

She said, "No, but I just had a kidney transplant three months ago, and I'm hypoglycemic.

He asked, "Who is your doctor?"

"Drs. James and Hall are the Urologists."

The paramedic pulled another stretcher down from its latched place and had Mom sit on it. He said to Mom, "We'll notify them that you're coming in."

Paul had been sitting beside Mom so quietly, but was getting really pale again. The paramedic reached for an I.V., then looked at us and said, "Mom and brothers, this is just for precaution. He's a little pale right now and we don't want him to go into shock from the pain and worrying about his mother."

Paul was obviously trying to be calm for Mom, but he said, "I'm not going into anything but the hospital."

Dennis said, "Yeah, Buddy, and we'll meet you there."

I missed what Paul said until Dennis responded to him. I needed to get my worry reduced and stop thinking the worst for Mom and Paul. The paramedic said to the other one, "We can take off now."

He stepped out of the ambulance and secured the door. He turned to me and said, "I remember you. Several months ago, I was out to your farm and picked up your mother and Grandfather. Do you always have two patients at a time?"

I just said, "Yeah, it seems like it."

I walked back to the truck, thinking *lately life seems to be dishing out double doses of trouble.* Officer Blair's chuckle brought me out of negative thoughts when he said, "Boys, let's get these vehicles off the road."

I turned to Dennis and said, "I'll take the truck back home. Come and get me."

The ambulance took off and Dennis turned around in someone's driveway. I followed, and then Officer Blair did the same. He followed us, but turned another way before we got to the farm lane. I wondered if he thought he might catch us speeding again.

When I got out of the truck, I could hear a lot of commotion in the hen house. Steve stepped out of Mom's car and heard the loud squawking coming from the hen house. He said, "I'll bet that darn weasel is in the hen house again and I'm not plucking any more chickens today."

Dennis agreed, "Me neither!"

They both took off running to the chicken house. Jack came around the hen house with a dead weasel in his mouth. He looked at us like, "*I did my best, but I could only get one and what do I do with it now?*"

I said, "Jack, good dog... good dog!"

Dennis opened the door to the chicken house, and there was a weasel with a hen in its mouth holding it by the neck. He dropped it and headed for the open door. I've never seen Steve move so fast. He had his foot on that weasel so quickly. It squealed and Steve said, "This is for Paul and the chicken that I had to pluck."

He put all his weight on the weasel, and it died. I had a flash thought for some reason. *I wonder if city boys ever have to go through experiences like this one?* I shook my head and wondered, *now, what do I do? God, help me. Remember, I'm only eighteen.*

Steve reached down, took the weasel by the tail, and flipped it out of the hen house. The hen that the weasel had in its mouth dropped to the floor. It was dead, too. Dennis looked at Steve and they both looked at me. I looked toward the sky and said, "God will this day ever end?"

Dennis looked at me like, *what now?* But, he said, "John, we are with you. God knows we are only teenagers. You take Mom's car and go to the hospital. We'll put the water on to boil again—won't we Steve? Just don't tell Paul unless he wants to know where we are. Give us a call from the hospital."

I sighed and said, "Yeah, I will."

I took Mom's car instead of the old farm truck and headed for Cape Girardeau and St. Francis Hospital. I was careful and watched my speedometer. I didn't want Officer Blair to stop me a third time.

I arrived at the hospital about thirty-five minutes after Mom got there with Paul. Marianne was standing beside Paul in the emergency room. He was holding on to his broken arm with his good arm while the doctor was reading the x-ray of the broken bone. Mom was on a gurney in the next partially separated space. Her doctor was with her.

I was surprised to see Marianne. She said she had come to see Chelsey. Chelsey was working at the hospital. They were both Kaitlynn's friends and students at the Missouri Baptist University. Marianne and I seemed to be getting closer since she started her summer work at Calvary Church.

When Marianne said she had come to see Chelsey, I thought she was also a patient at the hospital, but Marianne explained that Chelsey is working at the hospital for the summer and heard the call from the ambulance that Mom and Paul were coming in. Marianne waited so she could greet Paul and Mom when they got to the hospital. I appreciated her for doing that.

When the doctor turned from the x-ray and saw me standing there, he said, "Haven't I seen you in the emergency room before? You bring them in two at a time, don't you?"

I smiled and said, "It seems that way. If this keeps up, I'm going to become a paramedic."

The doctor chuckled and said, "Why not a doctor?"

I paused before I responded, not really knowing what to say, so I said, "Because there would be no one to run the farm and take care of this young guy on the table."

I looked at Marianne, and she just smiled. I couldn't tell what she was thinking. Paul whimpered like his arm was really hurting, but he asked, "Where are Dennis and Steve? Why didn't they come with you?"

I should have known; the "all for one" was still on his mind. I envisioned Dennis and Steve home plucking a chicken and had to think quickly. "They will be along shortly. They're home finishing up a chore."

The doctor stepped over, looked in at Mom on the bed in the next cubicle, then turned to me and said, "From looking at the x-ray, John, this break is going to require surgery." He quietly asked me, "Do you think your Mom is going to be well enough to discuss this with me."

I peeked around the curtain at Mom, and her face was still pale. Mom saw me and raised her hand. "Carry on, John. I'll be okay in about an hour."

Paul's doctor asked me to look at the film with him and he showed me two breaks.

"If I pull this bone to realign it, I will make this bone worse, so I'll need to go in and stabilize the breaks with pins or put a rod all the way through both of them. His arm will be growing, so a rod isn't the way I want to go. We may have to put some external support on them that can be taken off later."

I wasn't sure what he was talking about, so I said, "You do what you think is best."

The doctor turned to Paul and said, "Young man, my name is Dr. Lynn. We're going to push that bed with you on it, down to the surgery room, and fix that arm. Are you okay with that?"

Paul's pain medicine had taken effect, and he had his eyes closed, but answered, "Yeah."

Marianne smiled and said, "Doctor, aren't you my mother's cousin? Mary Weber is my mother."

Dr. Lynn looked at Marianne, briefly started toward the door, but turned back and said, "Little Marianne!"

He was surprised and said, "I haven't seen you since you were twelve or thirteen years old, and then you hardly had a word for anyone. It seemed to me, at the last family reunion, you were off sitting in a hot car sulking because you wanted to go somewhere else with a friend."

Marianne looked at me like, *I wish he hadn't said that*, but she followed up with a nice testimony. She said, "Yes, I was a selfish, egotistical child, but God took me to task and changed me from the inside out. Then I met John here, and his sister, Kaitlynn, and they have helped me grow spiritually. I'm a different person now."

Dr. Lynn was about to say something, when Paul opened his eyes and said, "John, you didn't tell me what the chore was that Dennis and Steve were doing."

I said, "Paul, they are home guarding the hen house. Jack caught a weasel, and Steve caught one too, so they thought it best to stay home awhile and make sure there weren't anymore. If they can, they will come up in the truck a little later."

He closed his eyes and said, "–dumb weasels."

Paul made me smile, and I needed that. The doctor looked at me with a big grin and said, "Yeah, dumb weasels." He pushed the curtain between Mom and Paul all the way back against the wall and explained what he was going to do.

An orderly moved the bed so Paul could see Mom. Mom's color was better. Her urologist was just leaving. Dr. James said to me, as I was walking out of the room behind Marianne, "Your mother threw us a scare. Her kidney is doing very well, but I am going to recommend she work part time. In fact, I will insist on it. Getting overly tired, not eating three healthy meals a day, and the stressful dispatcher's job put her right where she is right now. Four growing sons are enough stress."

Mom interrupted him and said, "You don't know my sons. They give me peace. There are none like them. They cook, they wash, and they pamper me." Mom's doctor just said, "Mrs. Moore, please think about what I said." He tapped me on the arm with his chart, as though he was saying *make sure she listens to me,* and walked on down the hall. Dr. Lynn walked on past us. He was in a hurry. The orderly had unhooked Paul's bed and started to move it toward the door. Paul saw Mom. He raised his head up and said, "Hi, Mom, are you okay now?"

He laid his head back down and said, "—dumb weasels!"

Mom looked at me like *what is he talking* about? I couldn't help myself. I laughed at Paul even though I knew his arm hurt. I told Mom, "We caught two weasels in the hen house, rather Jack caught one and Steve caught the other one when we took the truck back home. Dennis and Steve are taking care of the situation and will be here soon."

The orderly had Paul's bed almost out of the door when Paul raised his head up again, looked at Mom, and said, "All for one." I winked at Mom and put my finger to my mouth like *shhh,* so she wouldn't say anymore. Mom said, "Paul, I'm feeling much better now. Why don't you relax now and go to sleep?"

He said, "Ok-a-y," with a big yawn. I glanced at his arm and wondered how anyone could go to sleep with that kind of broken arm. The orderly pushed the gurney on out and went in the direction Dr. Lynn had gone.

∞

A girl came in with papers to sign. It was Chelsey. Marianne said, "Hi. I wondered if I would see you again this evening."

Chelsey looked at Mom and said, "These are permission papers to do surgery on Paul's arm."

Mom said, "Oh," and reached for the papers.

Chelsey said, "They are standard permission slips so the doctor won't be sued, if he breaks the other arm instead of setting the broken one."

A nurse had come back to talk with Mom. I saw her frown. Chelsey did, too. She looked at the nurse and said, "I'm sorry. That really wasn't funny."

I felt I needed to come to her rescue, so I said, "Ma'am, Chelsey is a friend of our family. She wouldn't say that to just anyone."

Mom signed the papers, and the nurse said, "The doctor said you are free to leave now, and go to the surgery waiting room."

She got down off the table with a nurse's help and we walked out into the hall. Paul hadn't left the area yet. They were waiting for the signed surgery papers. Mom gave Paul a hug the best she could and kissed him. Paul raised his head up and said, "I love you, Mom, but I don't love those damn weasels."

Mom's eyes got big. She raised her eyebrows and looked at me like *I* had taught him to talk like that. I shook my head and said, "Satan's been working today."

The orderly said, "It's the medicine they gave him. It causes people to say things they would never say under ordinary circumstances. He won't remember, after this is all done and the medicine has worn off."

I looked at the little guy on the table and said, "See you later, Paul."

I patted his shoulder, but had a feeling that I wanted to pick him up and somehow take all his pain away. I wondered if that was how Dad might have felt when we got hurt as young kids.

The orderly took the papers and moved Paul through some double doors, and we followed the signs that said, "Surgery Waiting Room." Mom's color was looking good, and she was ready to go the surgery waiting room. Before we got there, Mom's doctor came out of another area and said, "Bonnie, you cannot leave this hospital without going to the cafeteria and getting a full meal. You know what you can and cannot eat."

She looked at the doctor and meekly said, "Okay."

I assured him that I would see to it that she had some food as I was driving and she wouldn't go home until she had eaten.

We left and called Dennis and Steve. They said they would take the truck and go get a hamburger at the Cafe. Mom talked to them and laughed about whatever they were telling her. After she hung up, she said, "I understand I have two more chickens to cook."

I smiled and said, "That's if Paul doesn't find a poor family that needs them. I suggested to him that he could give the first chicken to a poor family when he discovered his chickens could be sold for meat." I also told Mom that he'd said, he would never eat chicken nuggets again.

She laughed and said, "I'll talk to Paul."

We walked down to the hospital cafeteria. Marianne went with us. There were several nurses in the line ahead of us. Mom looked up at the wall menu and said, "They have chicken strips tonight, son. Shall we have some?"

Marianne giggled, and I said, "Mom, I love you, but I don't love those damn… I mean dumb chickens."

The nurses in the line in front of us turned and looked up at me, and Mom said, "Son, watch your mouth or I'll wash it out with soap when we get home."

We were laughing then. The lady behind the counter asked, "May I help you?"

I answered, "Chicken strips, please."

The nurses were amused and walked to a table, but looked back a couple of times. Marianne was amused, too. She told me this day would be going down in her diary as a day to remember. I thought to myself, *she means a day to forget,* but I said to her, "Humor is the only way to get through a day like today."

Paul's surgery was supposed to take an hour to two hours, so we lingered over our supper. I wanted to make sure Mom ate a good meal and had time to relax. I couldn't believe that two hours before she had come to the hospital in an ambulance. Her color was good, and she ate a good meal of meatloaf, mashed potatoes, green beans, and peach pie.

I asked mom about what the doctor said about insisting she work only part time. She frowned and said, "The doctor thinks my job is a high stress job and my home life is also."

I looked at Marianne and then Mom. I said, "Well, I can vouch for the home life stress. Today was anything but calm. Mom, did you know the hen house floor had not been cleaned since Grandpa died?"

Mom can get this funny questioning look on her face, and I knew from reading her face, that she didn't know or had not even thought about the farm work. With her illness, working, four boys, Kaitlynn's marriage to Matthew, and Matthew's cancer, it is a wonder her doctor didn't say for her to quit her job altogether instead of working part time, so I didn't wait for an answer. I told Mom and Marianne that Paul didn't want to ask for help because we were all busy with our own projects.

Mom said, "I gathered as much when you came by the dispatcher's office today."

Marianne just listened. She had something on her mind. I didn't want to ask what it was until Paul was out of surgery and the family was home safe and tucked into bed—Mom and Paul especially.

After eating, we made our way back to the surgery waiting room. Dennis and Steve had finally arrived. It wasn't long before the hospital volunteer called our names to go to the consultation room to talk with the doctor. Paul was out of surgery. It seemed like it was only yesterday we had been called together at Barnes Hospital where Mom had her kidney transplant. Now, we are waiting for Paul's surgeon down here in Cape Girardeau.

I thought about my sister, Kaitlynn, and Matthew. They were in and out of the Barnes Oncology Hospital with Matthew's cancer treatments. I wondered if he was done with the treatments. I needed to call Kaitlynn and see how they were doing. Matthew was going to take a job at the Fee Fee Baptist Church as a temporary, summer, youth and children's music director. I wondered if that job fell through. I hoped not. Matthew would be good at a job like that. Marianne enjoyed working with the children at Calvary Church.

The doctor came in and sat down with us. He explained Paul's breaks again and how he fixed them. He said, "The arm will be very sore for a while, but it probably won't hurt as much as it did before it was braced with pins."

"Dr. Marshall Lynn" was embroidered on the doctor's white jacket. I thought that was nice because I had already forgotten his name.

Dr. Lynn said Paul was very lucky. He questioned me about the fall again. I repeated that he had carried a load of clothes from upstairs to the laundry room downstairs, and the load was too big for him. He stepped on a towel or something that was hanging under his load, and it tripped him from about the second step from the bottom. Dennis was yelling at him from upstairs that he was dropping things. I went to see why Dennis was yelling and saw Paul fall, but I wasn't close enough to catch him, and he fell on his arm.

Dr. Lynn was looking at us with a doubtful expression. He looked at Marianne a couple of times as though he was waiting to see if she would back up my story. I felt uneasy being doubted, so I added, "Dr. Lynn, don't you believe it happened like that?"

He said, "Yes, but I have a hard time believing that *two* breaks in his little arm could have happened to a healthy boy from a fall such as you described."

Dennis spoke up and said, "I can vouch for what John said. Paul decided he was going to take a huge load of laundry downstairs. I was behind him about six steps picking up what he dropped."

Dr. Lynn raised his eyebrows and glanced at Marianne again. Then he said, "I would like to keep Paul overnight and run some studies on him, if you don't mind."

Mom looked at me. Steve and Dennis looked at Mom and then at me. I could see Paul staying a few more hours. After all it was only seven-twenty p.m. according to the clock on the wall. He probably would be waking up and I suspected that by nine o'clock he would be saying, "I want to go home."

I looked at the doctor and wondered what was on his mind. Mom said, "Dr. Lynn, unless you have some valid suspicions, let us hear what they are, otherwise Paul will go home with his family. We aren't in the habit of over-riding sound medical advice, so talk to us. What studies and why? What are they for?"

Mom's voice quivered, but she went on and said, "In our family we have a motto, *all for one and one for all*. If there is one family member that has a need, the rest of us will rally around that one and support him or her. The boys also know that each individual does not make decisions that will affect the family, unless it's for the benefit of all of us, or at least discussing it with the rest of us."

Dr. Lynn said, "That sounds a little like communism, Mrs. Moore, or else a strong Christian family."

Steve was fidgeting in his chair and I knew he would not be quiet for long. He spoke up and said, "Absolutely not communism, sir. We are encouraged to be individuals. I raise Hereford beef and sell some prize animals. Dennis farms ten acres of soybeans, and John farms fifty acres of winter wheat and corn. We have ten acres of pasture land for my cattle. Paul raises chickens and sells his eggs. We give ten percent to God and ten percent to Mom for our needs. We consider it the family bank."

Steve was talking nervously and the doctor was looking at him like, *Where is this all coming from?* Dr. Lynn looked at me, and I just grinned and shook my head.

I was surprised at Steve for talking as he usually lets me or Mom do all the talking, but he kept on by saying, "By giving like we do, it has taught us to be good stewards of God's blessings. The rest of our earnings are ours to do with whatever we want, but it had better not be something that will bring harm to anyone else in the family. Paul gives his money to less fortunate people and has learned to reinvest his money in chickens."

Dr. Lynn winked at Marianne and said, "It still sounds like communism to me."

I saw Marianne give him back a very stern look. Steve's face lit up with either anger or his frustration of the day had reached its peak at that moment. He looked at Mom, and Mom patted his leg and said, "Steve, I appreciate what you just said, but I don't think Dr. Lynn is being serious."

I guess Steve's speech and the tension of his day made Dennis speak up also. Mom just sat there shaking her head occasionally and glancing at me and Dr. Lynn. She couldn't believe her boys were spouting off like they were, but she liked hearing what her sons were saying, so she didn't stop Steve or Dennis.

Dennis said, "And I have learned to take my earnings to learn more about soybeans and John here does very well with his wheat and corn. You may just think this family is different, but I can tell you—we are! John and I work hard, but we are learning to play the guitar." He pointed to Steve and said, "He sings. and Paul plays the trumpet. Whatever we do, it is for our creator who has blessed us and then it is for others—our family first."

The boys had observed the doctor just like I had. He was being or acting suspicious about something, and he needed to spell it out. Mom finally said, "Doctor Lynn, all my boys are very special to me; each in their own way. If there is something more than a broken arm, we need to give Paul all the attention and support we can possibly give him. With God as my witness, I have not seen anything of or about Paul that would give me an indication that some infection or disease might be lurking. No fever; he has energy to spare; he eats well, and he sleeps well. He is a very self-motivated child and he has a tremendous giving nature. What more could a mother ask for?"

Steve giggled and said, "Good beef."

That remark broke the tension and Dennis started laughing, too, and added, "Paul wants a clean chicken house and no weasels."

The doctor finally laughed and said, "Paul mentioned a couple of times that he hated the damn measles."

Steve and Dennis hadn't heard about what Paul said before his surgery and had a surprised, puzzled look come on their faces. The doctor got serious again and said, "Never the less, I would like to run some additional tests on Paul."

I could see Mom's face show some fear, so I said, "Dr. Lynn, tests are expensive, and when they're done someone has to pay for them or insurance does, then the premiums go up. If there is just cause to run the tests, than we will agree to them, but let us think on it for a few days. If it isn't an emergency, then as soon as Paul is ready to go home, we will take him with us. This family doesn't mess around when it comes to our health."

Dennis said, "Way to go, brother!"

I think the doctor thought we were a little nuts or else he didn't know what to make of us kids. We really are a pretty solid family.

We thanked the doctor and went back to the waiting room. In about an hour, Mom was called. Paul was awake and asking for her. The doctor was standing beside Paul talking to him. He was asking Paul how he broke his arm. Mom told us later that Paul was looking at him like, *don't you know?*

Paul looked at the doctor and said, "You asked me that when I came in. I told you. John told us boys that it would be twenty minutes before Mom would be home, to go check our rooms and get the dirty towels from the bathroom. I decided to take all the dirty clothes downstairs to the laundry. I should have let Dennis or Steve do it. I tripped on something I was carrying. I didn't drop anything else though. I held on to John's long legged pants. Doctor, have you ever heard our family motto…*all for one and one for all?"* Then he reached for Mom's hand, closed his eyes, and drifted back to sleep for a few minutes.

The doctor finally smiled and said, "Paul! Paul, open your eyes. You can go home in two hours. Can I go with you? I like your family."

Paul opened his eyes, looked at Dr. Lynn, and said, "They're the best. They caught two weasels in my hen house."

The doctor left the room laughing, and Paul wanted to know what was so funny. She told him that the anesthetic made him call the weasels, 'damn measles' before he had the surgery.

Paul looked at her with horror on his face and said, "I don't talk like that."

She said, "I had to laugh, too."

Anyway, Paul went home six hours after his surgery. It was after midnight. I asked Mom after the boys had gone to bed, "Mom, what about your health? You were taken to the hospital in an ambulance last night and two hours later you were eating in the cafeteria with Marianne and me. What happened?"

Mom admitted to me that she just didn't know, other than the fact that she only drank juice and ate a piece of toast in the morning. The dispatcher's phone was busy all day long. It was one of the highest freight-moving days since June three years ago. Someone shared an apple with her at noon, so she didn't have lunch.

She said, "The stress of the day and coming home to the middle of more stress— my body just refused to go on without food and rest. Just the fifteen minute ride in the ambulance and the glucose that the paramedic gave me made me feel so much better. I really felt good after lying there in the emergency room, even though I was worried about Paul. I felt even better after eating supper. I understand what the doctor said about working less, eating regularly, and avoiding stress. I will think about my job. I'm afraid to quit or go part-time for fear it will jeopardize our insurance again."

Mom asked me to pray about her job. I told her to get on to bed and not bother even washing up. She needed rest now more than anything else. She kissed me goodnight and said, "I think you are right... I will."

I made a quick trip to the barn and chicken house to make sure the neighbors or Dennis and Steve had taken care of the chores out there, and then I headed for my bed, too. I felt good to just get my feet off the floor. I decided not to even think about what we needed to do tomorrow.

Mom got up the next morning tired, but she said she felt refreshed. When I heard her moving about in her room, I got up, started the coffee pot, and made some pancakes, sausage, and juice. Mom was not going to work without eating. She came downstairs to the kitchen, gave me a hug, and said it felt like Grandpa was here again. When she left for work, she said she was going to ask for a week off to care for Paul and rest. If they wouldn't let her, she would hand in her two-week notice and go back to work part-time at the Café. I told her that now that I was home full time, perhaps I could do more on the farm to bring in more income. She kissed me and said, "I must have done something good to have a son like you." She went out the door singing the song from the Sound of Music.

Mom really would have liked to be home all summer with us boys. I had already decided that she *needed* to be there. I think after the previous day, I wasn't cut out to be a mother or a father—at least not yet. I didn't realize how much Grandpa had stepped into Dad's shoes, and how much we gleaned from his wisdom when he lived with us.

It's days like those that reminded me that I was only eighteen... well, almost nineteen. It would be nice having Mom home. I knew she needed time off from work just to sort through all the stuff from her parents and Dad. All three of them were in heaven and had no need of all the stuff in Grandpa's room. The attic is full, and we all have a box or two stored in our closets. Kaitlynn was going to come home and get Grandma's dishes and quilts, except for the quilts Mom was saving for each of us boys. Grandma used to sit and hand-stitch quilts for hours. She made two each year for years. Grandma died a year after Dad died. I wasn't very close to her.

I know it bothered Mom to have Dad's things still hanging in her closet. I decided to ask her if there is anything Dennis or I could wear. Dennis could probably wear some of Dad's sport coats. Dad had been six feet tall, and Dennis was six feet also. I took after someone. I guess Uncle Al. He was tall.

Uncle Al was Mom's retired physician brother. She met him when she found her biological family. He was helpful to our family when Mom got sick and had to have her kidney transplant. Uncle Al was Mom's oldest brother. When Mom's biological mother died, while giving birth to twins—Aunt Barbara and my mother, Bonnie—Uncle Al thought he would take care of the babies even though he was still a little kid himself. His grandmother couldn't take care of all six children, so his Dad gave up the twins to two families that he knew from his job on the railroad. They both wanted a baby. Grandpa and

Grandma Ross had lost two baby boys a few days after their births. They adopted Mom and never had more children. Grandma was really happy that my mother had five children. Grandpa called my sister, Kaitlynn, his number-two special girl. Mom was his number-one special girl. Grandma loved her, too, but Grandma really got excited about us four boys. She used to tease us about which one could be her boys that had come back from heaven.

I decided to let the boys all sleep in. I'll do most of the morning chores, too. Everything was okay out in the barn and chicken house. I took care of the animals and brought the milk and eggs in. I looked up at the kitchen clock, and at ten a.m. the morning was half over. I decided to go check on Paul and hit my bed for a little nap. Everyone else was still sleeping after coming in at almost one in the morning.

Paul was sleeping soundly. Mom had given him some pain medicine before he went to bed the previous night. When I had gone up to bed, Paul groaned and looked at the clock to see if it was time for more medicine. I covered him up. Steve sat up in his bed because he heard something. He said, "John, go on to bed. I am watching him."

I said, "Thanks buddy, see you in the morning." I went on to bed and slept soundly for four hours, but I woke up at my normal time, and so did Mom.

On Sunday morning we all got up at the same time. Steve and I headed to the barn to do our chores. He reminded me that this was Youth Sunday, and we had missed a practice session Friday night. Dennis and I were supposed to play our guitars, and Steve was going to sing with four other kids. Marianne was going to play the piano. Paul was looking forward to playing his trumpet. I didn't think he should even *go* to church... Mom either.

Steve was talkative. He said, "John, as early as we got up, maybe we can hurry the chores and have a practice at the church at eight o'clock. Call Marianne. Do you realize *she* missed practice, too?"

I suspected since Pastor Bishop knew what happened Friday night, Marianne told him to cancel the practice. I told Steve, that I had not thought about practice until he said something. I said, "I'll call Marianne at seven."

Steve let his two prize heifers out to pasture, mucked out the stalls, and put fresh straw down. The stalls were ready for the animals to come in at sundown. He filled the outside feed trough with feed and went to the water trough. It needed cleaning out, so he attached a short hose to the trough, got a suction going, and drained it. I hated to see him doing that on Sunday morning, but I wasn't going to discourage him. Grandpa had taught Steve how to clean the tank. The tank would get slimy green when the water just sat in the sun. He hosed it out after it was a pretty empty and filled it with fresh water. Steve took good care of the heifers.

I milked both cows, and started toward the house with the milk. Dennis was just coming out to help us with the chores. It took a long time to milk both cows by myself. I let Dennis take over and put it in the refrigerator on the back porch and then go to the chicken house. I fed Dennis's cow and my cow while they were being milked, so I took them out to the pasture. I had cleaned their stalls and put fresh straw down so Dennis didn't have too much to do in the barn.

It always took Steve, Dennis, and I about an hour to do the barn chores. This morning though, we hurried the cleaning part. Dennis usually does more than he did this morning, but I wanted him to stay in the house and help with Paul if Mom needed him. All was done, so I headed for the house. As I neared the back porch, I heard a lot of racket and a voice. It was Dennis in the hen house. He was yelling at me to hurry up and get out there. Steve came out of the barn, and headed toward the chicken house, too.

Dennis was mumbling and saying, "I've scalded my last chicken. I'm going to sell Paul's chickens. These darn chickens aren't worth the work. Why did God ever create chickens?" Dennis' mouth was going a mile a minute with no thought about what he was saying.

I stepped in the chicken house door with Steve at my heels. Dennis said, "Look! Look at this!"

There were two dead hens on the floor and the chickens on the roost were very agitated.

I surveyed the situation and said, "We bury these two. They've been dead too long."

I took them outside; then told I Dennis to open the small chicken door and latch it open. I told Steve to get two scoops of mash, put in the chicken trough outside and spread it along the long trough. Then I took the hose and hosed off the floor again. The setting hens squawked each time a person got near them. There were only two eggs in the other boxes. Paul was going to be disappointed. It looked like an egg sucking snake had been in the nesting boxes. The same thing happened right after the hens finally got old enough to lay eggs. A snake had punctured the eggshells and sucked the inside out. A snake had also gotten some hens by the neck and did the same thing. I was just standing there thinking. *Satan is like that snake. After he gets ahold of people, he sucks the life out of their conscience, moral, or right thinking.*

Dennis was still muttering and shaking his head when he asked, "John, what do we do now?" Steve came back in and said, "I'm gettin' me a gun."

Dennis had calmed down some and said, "Do you think a younger dog would guard the hen house?" I hadn't thought of that and told Dennis it was a great idea.

"Let's talk with Mom and Paul about that. In the meantime, looking at my watch… it is seven forty a.m., we haven't called Marianne, and we still haven't showered or eaten breakfast."

I gave the two eggs to Dennis and said, "Take these eggs to Mom, tell her what happened, and then call Marianne."

"Steve, start digging a hole… anywhere, to bury those chickens. I'm going to look for that snake."

Steve took four big shovels of dirt up, dropped the dead chickens in the hole, and covered them up. I looked around the interior of the hen house and finally saw the snake coiled up. It was high-up on a rafter. I was mad! That snake was the kind that climbs trees or poles and robs bird nests of eggs. I yelled at Steve, "Turn the water on full blast and bring me the hose; we have a snake to kill."

Steve put the last shovel full of dirt on the dead chickens, brought the hose to me, and ran back to turn on the water. I squirted the snake until it slithered down a two-by-six truss. When it got to the bottom,

Steve held it down with the shovel until I could get it by the tail. I said, "No wonder God cursed the serpent, especially this kind. They aren't up to any good. I hate killing anything, but this time it is necessary."

Steve said, "It's like killing sin, isn't it? When we stop the reasons for doing bad things, we don't do it anymore, or something like that, right John?" We're killin' the snake, so we still have the good eggs and chickens."

I hadn't thought of it in that way, but said, "Right on, Steve."

We walked to the house in a hurry. Mom reminded us to take our boots off and go get in the shower. Dennis was just coming out of Grandpa's bathroom with a towel around him. He said, "Marianne already called and told Mom she was going to have the girl's trio sing this morning. They were ready. She said, if we have time, we can practice again during the week for next week. She said she would like for Steve to sing, though, if he can get there by eight thirty."

Being Youth Sunday, Marianne thought the girl's trio and Steve would be enough. I told Dennis, "She is the director, we'll do what she thinks is best."

I yelled at Steve as he was hurrying up stairs, "Steve, did you hear that?"

"I heard," he yelled back.

I went upstairs, got my clean clothes, and came back down to Grandpa's bathroom. I could hear the water running upstairs, so I decided to sit down and eat. Mom had scrambled eggs and bacon. It sure was making me hungry. Biscuits were done in the oven, and I was hoping Mom had fixed Grandpa's white gravy, too.

We all sat down for breakfast about five after eight. Paul was talking about Dr. Lynn not believing how he broke his arm. I knew his arm hurt. Mom gave him some pain medicine to take with his juice.

I said, "Paul, what do you think about getting a younger dog to guard the hen house?"

His eyes lit up and his expression changed. "Can we?"

Mom smiled and said, "Paul, it looks like we are going to have to do something to protect your hens. Some dogs are bred to be ratters. I think a dog like that would chase weasels, too, or it would bark enough for us to go find out why it was barking."

I watched Paul, and he was not thinking about his pain. So I added, "Let's call the vet this afternoon and see what he can tell us."

Paul frowned and said, "But, John, today is Sunday. He won't be in his office today."

I assured Paul he wouldn't mind if we called him on Sunday afternoon, or we would just look on line. One of us can check on our computer. I looked at the clock and realized I needed to get in the shower as it was time for Dennis, Steve, and me to leave.

I took the shortest shower I've ever taken. I came out of the bathroom and Mom was saying, "Did you brush your teeth" to Dennis and Steve. She has that phrase on an automatic button. She must say it to each one of us four boys four times a day—breakfast, lunch, supper, and bedtime. That's sixteen times a day. Often she reminds us twice, so it is more like twenty times a day. I said to her, even though she wasn't talking to me, "Okay, I'm headed upstairs."

Steve, Dennis, and I took Grandpa's old truck and hurried on to Church. We got there right at eight-thirty-five. Sunday School didn't start for about an hour, so I relaxed.

Mom said she wasn't going to Sunday school. She didn't want anyone bumping into Paul's arm since the surgery incisions were so new. They would come to the extended worship service a little early, so Paul and she would be seated before people started coming into the auditorium. I think I would have kept Paul home, but Mom felt he needed to have a fresh memory of something other than the hospital experience, and she knew people would make over him. I could see her wisdom in that. He was feeling bad about falling and thinking he had made Mom sick. She wanted him, also, to see that *she* was well enough to go to church. She probably didn't want to miss Steve singing either.

Chapter 5

Marianne looked especially pretty when I saw her come in the church side door. I couldn't help myself. I like her more each time I am around her. It seems as if I have always liked her. That morning, her pink dress and her dark eyes made me want to think of her as more than a friend. She seemed radiant. A sensation came over me when she smiled and said, "Hi."

I was thinking, *Man, she looks good.*

I sat there listening as the girl's trio practiced and Steve went over his song, *The Wonder of it All.* Steve chose an old song. Maybe even over fifty years old. Grandpa would sing when it was a beautiful morning and we were walking out to the barn together. The sun would be coming up over the wheat field and Grandpa would sing, "There's the wonder of sunset at evening. The wonder as sunrise I see; but the wonder of wonders that thrills my soul is the wonder that God loves me." George Beverly Shea wrote the words and the music in 1957 but it was put back in some current hymnals.

Steve really does have a nice voice. It was more mature than most boys his age. Matthew and Kaitlynn would be pleased to hear him the next time they came down to visit.

At ten after nine, Marianne came back the ten pews that separated me from the piano. She sat down sideways in the pew in front of me and said, "Hi" again. I just grinned a silly grin. She asked, "What's funny? What are you thinking about?"

I was embarrassed to answer. I looked around at who was near us and might hear me but said, "Umm, Marianne, Did you know you are very talented and you're a deep spiritual person, too? You care about people—but this morning,"

I leaned closer to her, "I am noticing something else. You're beautiful. In fact this morning you are radiantly beautiful."

I had never seen her blush. She was at a loss for words, and I seemed to be making up her uncomfortable. I asked, "Marianne, am I embarrassing you?"

She put her arm on the back of the pew and leaned her head down on her arm. I said, "Marianne, have I upset you?" She didn't lift her head.

Dennis came in the side door and headed for us. He said, "There you guys are!"

From his direction he could see Marianne dabbing her eyes, and he looked at me and said, "What's wrong? What did you say to her?"

Marianne stood up and still didn't face me. I thought she was going to walk out, but instead, she turned around and faced me. She shyly said, "Thank you, John. I needed your compliment this morning. I had better get myself together and get over to the children's department."

I didn't know what to do… or say, so I just said, "Okay, I will talk to you later."

Marianne walked out the right door of the auditorium. I wanted to walk with her. I really wanted to take her in my arms and soothe all life's hurts away. I wanted to protect her. It finally dawned on me that I had gradually fallen in love with Marianne. She always seemed to be there when my family needed her—whenever I needed her, too. I had to pray and say, *Father, God, Thank you for Marianne. If anything is to become of our relationship, let it be with your direction and your blessing.*

It was nine-thirty a.m. and people were beginning to come in for Sunday school. I got *my* head together and decided to head for the youth department. Several elderly ladies were coming in the big doors at the front of the church. They seemed to be so frail, so much like Grandma had been before she died. I grabbed the door and held it. Each lady gave me a smile. One said, "John, if I was only…" she paused, "…sixty years younger, I would set my cap for you and never quit."

The other ladies giggled like teenage girls. I smiled and thought… *set my cap, I wonder what that means. Mom will have to explain that line.*

The last lady in the door said, "Thank you, John." I went on to the youth department wondering how they knew my name. I sure didn't know theirs. Maybe I need to pay more attention to other people besides my family and my work at home.

I walked past the children's department where Marianne was working. The children were gathering for an opening assembly. Marianne was talking to a couple of children. She had a smile on her face, and I thought, *she's good with children, too.*

Where did that thought come from? *Lord, are you speaking to me?*

Just two rooms down the hall of the church education building was the youth department. I could have followed the noise and known where the youth were meeting. I could hear Dennis and Steve talking to their friends—or so I thought. There sat Kaitlynn and Matthew. I stopped in the doorway. Kaitlynn saw me and jumped up. Matthew followed. Both of them gave me a big bear hug. "What are you two doing here?" I asked.

Matthew said, "We got up this morning, looked at each other across the table, and Kaitlynn said, 'Let's get dressed and drive down to Chaffee,' so, I said, 'Let's go.' Forty minutes later we were headed down highway fifty-five and going south."

I asked, "Does Mom know you are here?"

Kaitlynn chuckled, "She doesn't know yet. We wanted to surprise her, too."

I frowned and looked at Dennis and asked, "Did you tell them about Mom?"

He glared at me like I had said something I shouldn't have said, but he answered and said, "No, I only told them about Paul."

I looked at my watch. We had five minutes until starting time. Kaitlynn and Matthew both had a serious frown. Kaitlynn asked, "John, what is it?"

I told them, "Let's sit back down. Mom's okay now. She scared us Friday night. She fainted when she came home. Her blood sugar was so low when she got home she fainted when she saw Paul's broken arm. Her doctor recommended that she quit that high-stress job or eat properly. She was okay after we took her to the hospital cafeteria and she ate a full meal.

I paused, as I was thinking back over that whole evening, but went on talking, "I would like for her to quit and not work for a full year. She needs to relax and work at home disposing of Dad's and her parents' things. We've had so much stress on the farm lately, she doesn't need her work stress added to it."

Kaitlynn said, "I agree. I'll talk to her."

I asked Matthew if he knew it was youth emphasis Sunday and that Steve was going to sing. I didn't even wait for an answer. I just went right on and said, "Matthew, would you convince Steve that a voice is an instrument and it needs training and practice, also? Maybe you can give him some lessons."

Matthew looked at Steve and said, "Buddy, I'm proud of you. I look forward to hearing you sing today."

I realized I had my big mouth open when it shouldn't have been. I decided to say no more to Matthew or Steve about that. Steve and Matthew could develop their own relationship on their own terms.

Our youth minister walked in and greeted us. He saw Kaitlynn and Matthew and shook their hands. He welcomed them back home to Chaffee. I was sure after our opening assembly they would want to go to the young married couple's class. David, our youth minister, went to the front of the long room and greeted the youth. He looked over the group and reminded them that there were still a few opening spots for youth camp. He reminded us that there were three fund raising activities coming up. A bake sale would be in front of the café in downtown Chaffee the following Saturday, and the youth needed to talk to their parents and friends to go *by and buy.* He laughed and said, "I mean go b-y and b-u-y. At the same time, some of you will be on the parking lot here at the church washing cars. Also, the greeting cards have come in. Please sell as many as you can, but not here at the church." He paused and said, "Remember the only money exchanged in the church building is money gifts to the Lord. Get church members' names and phone numbers' and call them off the church campus." He looked around at the youth group and said, "Agreed!"

I felt bad that my brothers weren't going to youth camp. I sat there thinking about my brothers, Steve and Dennis, and their farm work. I decided to talk to them that afternoon. We could work out some kind of help in their place. I suspected they didn't even consider allowing themselves to go. I was never able to go because Grandpa and Mom needed me, but I thought Steve and Dennis probably could. I decided I would talk to the youth minister and Mom.

We sang a chorus, had a prayer, and then we all went to our Bible study classrooms. When I walked out of the youth assembly room, Marianne was standing in the hall waiting for me. She saw Kaitlynn and Matthew behind me. Her face lit up. She hugged them both, and then I was ignored. Kaitlynn took them to her college-and-careers class. I wondered if she realized what she had just done. I was a little offended but asked God to keep my thoughts and heart pure.

I wondered what was going on with Marianne. Maybe after church she would allow me a few moments to talk with her.

A teacher had come to our class before our regular teacher started and said, "This morning, we are exchanging students. I'm bringing five high school juniors in here."

Dennis was one of them. Then the teacher said, "I'm asking all seniors who graduated this year to come with me."

He read off the names. There were four of us. As we walked to our new classroom, the man said, "This is promotion day of sorts. Since it is youth Sunday, we will be recognizing all the graduating seniors in the church service this morning."

He took us to a classroom upstairs over the youth department room. My six-foot-three inch frame towered over the other graduates. They were girls.

I stood back and let the others go into the room first. Kaitlynn, Matthew, and Marianne were sitting together, so I sat down with the girls. I smiled at Kaitlynn. Marianne still had a serious face. She didn't act like our walking in the room was any big deal. Her face looked like her mind was a mile away from the Sunday school classroom. What was wrong with her?

The teacher welcomed us and went on with the Bible study reading from Jeremiah 35:1-19. The lesson was on leading a godly lifestyle for ourselves that would carry on into establishing our homes. That was one thing I really appreciate about my parents, but I couldn't keep my mind on the teacher's message. He asked several questions which led to discussion. I just sat there thinking about Paul and cleaning out the chicken house, the weasels and snake we had killed, and Paul getting his arm broken. I thought about how Sunday, which should be a day of rest, had started by burying two dead chickens, killing a snake, remembering a group music practice that we had forgotten, the previous night, and then upsetting Marianne. I wondered if God meant for Sunday to be a mental and emotional rest, too, or just a physical rest. I think God does mean to get rest from all the weekly duties and other stuff that goes on during the week, however, I seemed to accumulate a lot of concerns. I tried to meditate on a specific Bible verse, while I am milking the cows, and it helps. I kept a box of verses on a shelf in the barn. That Sunday I needed a Bible verse to bolster my ego. I didn't know why Marianne had my confidence level very low and my worry level high. That morning I missed reading the Scripture because we were in a hurry.

The buzzer in the classroom rang a five-minute warning bell. I had to say, *Lord, fill me with your Spirit. I need to feel your presence. Remember, I'm only eighteen and sometimes I feel very inadequate for so much responsibility, but I know you know about that. Help me to be as you want me to be. I need your strength.* The second buzzer rang, and the teacher led in a closing prayer. I was a bit slow in getting up. Matthew put his hand on my shoulder and said, "Time to go, buddy."

I said, "Yeah, man" and got up. I walked out behind Matthew, Kaitlynn, and Marianne. Matthew stepped back with me, leaving Marianne and Kaitlynn together. I thought to myself, *maybe that's what Marianne needs... some girl talk.* That's what I have always heard; girls like to share with one another. Guys have a hard time sharing problems. Matthew was talking to me, and I wasn't listening. I guess he could tell it, because as we started down the stairway, he said, "John." Then I realized he was saying it a second time.

"John, my brother, is there something I can help you with?"

I said, "Nah, my days lately have had twenty six hours in them. I'm fine."

Matthew started singing, "God will make a way..."

I laughed and said, "And he will. He always does."

Kaitlynn overheard Matthew. She turned around, and said, "John, do you need for us to come back home for a few weeks and help?"

I first started to say yes, but realized she has a home of her own now and must work to pay her bills, so I said, "That would be nice, Kaitlynn, but your home is your first priority now and Matthew, too."

Matthew said, "My treatments were done last week and I am feeling great right now. My dad has been carrying the financial load for us. My sister, Julie, is getting married in three months to the young doctor she met when I was in the hospital. He was there at our wedding, too, if you remember. Julie won't need Dad's support. My summer job is tough, not feeling well from time to time, but the Fee Fee Baptist Church has been patient with me. I only missed last week's practice, and Kaitlynn filled in for me. She's really been a helpmeet to me in many ways."

I admitted to them that it would be nice having Kaitlynn back home for a week, but she really needed to talk with Mom first. Then I asked, "Doesn't Kaitlynn have a job to think about also?"

Matthew didn't get to respond to my question as we had stepped down the last step and went through the door to the short hallway to the sanctuary. Kaitlynn stepped back and waited for Matthew to take the few more steps to join him. When she did, that put Marianne and me together.

I said to Matthew and Kaitlynn, "Mom should be in the auditorium with Paul. I'll join you in a minute."

I looked down at Marianne, and I just couldn't read her expression. She slipped her hand into mine and said, "I really need to talk with you after church. Can you wait for me? Will your mother mind?"

I put my hand to her waist in the back and patted her back. She looked up at me with a look of a frightened kitten. It worried me. We stepped into the sanctuary and she said, "I'll see you later." She left me, walked across the auditorium, and sat down with Steve and the girls' trio.

I walked back to where Mom and Paul were sitting. Mom and Paul were already explaining Paul's surgery to several people standing in the aisle. They had heard on the prayer chain about Mom collapsing and wanted to know how they both were doing. Mom saw Kaitlynn and Matthew approaching them. She couldn't believe they were in the church. The people in the aisle turned to see who had caught Mom's attention, and the frowns turned to smiles. I'm glad Kaitlynn and

Matthew had made such a good impression on our church family. That was important to me.

As I stood behind Matthew, waiting to sit down, I glanced over the auditorium. Dennis was coming from the back of the auditorium and pointed to someone. It was Officer Blair... not in uniform. He was looking at me with a look of disdain. It made me wonder what I had done now.

Dennis came up and said, "It's crowded over here. Let's go sit about two pews behind Marianne. I think she needs our protection."

I wondered why Dennis said Marianne needed our protection but I told Matthew we were going over to the other side and sit. He said, "Ok, See you later."

When we sat down, it was close to the time for the service to begin. Dennis said in a half-whisper, "The scuttlebutt talk in the youth class was that Officer Blair likes Marianne and is calling her every day. Her parents really don't care. They think it is you calling."

I remembered Marianne's brother is in that department. Marianne must have told him, and he wasn't too careful about who or what he told, unless he was asking for prayer for her.

I said to Dennis, "I'm younger than Marianne but he's *much* older."

Dennis had a disgusted look on his face and added, "They say he's thirty-two and divorced. Marianne talked to him on the phone, but that's all. She's afraid of him. That's what the girls in the trio told Steve. You had better keep your eye on him. He's already stopped you twice."

The organ started playing. I looked at Marianne sitting up at the piano and thought about what Dennis had said. I decided that since I am tall and have good muscles, but am not looking for a fight, I should pray for Officer Blair's salvation. God was still in our presence. I was still upset, though. I couldn't decide if my feelings were anger or just plain jealousy.

The service began, and after a couple of hymns were sung, the pastor asked the youth director to come up and recognize all the high school graduates and those promoted into the youth department. I went up to the front of the church auditorium with the other high school graduates. We received a new study Bible with our names engraved on it. I could see Officer Blair, but he wasn't looking at me. He was watching Marianne over at the piano. After the graduate's recognition, Steve got up and sang his solo. He was very poised, and sang the song like he had done it many times. Marianne's piano accompaniment made him sound almost professional. I was so proud of Steve. The audience clapped while Steve made his way back to sit with Dennis and me. Several said, "Praise the Lord."

The Pastor read some scripture, prayed, and then the girl's trio sang their song. Marianne had really done a good job working with the music in the church. After another hymn and the offering, Marianne came from the piano looking for a place to sit except on the front pew. She was looking my way. As she got closer to us, I stepped out in the aisle and let her sit between Dennis and me. I put my arm on the back of the seat and patted her and said, "Great job."

She whispered, "Thank you."

I wanted so much to look back to see if Officer Blair was watching us, but I didn't.

The pastor had a good sermon on the same theme as our Sunday Bible study class had the hour before the church service. It was on the lifestyle of the Christian. He really stressed the fact that Christians set examples for the world to see, and because it was the Youth Sunday emphasis, he told us we should pursue righteousness, faith, love, and peace as it says in 2Timothy 2:22. I told myself to remember the verse and it would be easy to find because of the 2 and the 2:22. I looked it up in my Bible as the pastor was speaking and it says, "Flee the evil desires of youth, and pursue righteousness, faith, love and peace, along with those who call on the Lord out of a pure heart. I read the next few verses, and started thinking about Officer Blair. I thought, I shouldn't quarrel with him, but do as the scripture says, "instead be kind, able to teach, not resentful, so that the knowledge of God will grant them repentance leading to a knowledge of the truth and that they will come to their senses and escape from the trap of the devil who has taken them captive to do his will." I was amazed at how God always comes through with some of his word, whenever we need the appropriate verses.

I really hoped Officer Blair was listening to the sermon and realizing that the youth in this church were some of the best youth Chaffee ever had. I wrote a note to Dennis and said pass it on to Steve. The note said, "Pray for Officer Blair." Marianne saw it and she looked like she was going to cry. She adjusted herself in the seat and opened her Bible. I wished I knew what was troubling her. Officer Blair couldn't be that bad. He was patient and kind to me whenever he stopped me.

We heard someone's cell phone ring; Mom would have scolded us for not turning our phones off before we entered the church building. I was sitting slightly sideways with my arm on the back of the pew. I turned and looked to see who was getting up and leaving the auditorium. It was Officer Blair. He was leaving the church quickly. I chuckled to myself because I knew God does answer prayer and intervene when we pray. I was amused and hoped that he wouldn't be outside waiting. I know Satan is persistent, so I should continue to pray for him.

A police officer is sworn to uphold the law, but there is no guarantee that his personal life is a God-fearing, law-abiding one.

After the morning service, several people told Steve and the girls in the trio that they sang beautifully. Some of them told Steve that God gave him a gift and he should sing more often. Steve was feeling good about himself and I was proud of him. I told him, "Buddy, you done good!" He just smiled and said, "Thanks."

Marianne whispered to me, "Can we talk now?"

I said, "Yes."

I told Dennis to take the truck and drive it home with Steve, but Marianne said, "No, I want all of you to follow me home."

I was puzzled, but said, "Okay, but why?"

"I'll tell you when we get outside. Dennis and Steve, you come too."

When we got to the parking lot, Officer Blair was standing by his personal car. It was parked two vehicles from Marianne's car, and we couldn't avoid walking past him. Marianne reached for my hand. Dennis and Steve were behind us. I wasn't aware of what was taking place, only what Dennis had told me, so I was very apprehensive. Marianne's hand was trembling a little.

Officer Blair approached us, and looked at Marianne. He said, "I was hoping to take you out for Sunday Dinner, Marianne. As much as we talked this week, I know you wanted to have a special dinner with *me*."

I could feel Marianne's tension. Her hand was beginning to sweat. She said very meekly, "I'm sorry, not today."

It didn't seem to bother him that Marianne was holding my hand. I thought *he sure has nerve*. Dennis spoke up, and very emphatically said, "She's invited to our house for Sunday Dinner!"

Then Steve followed up with, "Won't you join us? There is always room for one more, right, John?"

If there had been a way to tell Dennis and Steve to keep quiet, I would have, but I just said, "Steve, go check with Mom."

Steve took off running to catch Mom's car. He came back and said, "Mom said, sure."

I didn't know Pastor Bishop had approached us from behind me. He said, "Officer Blair, these young people need to be on their way home. Come to dinner at my house. My wife already agreed this morning to have any visitors come home for dinner today. We're happy to have you in our service today."

Officer Blair looked sheepish and said, "No, I just remembered, I was to be somewhere else. Thank you for the invitations."

He turned and walked toward his car, and I thought to myself. *That was a bold-faced lie, and Satan said it so sweetly.*

Pastor Bishop turned to me and said, "John, see that Marianne gets home safely, and stay away from that man. I've put in a call to his superior officer, and if I have my way, he won't be in this town long."

I looked at Marianne, and her face was flushed. I asked, "Are you okay?"

She let a tear fall and said, "Yes, but follow me home."

I still didn't know the full story of Blair, and decided I would drive her home. Dennis and Steve could follow. Pastor Bishop thought that was a good idea.

We left the church, and Marianne told me that Officer Blair had been calling her, saying he was *John* and her mother or father would hand the phone to her. It would be Officer Blair and not me. He would make all kinds of innuendoes to her and even threatened rape if she didn't at least go out with him once. She said her parents didn't believe that it wasn't me. They thought Officer Blair would be too busy to call so many times a day.

Marianne said, "Officer Blair called the church once when I was working. I wrote a note to the pastor and asked him to listen in on the other phone."

I asked her what the pastor thought. She said, "He was appalled at the things Blair said."

No wonder the pastor looked for him after the service and extended the invitation to the evil man. I understood why Marianne was frightened. I told her I would give her a code word or name, she was only to answer if I said it. The word was Lacey. She knew Dr. Lacey was the name of the president of her university.

Marianne was still trembling a little and with a scared voice said, "What am I going to do?"

I said, "For starters, Pastor Bishop needs to make a few more calls to more people than just Officer Blair's superior. He has been in that position too long *not to* know the full character of Blair. If the calls to your house continue, or if he is stalking you, get in touch with me. We'll get you out of town. Isn't Bethany, Kaitlynn's roommate, also home for the summer? Her mother would probably let you come to their place, at least until we can get a background check on Officer Blair." I thought to myself. *When I get home, I'm going to the computer and see what I can find on the internet.*

We drove the half-mile or so to Marianne's house. We were watching for Officer Blair and dared not miss any stop signs or go over the speed limit. I was glad that I had changed both light bulbs on the truck tail lights.

When we got to her home, her parents' car was not there. There was an old car sitting on the opposite side of the street. It was a vacant area where there were no houses beyond the old car. Marianne said she didn't know whose car it was. It hadn't been there when she left home this morning. Since her parents' car was not there, that meant perhaps no one was at home.

Dennis parked the truck behind Marianne's car in the driveway. I walked back to the truck and told the boys to keep an eye on the old car and any suspicious characters who might come and get it. I was going in the house with Marianne to make sure everything was okay.

I walked in front of Marianne into the house. It was quiet. She yelled for her parents, sister, and brother, but there was no answer. She said, "This is strange. They would never go anywhere without leaving me a note. Let me check upstairs."

I followed her upstairs. She opened her brother's bedroom door first, and there Robert sat tied to a chair with a gag in his mouth. Marianne screamed. I untied Robert, and Marianne pulled the gag from his mouth. He croaked, "Find Janet!" Marianne ran down the hall to her sister's room. Janet was lying face down tied to the bed. I broke the bed trying to get the ropes off. She had a gag in her mouth, but was all bloody. She had been raped. I wrapped her in a blanket, held her, and told Marianne to get her a drink. Janet was only fourteen and didn't need for this to happen. Robert leaned on the door frame and was crying like a baby, saying, "I'm sorry, Janet. I'm sorry."

Robert was sixteen and was obviously beaten. I asked, "Where are your parents?"

Marianne tried to hug him, but he hurt too badly.

He said, "I don't know. They got a phone call saying Marianne had been in an accident. The call came from the police department, so they took off." He swallowed a couple of times and said, "Something happened to them because it's been three hours since they left."

Robert hugged his ribs and acted like he was having trouble breathing, and Janet was crying. Marianne hands were shaking when I asked her if she had a cell phone, and she handed it to me. She said, "It has a strange noise in it."

Janet pointed to her phone, plugged into the charger. I laid Janet back on her bed, and Marianne sat down beside her. I picked up Janet's phone and took it apart. There was nothing in hers. I called Pastor Bishop's home and explained the situation. I asked him not to call the Chaffee police, but someone else.

Elizabeth Grace Jung

He said, "You kids sit tight. I'm going to call Scott City and see what they can tell me. I'll ask for an ambulance or have Scott City call for one and it'll to be a quiet call."

I didn't know what he meant by that, but guessed it would not be a 911 call because so many people have police scanners in their homes.

I told the pastor about the suspicious car sitting out front, and Marianne's parents were missing. He said, "Hang up and let me call for help. I'll call you back on Janet's phone."

Fifteen minutes had passed by while Dennis and Steve waited. They were out of the truck and leaning on it. It was just a few minutes later that a car drove up with Pastor Bishop and another man followed by an unmarked police car. The man with Pastor Bishop was a detective, and in the unmarked car were two individuals from the regional highway patrol department.

Marianne let Pastor Bishop and the detective in. One policeman talked to the boys outside in the driveway, while the other walked toward the old car across the street. He looked in both seats of the car. The car doors were unlocked, and there wasn't anything suspicious in the car. He walked back to Dennis and Steve and questioned them. Dennis told me later that he told the man that I had said for them to stay outside and watch the car because Marianne didn't recognize it. No one ever parks there. There's just a field and a vacant lot on both sides of the house, too. The police then came into the house. Marianne said, "We're upstairs" to the man at the bottom of the steps.

Pastor Bishop briefly prayed with us four kids, that God would protect the parents and would heal the young people in the house from this awful experience.

An ambulance arrived shortly after the first car. I carried Janet downstairs. I didn't wait for them in the house. Marianne had Robert's arm as they went down the stairs. She was talking softly to him, saying, "God will deal with the people responsible for this."

Robert looked at me. "One short man kept saying, 'Blair said not to harm them… just scare them." He asked Marianne, "Is Blair the boyfriend that keeps calling and saying he is John?"

I turned to Robert and said, "Blair is a sick police officer who is no one's friend, and he has crossed the line! I am John."

I didn't know what I was going to do, but it was something. I laid Janet on the ambulance stretcher, and the paramedics took over. Robert was put on another stretcher in the same ambulance.

I went back into the house and told Pastor Bishop I was going to take Marianne to the hospital to be with Janet and Robert. She was still hanging on to me out of fear. I asked Pastor Bishop if he had a cell phone. He said, "Not with me."

I told him to use Janet's cell phone as soon as they found out anything about Marianne's parents, and then I went back out of the house. I instructed Dennis and Steve to go on home and tell Mom, "We took Marianne home."

Both boys wanted to know the details of what happened. I told them, "You need to know some of the bad things Satan does to get his way." Dennis kept punching his fist into his other hand. I knew he was thinking angry thoughts. Steve said, "What a way to destroy a good day."

He had forgotten how the day started with the dead chickens and a snake in the henhouse. He was still feeling good about the church service. I told them they needed to go on home, but they should both control themselves and not ruin Mom's day with Kaitlynn and Matthew. "If you talk with anyone, talk with Matthew. Take him to the barn and tell him what has happened. He can use his judgment on what to say to Kaitlynn and Mom." I reminded them, it was less than forty-eight hours since Mom had collapsed.

I said, "Drive carefully. Officer Blair recognizes our farm truck and likes to stop it for speeding."

I no sooner said that, then there was the man himself in his personal car. He parked, rolled down his window, and said, "What's going on?"

I turned to Marianne and said quietly, "Run inside and get Pastor Bishop and one of the policeman." She ran, partly out of fear.

"Sonny, I asked you a question," Blair said. 'What's going on?"

His tone irked me, and I said, "If you're that interested, why haven't you gotten out of your car to see? Wouldn't an off-duty policeman have done as much?"

He looked at the ambulance pulling away with a look on his face I can hardly describe. Mean perhaps, but guilty as a weasel, and as low as one. I put my hand on his car door and wasn't going to let him get out, even if he had tried, at least not until I had the back-up of the policeman.

I told Dennis and Steve to go. "Mom's waiting."

They had fear in their eyes and were hesitant, but they did as I as I told them to do. Maybe they thought since Blair was with me they could drive a little faster to get home. They pulled out of the drive and left. I silently prayed, "God, go with them."

Officer Blair was watching them, so I said, "Blair, is this street on your regular route or were you coming to see Marianne?"

He looked straight ahead and said, "Do you have any objections?"

"Yes!" I said,

He looked at me and said, "Well?"

I had to think quickly. I said, "First, she is not interested in you, especially after you have been harassing her on the phone. Second, the injuries done to her family were done according to your plan. Apparently you picked two dummies to help you. Third, you still haven't stepped out of your car like an innocent man checking to see if he can help in a bad situation."

I was making him mad, and I knew it. I saw a gun on the seat beside him and decided to back off a little.

He said, "Sonny, if you will get your hands off my car, I'll get out."

I stepped back, hoping to block his view of the front door and anyone approaching us from the house. I still had not moved far enough from his car door for him to fully open it. He pushed the door hard on me and said, "Move!" I only stepped back another foot. I wanted him to get out of the car, but not get far away from me. I guess I was crowding him in his space and my body language was irritating him. When I look back on it, I wonder why he was so tolerant of me. He had the gun beside him, He was a policeman. He had authority, and I was a young kid. It must have been my six foot three inch frame. No, it was God.

Pastor Bishop stepped up beside me and said, "Officer Blair, is there something you needed?"

Marianne was beside him looking petrified. She said to me, "John we need to go."

"Sure," I said, taking her to her car and putting her in the passenger's seat. "Marianne, stay right here, I want to make sure Pastor Bishop is okay."

I walked toward the two men and noticed one of the undercover policemen was standing at the corner of the house. Pastor Bishop was stepping toward me, as though he was trying to get Blair to turn his back to the man. I said, "God, help us."

Why I said what I said next, I will never know. God was in control of the situation. A verse from the Bible popped into my mind. Psalm 27:1b, "The Lord is the stronghold of my life of whom shall I be afraid."

I said, "Officer Blair, I have a challenge for you."

He looked my way, and I decided he could come my way, so I stopped in my tracks. I looked at Pastor Bishop, and he was frowning at me, but I went on.

"The two dummies you sent to do a job for you made the mistake of mentioning your name while they were talking. If you were not involved in what happened here, prove it to us. You have always been good to me, but right now, Marianne's parents are missing, and you know where they are. Tell us who raped a 14 year-old girl and beat up her brother. Tell us where you think the parents might be."

I was making Officer Blair angry, but it was giving the policeman behind him time to walk up behind him. Blair took a step toward me and said, "You may be tall, but you are still a punk, kid. Not any different than those punks that hang out on the grocery store parking lot. Who do you think you are challenging me? You aren't any different than those two dummies, as you called them, who couldn't do a simple job without messing it up."

I said, "So you do know them! Well, I will tell you what, tell me where to find them, and I'll go get them for you."

The man behind him said, "No, Blair, you can tell me."

The policeman grabbed Blair's arm and put it up behind him forcefully. Officer Blair was well trained. He quickly turned and came back with a hard punch to the officer behind him. The officer was stunned for a second. I knew I had to do something. Blair didn't look any harder to rope than a rodeo calf. I just reached around him with both arms and locked my fingers. His arms were down at his side and locked in position. He kicked, so I put my knee in his lower back so hard, he couldn't remember which foot was on which leg.

"Okay, son, I have him," the other officer said, locking the handcuffs on one wrist. I pulled that wrist behind him and locked it on the other wrist. The officer said, "Blair, you are a disgrace to the uniform you were appointed to wear. We've been watching you for some time, but right now, I have one question. *Where* are Mr. and Mrs. Weber?"

That car," he sheepishly said, "the trunk!"

I started running toward the car. One of the officers who had come out of the house yelled, "Boy, wait!"

I opened the rear door and started yanking on the rear seat. It had a latch on one side which only took a second to figure out. I lifted the seat out of the car and threw it to the street. It barely missed two officers from Chaffee who had joined the others.

Inside the trunk, Marianne's parents were bound, gagged, and barely alive. I pulled Mrs. Weber's gag out. When Marianne saw that Blair was locked in the police car, she came running for her mother. Pastor Bishop was calling for another ambulance. I lifted her gently out for the officer to use a knife on the cords. She kept saying, "My children. My children!"

I said "Ma'am, all your children are safe."

She saw Marianne and started shaking. Pastor Bishop led her across the street and had her sit on a step.

Mr. Weber was a bigger man and was wedged in tightly. One of the policemen had gotten into the back seat and pulled out his gag. Mr. Weber said, "I'm wired to the key mechanism. Don't open the trunk. Don't move me." He could hardly speak.

I heard what the officer said. He walked a distance from us, so Marianne and her mother couldn't hear. He was explaining the situation to someone on his shoulder radio mike. He came back and told the other officer and the detective that someone would have to come from Cape Girardeau to defuse the car. It might take thirty minutes for them to get here.

An ambulance arrived. Marianne had gone back into the house to get her mother a drink of water. When she came out of the house, her hands were almost shaking the water out of the glass. I took the glass from her and told her to go on to the hospital with her mother. I would come later with her dad. She didn't want to leave until her father was out of the car.

I put both hands on her upper arms and said, "Marianne, Janet and Robert need you. Your mother needs you. Pastor Bishop and I will take care of your dad."

I told Marianne her Dad was stuck in the trunk. "We are waiting for someone to work on the trunk lid. Right now he is fine," I assured her, but Marianne was not going to trust anyone. She looked around at all the men standing and talking to each other. She wondered why all those policemen couldn't open the truck. She said, "Doesn't someone have a key that will work?"

I said, "Marianne, look at me!"

She glanced up at me but looked toward the old car and then the ambulance. A paramedic put her mother in the ambulance and started checking her blood pressure.

I finally said, "Marianne, please go with your mother. She will be shocked when she sees Robert and Janet."

She glanced up at me and tears were rolling down her cheeks, but she wasn't making a sound. I couldn't help myself. My tears came, too.

I said, "Marianne, I love you, and I don't want anything to happen to you or your family. I want to protect you as long as you will let me. Trust me and the Lord. We're going to get through this."

She put her arms around me and bawled. She tried to say something through her tears.

I said, "Come with me."

I walked her to the back of the ambulance and said to the paramedic, "Take her with you before she collapses."

The paramedic took one look at her and said, "Lift her in here."

I lifted her up into the ambulance. She was like a feather. The paramedic helped her sit down on a jump seat and put a seat belt on her.

The paramedic recognized me and said. "Oh, you are the 'two at a time' guy. Your name is John Moore, isn't it?"

I said, "Yes," shaking my head. "And this looks like the third time in the last six months that someone in my family had to call for help."

I wasn't in the mood to say anymore. I patted Marianne's arm and said, "I'll see you in about an hour. Tell Robert and Janet I'll be there for them, too."

She leaned her head back and cried. I heard her mother say, "Marianne, darling, we'll get through this."

I stepped out of the way, and the doors closed. The ambulance drove off. I stood there watching it drive down the street. When they turned the lights on, I felt like I should jump in Marianne's car and follow her, but the bomb squad had arrived. There were two men who were trained to handle situations like this. One man was inside the car assessing the situation. He wrapped Mr. Weber in some kind of insulated material. Mr. Weber was asking for a drink.

The officer said, "Not yet sir, but in about five minutes you will be out of here, and then you can get a strong drink. You deserve it."

They had a bright light shining into the trunk, so they could see the wires and all. A Chaffee fire truck had responded when the bomb squad was called. The firemen were standing by, and another ambulance had arrived, too.

A crowd was beginning to gather, and it worried the officers. Chaffee's remaining police officers had shown up to keep the crowd back. They did a good job of blocking off both ends of the street, but neighbors had called neighbors, and soon the press was there also. The TV men with big cameras on their shoulders were trying to get every bit of information they could out of the policemen and Pastor Bishop. I was upset about the invasion of Marianne's family's privacy, but I couldn't do anything about it. I just hoped the press didn't show up at the hospital for their story.

I talked to Pastor Bishop, and asked, "Do you think we should leave the house unlocked?"

One of the officers from the area office said to me, "Young man, I've been watching you. You are calm in a crisis. You think fast, and your pastor tells me you are a hardworking man. We need young men of your caliber on the police force. Think about it. When things settle down, give us a call. The police academy will be starting a new class soon. I can reserve a spot for you." I just looked at him and said, "With crops in the field, cows to be milked, and weasels in our henhouse, I'm not sure about that, but I will consider your idea, Sir. Thank you for the compliments. Right now my brothers don't have a Dad or a Grandpa, so I need to stand by and be a big brother for them."

Pastor Bishop said, "See what I mean!"

Pastor Bishop had no sooner spoken when the man from the bomb squad working inside the car, yelled, "Let her up!"

They opened the truck a little, and the man inside the car climbed out of the car's back seat area with three pieces of dynamite tied to some wire. The lid of the trunk went up, a few more wires were clipped, and the cord was cut off Mr. Weber's ankles and wrists.

I went over and said boldly, as if they were my younger brothers, "Stand back, men."

Later, I wondered why the policemen stood back and didn't interfere with me. They were watching me as though they were ready to help if I should need them. I lifted Mr. Weber out of the trunk and set him down slowly until he could stand on his own. His legs were weak from the position he had been in. I told him, "I'm Marianne's friend, John Moore. Mr. Weber, I am not the creep who has been calling your daughter or the one who harmed you and your family."

He asked, "Where is my family?"

I said, "They've gone to a hospital in Cape Girardeau with your wife, Sir. We have a paramedic here who will take you to join them. I told Marianne, I would come, too. Do you mind?"

The paramedic said, "Sir, we would like for you to come with us."

His legs buckled like his wife's did from the long hours cramped in the car trunk. A paramedic grabbed him and said, "Sit down, Sir."

He fell back on the gurney. They straightened him out and pushed the gurney to the back of ambulance.

Pastor Bishop said, "When the detectives are done fingerprinting, we'll lock up the house. Mr. Weber looked out the back of the ambulance and said, "Good."

I said, "I'll see you soon, Mr. Weber."

When the ambulance drove off, the firemen climbed aboard the fire trucks and left, too. A policeman was standing with the sticks of dynamite still in his hand. He was talking to a detective. I noticed the TV photographer kneel down and take a picture of the dynamite. Just as he snapped the picture the policeman laid the wires and dynamite on the trunk of the police car. I stood in the street and watched as the photographer walk toward his own car. My mind went from Marianne's family all in the hospital, to Matthew and Kaitlynn at home, to many other brief thoughts, when a tow truck came for the old car. They picked up the car seat in the street and rolled the car up on the back of their truck with a winch. I guessed it would be evidence. The neighbors began filtering back into their homes. Some had cheered as the ambulance went by with Mr. Weber.

I got into Marianne's car and just sat there for a few moments. I put my arms and head on the steering wheel, trying to get my head cleared of all that had happened since Paul fell and broke his arm. When I sat up, I said out loud, "Lord, this is only the end of June. What else do you have for me the rest of the summer? I need your strength, Lord."

I hadn't shut the car door, and one of the bomb squad officers heard me and said, "John? It is John, isn't it?"

I said, "Yes."

He said, "John, we need young men like you on the police force... especially young men who know how to pray."

I shook my head, thinking about my family, and said, "Thank you, Sir, but, right now I need to call my mother and let her know I'm fine, and I'll be home to milk the cows tonight."

The officer laughed and said, "A man after my own heart."

He shut the car door and walked away with a smile. I backed out of the driveway and said to myself, "I wish I could smile."

Then I remembered I needed to call Mom, so I pulled back into the driveway. Marianne's phone and purse were lying on the car seat next to me. I picked up the phone and started to dial, but I remembered what Marianne said about a noise. The phone might be bugged.

I jumped out of the car and went to one of the two officers standing in the yard. "This is Marianne's cell phone. She mentioned she thought her phone or the house phones might be bugged because Blair knew too much about where she was going and when she would be home."

I handed the phone to the officer, and he took it apart. He said, "Well, look here!"

He showed me a tiny device not any bigger than a dehydrated pea. It fit in the phone tightly.

I said, "Just leave it…its more evidence. Do you think it's safe to use the house phones? I need to call home and let my mother know when I will be home."

Another officer had joined us. They all turned and walked back into the house. I followed. They asked, "Do you know where all the phones are?"

I looked around and said, "I've only been in this house about three times in the past year and not very long, so your guess is as good as mine."

We walked into the kitchen and found the phone. There was a listening device in it, too.

I shook my head negatively, "Take it out, and I'll push the phone locator button. Look for the phones that are beeping." I said it as though the policemen and detectives were my younger brothers.

There was a phone in the living room, one upstairs in the hall, one in Mr. Weber's study, and one in the master bedroom. All five phones had a bugging device in them.

I blurted out, "Blair is not only a creep, he's stupid. The phones are all on one line. He only needed one bug or whatever you call it. I wonder how he got in long enough to put one in each phone. I'll bet he did it a month ago when Marianne was in St. Louis at the university. Robert and Janet were in school here, and Mr. and Mrs. Weber were at work. The creep!"

I looked at my watch and realized forty-five minutes had passed since we took Mr. Weber out of the car. "I really need to call home. Is it safe now?"

One of the officers said, "It's good. Go ahead and make the call."

I dialed my farm number, and Kaitlynn answered the phone. I said, "Kaitlynn, this is John. I'm sorry I haven't been there to visit. When are you headed back to St. Louis?"

She said, "Not until eight o'clock tonight."

I told her, "Good… Maybe I will get to see you at supper time. Is Mom available?"

Kaitlynn hesitated, but said, "She went upstairs fifteen minutes ago to rest. How's Marianne and her family? Matthew told me what happened."

I asked, "Does Mom know?"

Kaitlynn said, "When Dennis and Steve came home late and you didn't return, she wanted to know why. The boys couldn't lie to her, but just said Marianne's family was in turmoil and she wanted you to go home with her. Marianne wanted to talk to you and wanted the boys to pick you up at her house. They said you had asked them to wait twenty minutes, but then you told them to go on home."

I asked, "How much did they tell Matthew?"

"He only knows about Robert and Janet. Mom does not know anything"

I noticed the detective and police were looking at each other and listening to me, so I decided maybe I should get off the phone. I said, "Well, Kaitlynn, right now the entire family is at St. Francis Hospital and I'm going over now with Marianne's car. Tell Mom I'll be home before you leave. Use your judgment on what you tell her. I think they all should be released except Janet. They will need the car over there. Please pray for them."

Kaitlynn asked, "Do you think Marianne would mind if Matthew and I stopped by to visit them? I think it would be a good idea if Dennis and Steve visited Robert and Janet, too. I'll tell them what to say and what not to say. Janet probably won't want to face any boys or men after today."

I told Kaitlynn, "That would be great! Is Paul handy?" I waited, and Paul came to the phone. "Hey, Paul, "How's that arm?"

Paul wasn't talking much. He just said, "It still hurts a little, but it's better."

He needed to take a long Sunday afternoon nap, so I told him, "Paul, let me worry about your chickens, okay. You just get yourself a book or take a nap. You've been through a lot in the past forty-eight hours. I'll be home sometime before Kaitlynn and Matthew leave. Okay?"

I hung up the phone and said, "I'm out of here! I'm headed for the hospital."

I drove the fifteen or twenty minutes to Cape Girardeau from Chaffee, thinking over the past three days. It was quiet in the car except for the noise of the motor. I felt so alone. No brothers asking questions, and no Grandpa to worry about. Mom was resting, and Kaitlynn and Matthew were home to care for Mom. It was just me and God in the car. I had to talk to Him. I asked him again to help me. My body is big and strong, but in the moments on the highway, I felt weak. I know I must have told God many times over the past six months that I am only eighteen. From the way things have turned out, *He* has been saying to *me*, "I am God, trust me."

I thought about a lot of things on my way to Cape Girardeau. The idea that I should become a policeman was planted in my mind. Not once, but twice. I wonder why that seed was planted. I had to ask, *Lord, is this the direction you want me to take?* I thought about that the rest of the way to Cape Girardeau. The education wouldn't be as long unless I wanted a degree in Criminal Justice, and I could get that at Southeast Missouri University in Cape Girardeau. I could get a job locally as a policeman, and still farm the land. Then I would be able to help Mom with the boys. It began to sound like what I should do with my life. Dad worked on the railroad and worked the farm, too.

I thought about what the officer said, *we need people on the force that are not afraid to pray.* I liked that. I thought about the type of person Officer Blair was, and I could understand how important it would be to have people on the force that would not only uphold laws, but would have a personal life that was honest and dedicated to a good moral code. As far as I am concerned, God is the Supreme Being, and a person dedicated to him will have integrity that manifests itself in a moral lifestyle. Officer Blair may have upheld the law, but he hired goons to break it for him. That doesn't show integrity. Maybe I *should* consider the police academy.

A thought popped into my mind. *Go for it!*

I almost stopped the car, just so I could think. I prayed, *Lord, you don't even give a guy time to pray about things, do you?*

My mind was made up in the space of four minutes. It was really made up for me, and somehow, I didn't have any negative feelings about it, only peace.

I know Mom has often quoted a verse to my brother and me, "Delight thyself in the Lord, and he will give you the desires of your heart." I wasn't sure it was a desire, but it was a big question in my mind. I had been thinking about what I should do after I graduate from high school. I guess it was a desire to *know* what I should do with my life. I thought again about the verse Mom quoted to us. "Delight thyself in the Lord, and He will give you the desires of your heart."

Mom learned that verse from the King James Version of the Bible. I know I have worried sometimes about leaving home, going away to a university, and studying something for two to four years. I've shared my feelings many times with God, but I hadn't made any decision. When I thought about the verse Mom quoted to us, I tried to think about my true desires. One desire is for everyone to love God, and get along with everyone else. To love each other would be best, but since Satan seems to control even weasels and snakes, I guess it would be impossible for everyone to love everyone else, unless they meet God and His son, Jesus, and let Him help us love others.

My thoughts went to Officer Blair. He sure needs a thorough do-over by God. Those thugs of his need to be punished for what they did to Robert, and especially Janet. Marianne and her family won't even want to go back to their home. I had to pray before I got out of the car. *Lord, what can I do for Marianne and her family? What can I say today, to help them?*

The first person I met in the hospital was the police detective who came to the house with Pastor Bishop. I thought I had left them in Chaffee, but I guess they left when I was talking on the phone. The Detective was wearing his badge, and I recalled what he said to me earlier. *They need hard working young men to become policemen.* I heard an inner voice say, *a policeman…you can do it.* I realized God was speaking to me again, and I shook my head like there was something on it that needed to fall off. I'm sure if someone saw me, they would have thought I was having a seizure. I couldn't believe that out of the crises of this day, I was hearing something that would affect my life and others.

"All things work together for good, to those who love God, to those who are called according to His purpose." That was another verse I had memorized that Mom had quoted many times after Dad died.

Pastor Bishop spoke, "Hello, John. You look like you're having some heavy thoughts."

"I guess I am. Where's Marianne?"

"Right now, she's in the conference room with her parents. Janet and Robert have been admitted for observation. The whole family is pretty shaken up."

I wasn't feeling too stable either, but asked, "What are they doing in the conference room?"

The detective said, "They are questioning them about *who* the perpetrators were. We will compare notes."

I had to ask, "Is this standard procedure?" You would have thought I was already a policeman using those words.

He said, "No and yes. Cape Girardeau has had two similar cases over the past year, and they need to find out all they can on this case. They might be related. The perpetrators sound like the same individuals."

I said, "Oh" just like Paul would have. I was standing there with Marianne's purse. Two younger women walked by and laughed. I wondered why they were looking at me with such a peculiar look. I thought to myself… *at least someone's smiling today.* Anyway, aren't some men carrying purses these days? I bet I would be completely ignored if the purse were a Bible. They'd think I was a preacher and go on their way without another thought.

Pastor Bishop interrupted my thoughts and said, "Robert could use a visit from you, John. Maybe Janet, too. She needs to know there are still good men in this world. Dennis and Steve might reassure her, too."

I told Pastor Bishop that Dennis and Steve would probably be up a little later, and then handed the purse to the detective and said, "Would you see that Marianne gets this?"

I started to walk away, but remembered the car keys. I stopped and said, "And these. Tell Marianne, not to worry. Kaitlynn and Matthew will get me home."

Pastor Bishop asked, "Don't you want to know the room numbers? Room 211 and 212."

I chuckled and said, "I guess I left my memory back in Chaffee. Thanks."

I headed for the elevator, went up one flight, and wondered what I should say to Janet and Robert. I prayed, *What should I say, Lord?*

A thought came back...*you'll think of something.* I answered and said, *Thanks, Lord, but I need something specific.* Then the scripture verse came to me, "Cast all your burdens upon Him for He cares for you." I wasn't sure what that meant, so I said, *Okay, Lord, whatever!*

I stepped off the elevator and went to room 211 not knowing if it was Janet's room or Robert's. It was Janet's. She was sitting on the side of the bed, wearing a hospital gown and robe on, crying. Her arms had bruises and her face was swollen. She looked so small. I asked, "Janet, why the tears?"

It was a foolish question to ask after all she had been through. She looked up at me and said, "Don't you know?"

I said, "What I know is there is a fourteen year old girl with a beautiful heart and mind sitting in this room crying. Satan was able to tamper with her physical body and is trying to work on her spirit, but we're not going to let him, are we? In less than a week, your physical body will be somewhat back to normal. A lot of the swelling will go away. Mentally, your healing may take a little longer. That's why I am here, Janet. I want you to understand that. I also want you to know there are wicked, bad, stupid people in the world, and sometimes they cross the line and hurt innocent, good people. You and your family are the victims this time, but there are also good people in this world. We need to stand together against evil. Are you with me on that, Janet?"

She stood with her bare feet and came to me. She wrapped her arms around me and cried. I didn't know what to do but hold her and say, "I'm here for you, Janet. Steve and Dennis will come by and let you know the same thing. Think positive. Your whole future will not be ruined because of this bad experience unless *you* let it. Do you understand?"

I patted her head and said, "Right?"

She was hesitant, but said, "Okay."

I pulled her away from me, looked her in the eye, and said, "Janet, make me a promise. Every day when you get up, look in the mirror and say, 'Good morning, God. Thank you for keeping me alive. What can I do for you today?' As your body heals, let God heal your spirit."

A voice from behind me said, "And who is this man with the Wisdom of Solomon?"

I turned to find Mom, Kaitlynn, and Matthew. Janet moved back to sit on the bed. I stepped aside to let them in. Kaitlynn had a cute little teddy bear. She gave Janet a hug and said. "Janet, I'm so sorry for the pain those people caused you. When you need a hug, hug this little bear."

Mom said, "Let's get you out of that drab hospital gown, so you can wear this bright, cheerful one."

She held up a bright pink knit gown that said across the front. "I am loved by family and friends." Then in small letters, it said, "and the rest can go where the *son* will no longer shine,"

Mom hugged her, too, and said, "That s-o-n means, Jesus. We're here for you, honey."

I gave Mom a pat and said, "There may be a Warden Jordon down the hall waiting to tell us there are too many people in this room. I'm going over to see Robert."

I went to the room next door and heard Dennis saying. "Look, Robert, your sister needs you more than ever right now. She needs to know all guys are not beasts like the two mad men who attacked Janet and you."

Steve said, "Robert, especially in the next few months, let her hear she's still your sister, and she's still very much a lady. Keep reassuring her. She may get upset with you a few times, but she needs to understand *family* is important, and you are going to stand by her."

Robert had fury in his eyes and said, "Who are you to tell me how to think—Counselor Dennis the psychiatrist and his associate, Counselor Steve?"

I stepped farther into the room and said, "No, three counselors! Steve is Dr. Steve, Dennis is Dr. Dennis, and I am Rev. John a Bible thumpin' preacher counselor. The Bible says to bare one another's burdens and we are here to lighten your load."

Robert grabbed his tissue box, threw it at me, and said, "Well, you three counselors need to be three detectives and find the thugs who did this to us. Preach to them. When I find them, I'm going to kill them for what they did to my family."

I thought about what Mom had said in the hall about us boys being Robert and Janet's peer group, and we could help them sort out this mess better than anyone. I thought about my life calling as an occupation and figured there would be no better time than now to share it with my brothers and Robert.

I said, "No, Robert, I'm not a reverend, and my brothers are not counselors, but I do want to share with you what happened to me at your house after you left. I graduated from high school less than a month ago, and I've been very concerned about what should be my next step. Should I go to school and study agriculture? Should I go away to school somewhere and leave Dennis and Steve fully responsible for the farm? Should I go to the same school as Marianne, Matthew, and Kaitlynn to study Bible and music? Southeast Missouri University and Missouri Baptist University had accepted me to be a student at their university, but I still didn't know what to do. When I was helping at your house after you left, one of the policemen said, 'John, I've been watching you, and you're the kind of young man we'd like to have on our police force. You're a quick thinker. You were calm under stress, and I've heard you are honest and a hard worker. We have a class starting soon at the police academy, and I'd be glad to reserve a space for you.'

"Robert, I was amazed or astounded that I was being watched with all that was happening at your house. Being a policeman had never entered my mind, so I thanked the man for his compliment and told him that going to the police academy wouldn't get the cows milked and crops harvested. He just said, 'Think about it.'

"Then, just before leaving the house, I sat down in Marianne's car and put my head down on the steering wheel. All of the day's crises that began at our house early this morning had finally hit me and I sat there for a few minutes with the door open. Then I said out loud, 'Lord, this is only the middle of June. What else do you have for me the rest of the summer? I need your strength, Lord.' I hadn't shut the door and I didn't hear one of the bomb squad officers walking toward the car, but he heard what I said.

"He said, 'John, we need young men like you on the police force—especially young men who know how to pray?'

"My response was, 'Thank you, sir, but right now I need to call my mother and let her know I'm fine, and I'll be home to milk the cows tonight.' The man laughed and said, 'A man after my own heart.'

"Guys, on the way up here I thought about a policeman's job and how I could do that and still work the farm. A voice came from somewhere inside me and said, *go for it!*

"I told God, 'You don't even give me time to think about it or even talk it over with anyone.' So, Robert, the reason I'm telling you this is because those two bums, along with many others, are still out there doing their dirty deeds. You and I need to make a commitment to *not* become like them in our feelings of vengeance. We need to learn how to catch evil people and put them behind bars where they belong. We can do that legally.

"Robert, I don't know what interests you have or if you've thought about what career you might like to have, but I can tell you this, I'll need a good detective to work alongside me when I become a police officer. Officer Blair had his chance to make the world a better place, and he failed, so let's replace him with a couple of really good cops. Will you think about it?"

Steve and Dennis were quiet hanging on my every word. Steve finally said, "Wouldn't it be something if all four of us put on a uniform and went after the bad guys?"

Dennis said, "Yeah, I agree. We could still work the farm as policemen."

Robert laughed and grabbed his jaw. It hurt to laugh. He said, "You guys have gone from psychiatrists and reverends to being policemen. You almost make me want to go to the police academy, too."

Mr. Weber stepped in the room, took one look at Robert and started crying. Robert said, "Dad! I thought something had happened to you and Mom."

Dennis and Steve quietly stepped back into the hall with Mom. Mr. Weber wrapped his arms around Robert and said, "I'm so sorry I didn't believe Marianne about that rotten man—none of this would have happened."

Robert looked at me like, *what do I say?* He had never seen his Dad so upset about anything. I spoke up and said, "Mr. Weber, I think we've found a way to make something good come from this horrible situation."

Mr. Weber turned to me as though he had not noticed I was still in the room.

He said, "Oh, John." He pulled out his handkerchief and blew his nose. "I'm sorry you were involved in all this, but I'm glad you were—if that makes sense."

Mr. Weber must have been about five-feet-ten inches tall because I felt like I towered over him. He held out his hand and said, "I want to say thank you for helping my family today. I know Pastor Bishop and Marianne think highly of you. Thank you for getting my wife and me out of that trunk."

Robert's eyebrows shot up, and he asked in disbelief, "What trunk?"

Mr. Weber realized no one told Robert what had happened. I could tell that Mr. Weber was at a loss for words, so I said, "Those same evil men had your Mom and Dad bound and gagged in the old car that was parked across the street from your house. Fortunately, we found them and got them out. I've heard there have been similar cases. So, Robert, you and I have to commit ourselves to our education, so we can go after those men and others like them."

Robert said, "Dad, John says we're going to replace bad cops with some good ones. He thinks God let him know through our experience that he is supposed to go to the police academy and he wants me to become a detective. What do you think?"

Mr. Weber sat in the chair next to Robert's bed and said, "I think John would make an excellent police officer, and you too, Son. There's no time like now to start thinking about what you want to do after you graduate. You only have one more year to decide."

Robert elevated his bed, so he could sit straighter. He looked at me and said, "John, I'm like you, being a police officer never entered my mind. Do they take eighteen year-old kids?"

I thought for a moment. "I shrugged my shoulders while thinking but I said, "Robert, apparently they do. One officer said he would hold a place for me, and I am still eighteen. I'll check into it. The course may require a year or so studying criminal justice. I don't know. I suspect that in order to be a detective you might have to have some college education. Let me find out. In the meantime, please consider what Dennis and Steve said to you.

"Mr. Weber, if you don't mind hearing this, I'm going to give Robert a pep talk."

His eyebrows rose like Robert's did. He said, "John, be my guest."

Robert smiled the best he could with his swollen face and said, "I thought I already had my pep talk."

I swallowed, looked at Mr. Weber, and said, "I was raised on a farm. I have taken care of all the animals on the farm. I have assisted in the breeding of some of them and the delivery of the calves. When it comes to sex, I know all the facts. I have enough experience to know that the only humans who behave like animals are those who are incapable of having *consideration* for others, *loving* others so much that *their needs* become a priority, or having *happiness* and *joy* just being in the presence of another person. People were created to have thoughts that result in those feelings, and then good behaviors follow.

"Then there are people in this world who, because of something unfortunate that happened to them, shut out everything that is good and concentrate on all the bad they've experienced. Because they dwell on the negative, eventually they become unable to function in some areas of their lives."

Mr. Weber interrupted me and said, "Son, I don't want this to happen to Janet. John is right. Janet was a victim of animal behavior and she needs to know she's still a lovely girl, capable of having good thoughts in all areas of her life. The male people in her life, starting with you and me, need to be supporters. If you've been arguing with her, and I know you have, it's time to stop and find some way to talk to Janet that will make the difference. In the long run, it will affect how she responds to the men in her life".

I agreed with Mr. Weber and said, "My mother suggested something, and I was a little unsure of the idea, but it may be helpful to Janet and you, too, Robert. Mom thought it might be helpful for you and Janet to come out to the farm for a week to allow your parent's to regroup their emotions and think about what security measures they can take for the family and while you are with us, my brothers and I can help Janet by proving that *not all* men are like the men who attacked her.

"I was hesitant to put more responsibility on Mom, but she said, 'I have confidence in my sons. They will help Janet see what real gentlemen are like.' I think she's over-rated us, but I agree with her. My brothers will treat you and your sister with respect. Janet will have to eventually face her friends and peers. This might be the way to start slowly."

Mr. Weber was looking at me with his eyebrows still raised and he said, "I think that might be a real good idea."

He looked at Robert and said, "If you go to the farm your swelling and bruises will have time to heal. I'll have to talk to your mother, but maybe we can do a make-over in your rooms, so the memories won't meet you face-to-face when you come home. What do you think, Robert?"

Robert hesitated, but said, "I would be willing, if you, Mom, and Janet think it is a good idea. Maybe it's time for a family conference—something we've never had."

Marianne walked in the room, came up behind me, and put her arms around me. I could feel her shaking and sniffling. Mr. Weber got up from his chair, took her arms from me, and pulled her to himself. She kept saying, "Dad, I'm so sorry. I wished that I had gone out with the man. Then he would've hurt me and not the family."

"No, Sweetheart. It wouldn't have stopped with you. Blair had some hidden secrets that made him who he is today, and apparently whatever they were kept him from having consideration for others. He would've hurt you and eventually tried to control you. He would have hurt us all."

I thought about what Mr. Weber said and realized it was some of what I said just minutes ago. Mr. Weber reached over Marianne and held out his hand to me. He said, "Marianne, when you start looking for a husband, please look in John Moore's direction."

I shook his hand and smiled. Marianne started laughing through her tears.

Robert said, "Has she gone loony on us?"

I handed her a couple of tissues from Robert's bedside table and said, "Marianne knows how I feel about her, and right now, she deserves to act a little irrational."

Marianne laughed again and said, "Will you repeat what you said to me when you tried to get me to go to the hospital with Mom."

I glanced toward the hospital room's window, at Robert, then at Marianne and said, "I believe I told you, 'Marianne, please go with your mother. She'll be in shock when she sees Robert and Janet.'"

Marianne gulped back her tears and said, "Yeah, you said that. But, through my tears, I saw a tear fall down your face, and you said something else. Would you repeat it please?"

I grabbed her and laughed. "You are trying to put me on the spot aren't you, but that's okay. I'll repeat it as often as you want to hear it. I said, 'Marianne, I love you, and I don't want anything to happen to you or your family ever again. I want to protect you as long as you will let me. Trust me and the Lord. We are going to get through this.'"

At that moment, Mom and Mrs. Weber stepped into the room. Mr. Weber said, "Welcome to the family, son."

They both looked curious, but Mrs. Weber headed for Robert and gave him a big hug. Then she hugged Mr. Weber and said, "With God's help, we're going to get through this."

Mom asked, "Was there something going on before we came in?"

Kaitlynn and Matthew were pressed in together in the doorway. I looked sheepish, and Robert broke the silence for us. He said, "Oh, these two loony birds are in love, and Dad welcomed John into our family."

I said, "Now, Robert, you'd better be careful. You've only had sisters, and one day you'll have a big brother. and I mean b-i-g." I stood on my tip toes, and everyone laughed. Mom added, "A happy heart's like a good medicine. May I add my two cents in here?"

I didn't say yes, you may have the floor. No one else said anything either, so I said, "Mom, you knew it was coming. I've liked Marianne since I was a junior in high school, and I've always thought of her as a great friend. She's been there for us during some of our family crises, too."

Matthew was listening from the doorway and he chuckled and said, "And?"

I chuckled and looked at Marianne. I was a little embarrassed, but said, "And she's talented. She's intelligent. She loves music. She loves children. She loves our family and thinks we are special. She's a sweet Christian girl, who loves her Savior and Lord. Not only that, she is a good-lookin'gal. I have finally understood why I have such strong protective feelings for Marianne. She's more than a friend. I have fallen in love with her."

Robert laughed and grabbed his sides. Everyone looked at him. He said, "Oh, it pains me to think I might lose my big sister."

Mrs. Weber went to him and said, "Robert, relax, Honey. Let your breathing be relaxed."

I looked around and realized there were way too many people in the room, and I was about to turn and leave when Robert said, "John, write down all you said about Marianne, so I can use it when I find a girlfriend. No, when you have your first fight, I'll give it back to you to read." We all chuckled about that. I just said, "Good idea."

Everyone got quiet, as though they were thinking. Marianne said, "Don't start any wedding plans, yet. I have to get through school first."

I smiled at Marianne and added, "And I have the police academy ahead of me, but in time—God's time, we will be husband and wife."

Matthew interrupted, "Wow! Some great decisions have been made in the last hour."

Kaitlynn stepped further into the crowed room, and reached for Marianne's hand, and said, "Marianne, this is wonderful news. Let me know when you need my Sylvester/Tweety Bird Nightie."

Mr. and Mrs. Weber moved to the other side of Robert's bed. Mom put her arms around me. She hugged me, and then turned back to Marianne and gave her a hug. "John, Marianne, I had prayed that one day you both would see that God had already planned for you to be together as one. John, you know Marianne has already become like a member of the family. She fits in so well. I know, also, that the Weber family will be one of the best extended families we could ever have."

Kaitlynn added, "I've always wondered what it would be like to have a sister. Now, I'm going to have one."

Mrs. Weber said, "Wait a minute. This is unfair. We haven't had time to get to know John."

Mr. Weber looked at his wife and said, "When John pulled out the back seat of the car with such determination, took the stuffing out of your mouth, lifted you out of the trunk, and then went after me, I decided I wanted his help and protection for all my family."

He chuckled, but went on to say, "If I heard right, when I first came into this room our son, Robert, said he's going to help fulfill that position, too. Both these guys decided that the bad cop needed to be replaced with some good cops."

He looked at Robert proudly, and Robert smiled as best as he could with his swollen jaw. He said, "Well, John did a pretty good job of convincing me I should go after those thugs who hurt us, as a police detective, instead of going off in a rage with a gun. He told me God didn't give him time to pray about being a policeman—God just told him to 'Go for it!'"

Everyone was looking, at me waiting for a comment. "It's true," I said, "God has a way of taking unfortunate experiences that Satan dishes out and making something good from them. When I was at the Weber's, I was told not once, but twice, that the police academy was looking for hard-working young men. It never entered my mind that I could become a policeman and still help Mom with the farm. On the way to the hospital, God said, *Go for it!* I told the Lord He hadn't given me time to even think or pray about it. If Marianne will wait for me, I will enroll in the police academy for the fall semester, and I'll check on any junior program that might be available for high school students."

I glanced at Mrs. Weber and I couldn't read her expression. I know she was worried about Janet and Robert, and the fact that the men who hurt her children were still on the loose. She caught me looking at her. She smiled and looked down at her red wrists.

She looked back up and said, "John, I've only been around you for short periods of time, but each time I think: his parents did something right in raising him. You and Marianne probably have two years before you can even think about marriage, but like my husband, I welcome you into our family."

I held out my hand to shake her hand. She said, "No hug?"

I gave her a big hug and realized she was as tiny as Marianne. It made me angrier that those men dared to do anything to Mrs. Weber and Janet, but I said, "Thank you, Mrs. Weber, I promise I'll be a gentleman at all times around your daughter."

I looked at Mom and asked, "Where are Dennis, Steve, and Paul?"

Mom looked at her watch and said, "Dennis and Steve are next door with Janet, and Pastor Bishop took Paul home with him."

I glanced at the clock on the wall and realized it was getting time for the cows to be brought in and milked, so I said, "I think we ought to give this family time to be alone together, without a room full of people."

Looking at Mr. and Mrs. Weber, Mom added, "If you want, I can stay with Janet tonight." Mrs. Weber said, "Thank you, but my husband will be here for Robert, and I'll stay with Janet tonight. We'll talk about your invitation to the farm."

Marianne took my hand and whispered, "Where did you park my car?"

She handed her Dad her keys and said, "I think I'll go home with John, if you don't mind. I'll stay in Kaitlynn's room. I don't want to go back to the house for any reason tonight."

Kaitlynn responded, "Marianne, you're more than welcome to use my room. Matthew and I need to head back to St. Louis. We'll be putting your family on our church prayer chain for wisdom and strength. Okay? And I think we need to be leaving now. John, you be sure to keep us posted on Marianne and her family."

Matthew turned, and Kaitlynn followed him out the door. The rest of us followed Mrs. Weber next door to Janet's room and beckoned Dennis and Steve to come on. Janet was laughing about something, and it made her mom smile and the rest of us to feel so much better. Mom was right. Her boys, Janet's peers, would be able to bring healing to Janet.

As we walked out the revolving doors at the front entrance of St. Francis Hospital, it occurred to me that Mom had fainted from low blood sugar and stress three days ago. I asked Matthew if he and Kaitlynn had time to go to the Pizza Inn before leaving. We all needed to eat something, especially Mom. I couldn't have her passing out on me before she got home.

"We really need to hit the road," Matthew said. "We can stop later for a burger or something that's quick."

Dennis said, "The Pizza Inn is a buffet—you can eat and run quicker."

Kaitlynn agreed, but Steve said, "Dennis, they are driving home—not *running.*"

Dennis hit Steve playfully on his upper arm, and they both laughed. I'm glad they were able to keep some sense of humor after all that happened today.

Mom's Cell phone was ringing in her purse as we got in line for pizza. It was Paul.

His arm was hurting, and he wanted some medicine. The evening church service was to start in less than an hour. Mom told Paul we would pick him up before church started.

We didn't linger at the Pizza Inn. Dennis and Steve could eat almost a whole pizza in ten minutes. I ate only three pieces. I couldn't stop thinking about the day.

At the table everyone seemed quiet. I guess we were all thinking about the events that happened in the past three days—Paul's broken arm, Mom's fainting spells, Kaitlynn and Matthew's surprise visit,

Steve's solo in the church service, and the Weber family's horrific experience. Then to top it all, Marianne and I confessed our love for each other to the families, and God told me to become a policeman. What a weekend!

I looked at Marianne across the table, and she was picking at her food. I knew she was thinking about her sister and family. I couldn't wait to get her home and away from everything and everyone."

I said, "Marianne." She didn't hear me, so I repeated, "Marianne, are you okay?"

Mom looked at her and said to me, "I think we've had enough to eat. We need to get her home, and give her a sedative to help her relax and sleep. She needs to be rested for her family tomorrow. Marianne still hadn't answered me, so I reached over and took her hand. She looked up at me and I said, "Would you like to go now, or do you want to go back to the hospital?" She shook her head. I wasn't sure which question she was answering.

Mom said, "Let's go. We have a boy to pick up, and he's waiting."

We said, "Good-bye" and gave Kaitlynn and Matthew hugs. Matthew said to Marianne, "You know, I believe God prompted us to come down here today. I'm glad we were here for your family and ours."

Marianne put both hands over her face and started crying. She took a couple of gulps and said, "Kaitlynn and Matthew, seeing you and knowing you were here helped me. Thank you for coming down today of all days."

Matthew and Kaitlynn hugged her and Matthew said, "Do you mind if I pray?"

Matthew prayed a beautiful prayer for the safety and healing of both families and a safe return to St. Louis. Matthew laid his hand on Kaitlynn and Mom. We all said, "Amen," and we smiled when we said, "Good-bye."

God sure knows how to put healing words into someone's mind and mouth. I took Marianne's hand and walked her to Mom's car. Dennis and Steve drove Grandpa's truck.

Mom handed me the keys and said, "John, you drive, and Marianne can sit up front with you. Paul will be more comfortable with me in the back seat."

It was dark by the time we left the parking lot and headed south for Chaffee. Paul was waiting on the church front step for us as he was told to do. Mrs. Bishop was with him. Mom got out and gave her a brief update on how the Weber family was doing, and then we left for the five minute drive to the farm.

By the time we got inside the house, Paul was whimpering. He was long overdue for rest and pain medicine. Mom helped him go upstairs and get into his pajamas after giving him the medication for his pain. I felt so sorry for him, but I had to go out to the barn. I told Steve to go take care of the chickens. I handed him Paul's old, stained, pink plastic bowl and said—"Collect the eggs. I suspect the hens will all be inside on the roosts, so don't worry about feeding them. Make sure the small door is closed, and the big one, too."

Steve looked at the bowl and shook his head. He finally said, "If there are any weasels, snakes, or dead chickens, *you* are going to deal with them."

I said, "*Go!*"

Dennis and I headed out to the barn and got Steve's heifers fed, watered and into their stalls. We milked the two cows, too. Dennis was quiet. I asked him how Janet was doing. He started laughing, and I wondered what was so funny.

He said, "Steve and I gave ourselves the name "Bobbies" as they do in England for policemen. We told Janet no one at school would bother her as long as Chaffee had two Bobbies. It took Janet awhile to relax with us in the room, but she finally laughed, even though it hurt her bruised face."

Dennis got serious and said, "John, Janet is a very sweet girl. I hope Steve and I can help her. I don't want her to feel like all guys are like those evil men. If she comes out here to the farm next week, we'll show her that we are gentlemen and so are most other boys or men."

We finished milking with the quiet sounds of the cows chewing their cud and a couple of barn cats mewing for a taste of fresh milk and food. They wanted our attention and petting, too. I took the milk to the strainer, ran the milk through it, and then carried it to the refrigerator on the back porch. Mom was sitting at the table with Steve and Marianne. It was getting close to nine o'clock, and I wanted to lie down somewhere in the living room, but Marianne looked at me and said, "Do you mind if I go to bed? I need to be alone."

Mom patted her arm and said, "You go on. I changed the sheets on Kaitlynn's bed when I was up there with Paul. There are clean towels and a nightgown on the bed."

Marianne stood up and started to turn. Suddenly, she grabbed the table and sat back down again. Steve quickly reached for her and surprised me.

Mom said, "Looks like this day is over for Marianne, too. John, you help her up the stairs. The sedative is working, already."

Marianne stood up again and said, "I'm okay."

Her face went white, and Steve said, "She's going to faint like Mom."

I took one look at her and said, "All right, this day is over." I picked her up and carried her upstairs. Mom and Steve were on my heels following us.

Dennis came in from the barn, saw us all going up the stairs, and asked, "What's going on?" I guess he was curious because you'd have thought there was a magnet attached to the back of Steve, as Dennis followed us up the stairs to Kaitlynn's bedroom.

I laid Marianne on Kaitlynn's bed. and Mom said, "Let's just cover her up and let her sleep. She's had a trying day. I'll check on her when I go to bed."

Steve was pulling off her shoes, and Mom was removing the towels and nightgown from the bed. Dennis had taken a quilt from the back of a chair and handed it to me. The whole scene was surreal. It was as though Marianne was already a sister and needed her brothers desperately. I remembered what Matthew, Kaitlynn's husband, once said, "This is what love is all about—seeing a need and doing something about it."

I said to Mom, "Do you think we should try to wake her and make sure she's okay?"

Mom felt her forehead and checked her pulse. She looked at me and quietly said, "I think she'll be okay? I'll sit here for a little while and watch her. Paul's already asleep."

Marianne stirred, and I said, "Marianne..." She opened her eyes, looked around at us, and smiled. She didn't see Mom on the other side of the bed. She closed her eyes and said, "I didn't know they had an all-male choir in heaven."

Mom laughed. "See, boys, she'll be okay."

Dennis and Steve walked out of the room laughing, and I sighed deeply. Mom linked her arm through mine and pointed to the door. We walked out of the room, shut the door, and giggled, too. We were both glad the day was almost over.

Chapter 6

A week has passed since Janet and Robert were admitted to the hospital. They were both kept for two days to make sure their bruises hadn't hidden something deeper. I was glad because it gave Janet and Robert two days together, and Mr. and Mrs. Weber two days to sort through their thoughts. Pastor Bishop visited with them, and Robert gave his life to the Lord. Janet was still fearful of everyone who walked in her hospital room.

Marianne spent one night and part of the next day with us. She woke up refreshed and said she hadn't slept that well since she was a little kid. She went back to work at the church the following day, which was Tuesday.

Mr. and Mrs. Weber allowed Janet and Robert to come to the farm for a week—even longer if they were hesitant to go home. Marianne and her mom came out to visit every day. They were secretly stripping everything out of Robert and Janet's rooms and switching them. They already had the walls repainted in different colors. Janet had to get a new bedframe because I had broken her bedframe trying to help her.

Mom gave Mrs. Weber money from my deposits in the family account for the bed or whatever she wanted to get in Janet's room. Mrs. Weber didn't want to take the money, but I told her, "I would feel better knowing I had a part in helping Janet recover." Marianne convinced her mom to take the money and use it to get a new bedspread and drapes.

Mom called the railroad office and took a week's vacation, so she could be home with Paul. It worked out well for everyone. She worked on Grandpa's room, boxing things up. I knew it was hard for her, so I was glad Janet and Robert's presence provided a distraction.

After Janet and Robert had been with us for a couple days, I put them on a work schedule with the rest of us. They both thought I had lost my mind, but they cooperated. Janet's first job was to collect the eggs and feed the chickens. My brother Steve's job was to show her where everything was and teach her to reach in the boxes for the eggs and leave the setting hens alone. Steve had to clean the floor of the hen house before Janet went out.

When Steve came back in the house, he said, "I'm praying for Paul's quick recovery. He can have the chickens. I'll take my heifers any day."

When he got the stained, pink plastic bowl to show Janet how to gather the eggs, he said, "This bowl has to soak in bleach, or I'm going to pitch it."

Mom told him to calm down. She'd had the bowl since she got married. Mom took the bowl from Steve and handed him another plastic bowl. She said, "Wait a minute." She took the bowl away from Steve and walked over to the little table under our wall phone. With a marker she wrote, *Paul's egg bowl*. She handed it back to Steve. He walked back out of the kitchen to the back porch and I heard him say. "This is better… more my style."

Mom laughed and I said, "Whatever that meant." I had to laugh, too.

Paul came to the kitchen and sat down at the table, dropping his shoes on the floor beside him. He grimaced as he turned toward me, and said, "I like the pink bowl." He had such a serious look on his face when he added, "Mom, I was thinking about my broken arm and Janet and Robert's bruises. Sometimes we hurt ourselves by our own stupidity, and other times we're hurt by someone else's stupidity. I'm right. Aren't I, John?"

Mom answered for me. "Paul, you are right, but we have to love those stupid people as God loves us. God doesn't like the things they do, but he still loves them. When they confess their wrong doing, God will forgive them. We should, also."

"Yeah," Paul said, "but it's hard."

I said, "Paul, you're right, but keep your thoughts between us until Janet and Robert have healed, okay? Besides, your baby chicks are being born, and Janet has gone out to watch."

Without saying a word, Paul jumped up and grabbed his shoes from the floor, and put them on with one hand like a million dollars was waiting for him in the hen house. He left the kitchen with both shoes untied.

Mom and I both gasped, but I said loudly, "Wait, Paul!"

I was going to tie his shoes for him, but when he got to the three steps going out the back porch, he stopped. Mom was after him in a second. She tied his shoes and gave him another warning. "Don't get your arm dirty or it will get infected."

He said, "I know," and hit the porch steps in a hurry. Mom shook her head and said, "Thank you, Lord."

I said, "Yeah. I thought he was going to skip that last step, like I do."

It took about a day and a half for the setting hens to give us thirteen new baby chicks. Paul and Janet were excited and were already counting the eggs the chicks would give them when they were grown. I don't know what conversations were going on between Janet and Paul in the hen house, but they both seemed to be healing physically and emotionally.

Steve was another story. He had to clean the hen house twice for Paul and was beginning to complain. I decided it would be my turn to clean it next time.

Dennis became Robert's overseer. I gave Robert the job of feeding the barn cats and helping milk the cows twice a day. He caught on quickly to the routine of putting feed into the trough and cleaning the teats, but his hands were still sore from his fight with those thugs, so Dennis and I did the actual milking. He still couldn't use his arm muscles very well either. I hoped that someday we could afford the milking machines, but with only two cows it wasn't worth the expense.

Mom decided that Robert should help with the cooking and baking. She was surprised by his desire to learn. Mom was so good at complimenting and encouraging Robert, he wanted to prepare a whole meal for his parents. He was almost silly about the rest of us appreciating his efforts.

Steve told Robert, "I think it's time for me to go back to helping in the kitchen."

I told Steve, "Your turn won't come again, at least, for another week."

Cousin Stacy came out to the house for four dozen eggs and three apple cobblers. After she paid for them, Mom told Paul to tell Janet and Robert what is done with the money. She had already told Paul to share his egg money with Janet because she was going to share her cobbler money with Robert.

Paul got sixty cents from each dozen eggs, so he gave half to Janet. Cousin Stacey paid two dollars and fifty cents for each cobbler. Robert said, "I can't believe that's all that lady pays for the cobblers because the price at the café is at least a dollar and twenty-five cents on each order." He was thinking and added, "Each pan has six or seven servings.

I watched Robert's face, and he finally said, "Wow, she is making a profit of over six dollars per pan."

I didn't have the heart to tell him that the pans were extra-long and had more like ten servings. I just said, "Robert, that's the way of business. You buy low, and sell high. You buy wholesale, and sell retail."

"When will she be back for more?" He said with a grin.

Mom heard the conversation and said, "Not until next week. Cousin Stacy still has a peach cobbler in her freezer. She'll put two of the apple cobblers in the café refrigerator today, so she'll have those for the late dinner crowd. She said our chocolate cream pie was a big hit. Maybe we can bake two tomorrow and take them into town. We usually don't bake pies unless she calls and says she's behind in her baking. Remember, Robert, we have to charge for the ingredients in the baked goods."

Robert sat there thinking for a second. "You don't take anything out for your work?"

Mom looked at me for help answering his question, so I said, "Mom's very gracious to Cousin Stacey and doesn't charge very much for the ingredients in the baked goods because Cousin Stacy is always ready to help us when there's an emergency. She and her husband took care of Grandpa Ross when Mom was in the hospital, and sometimes she hires Steve at the café when she needs extra workers. She's family, and family helps family out. That's what caring is about."

Robert looked at me thinking intently and said, "Well, you folks know how to do it, don't you?"

I chuckled and said, "Now, that's a business that pays off in rich dividends."

Mom was doing something at the sink and she turned around and said, "John, I could not have explained it any better, myself."

Robert asked, "What do you mean by rich dividends?"

Mom was waiting to see what I would say. I looked at her for help to answer the question, but she just smiled. I decided it was time for Reverend John to step up to the plate.

I said, "God tells us to cast our cares on Him because He cares for us. The best way we can show our appreciation for God's help with our problems is to help other people. By caring for others, God is able to use us to bless others. We become a channel for blessings that flow from God to others. God hasn't failed to stand by this family. After Dad died, Grandpa became our channel of blessing. Since he died, there have been many others, like our neighbors the Jenkins and Cousin Stacy, who do things for us. Hopefully, you will understand that we—the Moore family—are being that channel from God to help your family. That's the way it works."

Janet walked into the kitchen while I was talking and said, "You're a rare family, though."

"No, we're not, Janet. Just wait and see. When you love people and do as God tells you, they don't always return the love, but God always does. That's what I mean about caring being a business that pays big dividends. God is the master banker, the master of everything, and the master at loving us, so why wouldn't He bless people who honor and love Him?"

Robert decided he'd heard enough, I guess. He got up from the table and asked, "Where's Dennis?"

I told him, "Out checking his soybeans."

As he was walking out the door, Robert said, "When we become police officers, I want you to work with me, John. With your life-line to heaven, I want *you* by my side."

Janet and Mom chuckled, and I said, "Sounds like a good deal, Robert."

Janet sat in Robert's vacant chair and asked, "Can I call my mom?"

I reached for the kitchen phone and handed it to her. I smiled and said, "We have a time limit of five minutes."

From the expression on Janet's face, she didn't know whether or not I was serious. She looked at Mom for approval, too. Mom said, "Janet, you can talk to your mother as long as you want and as often as you want."

I chuckled, and Janet said, "Oh," as she put her home number in the phone.

Since it was a nice clear day, I decided to leave the kitchen, and go out to the cornfield. It looked like some of the corn was ripening too quickly or else drying out. An irrigation system would be necessary one of these years. I didn't want to be caught without a corn crop because the soybean and corn crops pay most of the farm bills.

As I was walking toward my cornfield, I saw Dennis in his soybean field talking to Robert.

I said a prayer for them and asked God to help them communicate. They were both going to be seniors at Chaffee High this fall. They were in many of the same classes, but they had different friends, so they didn't know each other very well. Dennis turned seventeen last March, and in just a few days, Robert would be the same age. I was hoping they would become friends, and Dennis would help Robert in his walk with the Lord.

Dennis just handed Robert something. It looked like one of his scripture memory cards. I know Dennis does his memorizing when he goes out to walk around the soybean fields. I had to say, "Thank you, Lord."

∞

I checked some of my cornstalks, and the dry weather had done damage already. I was going to check on our neighbor's irrigation system, and it would have to be soon.

"John! John!" Steve came rushing out of the barn and was yelling at me. My thoughts of irrigation systems, Dennis, and Robert left me. Steve yelled to me, again. "John, come quick!"

Steve was excited or alarmed about something. He yelled, "Hurry!"

I dropped the corncob with all the dry leaves and started running to the barn. Steve had hurried back into the barn. Dennis heard Steve, too, and started running toward the barn. He left Robert standing in the soybeans, looking at him.

When I went through the barn door, Steve was still yelling, "My prize heifer's delivering a calf. She's having trouble."

With all that had gone on lately, I had not noticed she was pregnant. I thought Steve was just fattening this particular female to sell. When Steve bought her at the 4-H sale, the owner must not have known either. I went out the back door of the barn to where Steve was in the barnyard. Dennis and Robert were behind me. Mom sensed something was wrong and followed us from the house. I yelled at her to go back and call the vet. Steve's cow was having a calf and having trouble. She went to the phone in the barn tack room. We keep the vet phone number beside the phone on the wall.

We took the cow into the barn and into a clean stall, and she laid down. I said, "No, gal, you can't lay down. You have a job to do."

I told Robert to take her head harness and pull her up, while the rest of us tried to lift her so she could get back up on her feet. This was all new to Robert, and his serious, bruised face showed some fear, as well as some concentration about what we were doing. I'm sure he had never experienced a situation like this. We worked and encouraged, and finally we got the cow up on her feet.

Mom came back to the stall with Janet and Paul. I reached for the long rubber gloves that Dad had purchased years ago, when he was helping to deliver calves. I don't know how I remembered them being on a high shelf in the stall. I was only twelve years old at the time, but Dad and the vet tried to get a calf turned around inside the cow, and I was watching. I listened to every word Dad and the vet said to each other. I remember the vet saying. "The calf was supposed to come out back feet first, but the calves back legs are caught up under the calf." The vet couldn't help that cow back then. He had tried to get hold of the calf's feet, but he couldn't, and we lost the cow. She died giving birth. Mom cried about that. She said she knew how painful births were. Now, here I am as an eighteen year old kid, no longer twelve and I'm in the same situation.

I looked at the gloves and put one on. I wondered if I should try and do the same with this cow, but the vet drove up beside the barn. Mom went after him. I was ready with the box of gloves, when he walked in and asked, "Have you checked to see if the birth is breech?"

"No," I said. "I got the gloves and decided to wait for you, since I had never done it before."

The vet glanced around at the audience sitting on the top of the stall's half-wall, or hanging over it, resting their chins on their arms. Paul and Janet were sitting on the wall, and Mom and Dennis were watching from the top. Robert had moved to one corner in the stall out of our way, and Steve had the cows harness. The vet said, "Well, let me see here."

He had greased his hand and arm with something and reached inside the cow. Paul, Janet, and Mom looked fearful. I said, "Mom, maybe you had better take the kids back to the house."

Janet raised her eyebrows. She looked at me, and then looked at Mom. She said, "Well, it couldn't be any worse than what happened to me. I want to get down there and comfort the cow."

I was surprised Janet said that. I knew her emotional healing had begun. She jumped down into the stall from the side railing, and she talked to the cow while petting her. I was amazed at the soothing sound of Janet's voice, considering she had been raped by evil men ten days ago.

I looked at Mom, and her mouth was moving. I knew she was praying for Janet and the cow. I remembered the talk I had with Robert less than an hour ago about being a channel for God to bless others.

God was using Mom to intercede and pray for Janet, and Janet was blessing the cow.

The vet was able to turn the calf around and bring the hind legs and feet down. We all stood around and waited. The cow tried to lie down again, but the vet said, "Keep her up." She was in such great pain, and she bellowed out several times.

Janet had tears rolling down her face, and she was saying, "You'll be okay. You did a good job. You'll be okay."

When the vet was finished with the new mother, he said to Janet, "You'd make a good veterinarian or technician some day. You have a very soothing voice, and animals are comfortable around people who talk in a way that is calm and gentle."

Steve stepped up and said, "Thanks, Janet."

Janet looked at Mom, and her face got white, her hand swiped her face and she grabbed for Steve. Between Mom fainting five-days ago, Marianne collapsing Sunday night, and Janet feeling and looking like she was going to faint, I am beginning to worry about the women in my life. There is always some kind of crisis on the farm, so it's a wonder we men don't become weary or faint in our spirits more often. Anyway, when Dennis saw Janet's face, he immediately picked her up, went out the wide front barn door, and headed for the closest water faucet. Mom was right behind him with Paul.

The vet had come out of the stall and was washing his hands in the tack room. He saw what happened and searched in his bag for something. He handed me a small bottle and said, "Here, have her sniff this. I keep it handy for my patient's owners who faint on me. It happens more than you'd think."

Janet was better with the cool water on her face, but I put the bottle under her nose, anyway. She took a whiff, and then really woke up. It was some kind of ammonia, and it worked. She looked at me, smiled, and said. "What did the vet say about me being a comfort for animals? You guys are really the comforters."

All of us, including Robert, were all standing outside the barn with Janet. Paul said, "Janet, in our family, the motto is 'all for one and one for all.' That's why we was all in there with that cow and we're here for you right now."

I heard Mom say, "Paul, we *were* all in there…" Mom was correcting his grammar, but Paul missed his mistake and said, "Yeah, Mom, that's what I said. We care about people like we do my chickens and Steve's cows."

Mom and I chuckled, but I said, "Paul, you are right, but I think I care more about people than I do your chickens. Well, maybe my corn and Dennis's soybeans are on par with your chickens."

Paul looked at Mom smiling and said, "Well-l-l, you guys know what I meant!"

Robert laughed and said, "Yeah, you guys know what he meant!"

I ruffled Paul's hair and chuckled. Mom told Janet and Paul to go back to the house with her, so I decided to go back in the barn to hear any instructions the vet would give Steve, but Steve had already gone back into the barn and came out with the vet. The vet said, "You have a fine calf there, but keep watch on his momma. Keep her in the stall another day, maybe two. She needs rest now. Keep a watch on them both."

Steve had some medication in his hand. The vet added, "See if you can get her to take some of that medicine." He looked at his watch. "Just squirt the medicine into her mouth. It has some added vitamins for the calf and a very mild pain medication. It shouldn't harm the calf."

Steve looked at the medicine in his hand and back at the vet, and said, "Okay."

I was glad that I heard the instructions. I would have worried and wondered what Steve was giving to the momma cow. On the farm, it is always good for two people to know what is going on, because we often have to step in and do someone else's job.

After the vet drove off, Steve and I went back in the barn to check the cow and her calf. Dennis and Robert had gone to the loft, and I could hear them talking. Robert said, "I'm not sure I could ever watch a woman give birth."

I was proud of Dennis when he responded. "Well, Robert, birth is the way God created for life to continue. Just make sure you never do anything to destroy it before it has a chance to live. Don't sleep with anyone but your wife—the person God wants you to live with and have a family with."

Elizabeth Grace Jung

There was a pause in Dennis and Robert's conversation, and I realized I had already forgotten what the vet said to Steve about the medicine. I glanced in the stall, and the little bull-calf was already on his feet. Steve looked at me with pride for his new calf. He was grinning from ear to ear. I suspected dollar signs were going around in his head, but I heard Dennis's voice again. He was saying, "Robert, pray for her, and if she is pregnant, remember God knows. Good people sometime get caught in the effects of other people's wrong-doing, and it wouldn't be Janet or the baby's fault. We would stand by her and give the baby all the love it could get, so it would never grow up to be like the evil men who hurt her."

Some bales of hay came down from the loft with a thud. I yelled. "Dennis, we are down here. Be careful."

He yelled down to me, "Oh, sorry. I thought you had gone to the house with the others. I thought since we were already out here I would throw down some hay for this evening's chores."

I just said, "Thanks."

Dennis and Robert came down out of the loft, and I heard Robert say, "Dennis, I agree. I know what you mean."

We left Steve in the barn and started toward the house. Mom, Janet, and Paul were still outside of the house. Mom was talking to them. Robert looked back at the stall in the open doors of the barn. I glanced at Robert, wondering what he was thinking.

When he saw me looking at him, he said, "I'm going write a book about my week here. There's always something happening here—baby chicks, a baby bull, both my sisters fainting."

I couldn't help but laugh. "You got that right, Robert. Maybe you better think about working with us the rest of the summer."

I was just kidding, but after I said it, it sounded like a good idea. Then again, I'm not sure if I can handle another responsibility. I'm only eighteen. Wait, I had a birthday, and I'm nineteen now. With all that's going on, I forgot the date, and the rest of the family did, too. My heart and mind immediately had to pray. *Lord, I need your help here. I'm not sure if I can handle Robert and his problems all summer.* I heard a voice in my mind again, and the voice said, *I am God. Trust me.*

I shook my head, and Robert said, "John, are you okay?"

108

I don't know why I did it, but I shared with Robert that sometimes things get pretty tense around the farm. I keep telling God I'm only eighteen—now I'm nineteen—and I don't think I can handle any more responsibility, but every time I think it, I hear a voice in my head saying, *I am God. Trust me.*

Robert was looking at me with a silly smirk on his face like he wanted to say something about me hearing voices.

He said, "John, you're not crazy. In school, the rest of us guys used to wonder how you were so good looking and yet so mature. We wondered why you didn't give the girl's a lot of attention. You seem to take all of life with confidence, as my mother would say. The guys admired you and Dennis. I'm sorry we didn't get to know you sooner. Now I know why you're more mature then most teenagers. You've trusted God every day for your crops not to fail and for things like that cow and her calf. We didn't have a clue about things like that. I guess with all that it takes to work a farm without a father or grandfather, you have to trust God to help you. Some of us haven't learned that. We still trust our parents or someone else to do for us. I've been thinking about that. I hope I can learn to trust God, like you do, and not get into the habit of expecting others to do for me when I'm healthy, strong, and capable of doing for myself. I think I've been pretty lazy at home. I'm going to work on that. Besides that, most everything out here on the farm is done for other people, too, not just for yourself. Your crops, your milk, your eggs and even Steve's cobblers feed other people. Most teens like me don't think about all the work somebody did, just so I can eat."

I started to walk back to the cornfield, but I stopped and said, "Robert, I appreciate what you said and your compliments. Thank you, but sometimes I fail. I have feet of clay—feet made of clay." I left him walking with Dennis.

Dennis heard what I had just said to Robert, and Robert asked, "He said he has feet of clay. What's that supposed to mean?"

I looked back at them and heard Dennis say, "That means he fails or makes mistakes sometimes. Like clay, he crumbles and breaks, too. We're not always as mature as the other kids think we are."

Like my little brother, Paul, would say, Robert said, "Oh."

I looked at my watch, and it was almost 3:00 p.m., and I really needed to go back to the house instead of the cornfield. I needed to rest for a half-hour. Mom insisted that we rest each day during the summer. She told each one of us, "You all need to take time alone and rest from your labor each day. It's best for everyone to do it at the same time so no one will be disturbed by others."

I thought Mom was treating us like little boys again, but I quickly learned that my alone time helped me when it came time to do evening chores. I found the rest time was, also, a good time to read some of my farm magazines, especially the latest on fertilizer and crop blights that had been moving our way.

Robert and Janet appreciated their time alone, too. They needed rest for their bodies to heal. Our thirty minutes of rest usually lasted an hour or two.

I searched through the mail for a farm journal, but Dennis had apparently taken them all upstairs to our room, so I went on upstairs and laid on my bed. As I was getting my pillow adjusted, Dennis came in and took one of the magazines off my desk. He sat down on his bed, but laid down his magazine and looked at me. I could see and feel him looking at me. "What?" I said. "John, I think I have feelings for Janet, and I wonder if it's because she's the only girl here besides Mom, or if it's because I've never dated and I'm curious."

I looked over at him and then I turned back and looked at the ceiling. I thought, *God, help me!*

I asked him, "Have you talked to God about your feelings? If not, that's the first thing you need to do."

"Briefly," Dennis answered.

I sat up on the side of my bed. I was searching for words, and a million thoughts came to my mind.

Finally I said, "I heard what you said to Robert in the loft. Let me put things in perspective for you. The way I see it, you were right about what you said to Robert, but you may be concerned about Janet for the very reason you told Robert. Those evil men who raped Janet could have gotten her pregnant, and a baby would come into this world. You, also, may *fear* that for Janet. She is too young to experience that and too young for the responsibility of a baby. Her whole life is in front of her, and a baby needs lots of love, care, and good teaching." I could hear my words and knew that what I was saying was coming straight from Grandpa and Dad. I understood now, what they use to tell me about girls, their age, the responsibility of bringing a baby into the world, and what a man's role in life should be.

I reminded Dennis, "Mom, Dad, and Grandpa did a good job of teaching us that we need to be spiritual role models for the family. We, also, need to be providers and protectors for the family, and that means for our wives, too. We have a natural instinct to protect women when they are in danger. Janet had something happened to her that shouldn't happen to any girl, especially one as sweet and young as she is. I understand how you feel. When Janet almost fainted, you realized how vulnerable she is. Your inner radar went off, and you wanted to help her. Your protective instincts kicked in. My suggestion for you is to be her friend and don't confuse physical responses with what your mind tells you and especially what God tells you. If you don't, what you feel might make you do something you would regret."

Dennis just said, "Yeah, I'm aware of that, also, but I have thought God could be telling me something, too. I noticed Janet long before she had anything ever happened to her and not because she is Marianne's sister, although, that is a plus or maybe a blessing, too. She's pretty and she's musically talented. I don't know, John, maybe we *are* more mature than our high school friends, but how did we learn as much as we know? Other kids have good parents, too. Do you think it's because we had to share responsibilities on the farm and café in town for the welfare of our family? I know I get concerned about mortgage payments, getting a good soybean crop, and if Mom will be okay with everything, if something happens to us. Most kids don't worry about anything except making good grades, winning the next football game, or who likes who in high school. I guess, I'm a worrier, too."

I cleared my throat, readjusted my pillow, and lay back down again. "Dennis, I don't know what you're really feeling or thinking about everything, but trust me when it comes to girls, Dad and Grandpa had some serious talks with me. Even though I adore Marianne and want her to be my wife, I have enough common sense to know that she needs to finish her education, and I need to get a job before I ask her to marry me. You're seventeen, and I'd urge you to think positively about your future before you let a girl turn you away from your goals—no matter how young or sweet she might be. Grandpa used to say, 'Son never let your body override your common sense. Even animals know when it's time to go back to the barn.'

"I've thought about his words many times. When there's a storm coming and the wind is picking up, the cattle face away from the wind. Watch them sometime. You'll see that almost everyone will have their back ends taking the brunt of the wind first. Then there will always be one or two that will have found a nice patch of grass and refuse to turn with the rest of them. People are like that, too. Some men defy the consequences of their actions just to get a pretty girl. Don't let your body rule your good sense, or you will be just like the stupid cattle, who would rather have a pretty blade of grass than protect his face from the storm.

"Sometime, Dennis, when I'm on the tractor, God speaks to me and explains things to me just like Grandpa used to do. I pray a lot about things. Sometimes I even feel so stressed out that I go to the bathroom and cry. Please don't tell Mom. She doesn't need a wimp for a son. She thinks I'm emotionally strong, but as I told Robert, I have feet of clay, and I don't like trying to be strong all the time. Dennis, I need you to be strong, too—even if it's just for me."

Dennis picked up his magazine from the bed beside him and chuckled. He said, "I'll do my best."

I opened the first page of my farm journal and looked at the index. There were several articles I wanted to read, but I heard Mom downstairs in the kitchen, so I stood and straightened out my bedspread.

Dennis stood, too, and said, "Hang in there, John. I'm here for you." He went to the bedroom window and looked out at his soybean crop. He said, "John, I'm going to lose all the soybeans if we don't get an irrigation system, and soon."

I looked at him, wondering how he could change topics so quickly. I thought about my corn and wondered how much I would lose this year.

I said, "Let's go downstairs and talk to Mom. Maybe the family account has enough money in it for us to do something, but with all of the medical bills piling up, I doubt it."

Janet came out of Kaitlynn's room as we neared the stairway. She glanced at Dennis and me. "Oh," she said, "You're going downstairs, too."

Dennis said, "Feelin' better, Janet?"

He stepped back and let her go down the stairs first. Janet said, "Yes, thanks," as she stepped in front of Dennis. All three of us headed to the kitchen.

Chapter 7

There was a big surprise waiting in the kitchen for Janet, Dennis, and me. Mrs. Weber was sitting at the table with Mom, Marianne, and Dr. Lynn. I was very surprised to see Dr. Lynn. He stood up and shook hands with Dennis and me. Janet had gone to her mom to hug her. She acted as though Dr. Lynn's presence was no big deal. My first thought was, *something is wrong,* but he answered my question before I asked.

Dr. Lynn pointed at Mrs. Weber and said, "I met Marianne and her Mom in the hardware store, and they said they were on their way here. I talked them into letting me come with them. You do remember, they are my cousins, don't you? Besides, I have a young patient here. It's still legal to make house calls. Isn't it?" He laughed when he said, "Isn't it."

I laughed and said to Mom, "Well, we've already had an animal doctor here today, might as well have a human doctor, too. Where *is* Paul?"

Mom said, "The last time I saw him he was headed to the barn with Steve to check on the new calf."

Dennis moved toward the door and said, "I'll go get him."

Janet said, "Marianne, you have to see the new baby calf. It's adorable. I helped deliver the calf by holding the cow's bridle and comforting her. The vet said I'd make a good vet because animals are comfortable around me. They know when people talk to them in a calm voice."

Marianne got up and said, "Let's go see that calf."

The girls joined Dennis on his way to the barn. I looked out the back door and started to go with them, but Dr. Lynn said, "John, you stay in here. I want to talk to you and your mother. I was planning on waiting a day or two to see what developed with Paul. He has a check-up on Friday, and I could wait until then, but since I'm here, we'll talk now while Paul is out of the room."

"I stopped by the office and picked up Paul's lab report," he said, as he took papers out of his pocket and handed copies to mom and me. It was Paul's blood work from when his arm surgery was done. I looked at it and didn't understand all the numbers. I said, "You'll have to explain this."

He pointed to Mom's paper and said, "Right here, it says, 'White count 15,000.' A normal count would be around 5,000. The red count looks like it's low normal for now."

I looked at Mom, and I could tell she didn't have any idea what it was all about, either, so I asked, "What would make a white count rise like that?" Dr. Lynn chose his words carefully and said, "Well, at this point we're not sure, but for a boy Paul's age, my first thought is Leukemia. I really would like to have Paul brought back to the hospital to run more blood tests."

Mom had a desperate look on her face. I said, "Dr. Lynn, would you like to see Paul right now?"

"Yes, if you don't mind."

I got up and put my hand on Mom's shoulder, patted her, and I went out the back door. All the boys, Marianne, and Janet were already heading back to the house. I stepped back inside the kitchen and said, "Mom, you should put more cookies out. They're all coming back to the house.

Mom got up, went to the freezer, and pulled out a plastic container filled with the cookies Steve had baked. The boys came into the kitchen one by one, greeting Dr. Lynn and Mrs. Weber. I was glad our long kitchen table seated ten people.

Robert looked at his mother and asked, "Mom, are you getting desperate for us to come home? If not, I'm thinking about staying here all summer and working."

Mrs. Weber was surprised and laughed, "Is my cooking that bad?"

Steve added, "I don't know about your cooking, but Robert's learning to cook food. It won't get an A-grade yet, but it'll pass."

Robert knuckled him on the arm, and Steve chuckled mischievously.

Paul was standing across the room by the cookie platter, looking at Dr. Lynn. He didn't seem to recognize him.

Dr. Lynn smiled at Paul and said, "You don't remember me, do you?"

Mom answered for Paul, "Paul, this is Dr. Lynn. He did the surgery on your arm. He's Mrs. Weber's cousin and he came out to see you this afternoon."

Dr. Lynn motioned to Paul and said, "Come here, son. I just want to make sure your arm has been taken care of by all your brothers. Have they been treating you well? Come here, and let me see."

Paul moved slowly to Dr. Lynn, but he was hesitant to get too close.

Dr. Lynn asked, "Have you been keeping your bandages dry?"

Paul answered, "Yes."

I could tell he was embarrassed to have everyone watching him, so I said, "Mom, why don't you and Paul take Dr. Lynn in the dining room and let Dr. Lynn take a closer look."

Paul didn't wait for an answer. He grabbed two cookies from the platter and headed for the dining room. Mom and Dr. Lynn followed, and so did Janet. I raised my eyebrows at Marianne, and she raised her shoulders, as if to say, *I'm not sure what she thinks she's going to do.*

Dennis poked Robert, "Do you think your arms can take shooting a few baskets?"

Robert got up and patted his Mom on the shoulder like I had done. He said to Dennis, "Bring it on. We'll see."

Steve got up, too. "Let's go."

They got three basketballs out of a bushel basket on the back porch and headed out the back door.

Dennis said, "I'll challenge you to…"

I didn't hear what the challenge was because Mrs. Weber said, "I'm glad we agreed to let the kids come out here. I'm sure my negative feelings about the disaster our family experienced would not have allowed Robert and Janet to heal this fast."

Marianne looked at her mother, and then me. She said, "John, I know the added responsibility probably isn't easy, but I'm grateful, too."

I shrugged my shoulders, but said, "Actually, Janet and Robert fit in well, and they have assumed a part in all the work around here. At the moment, I'm pleased with them, but I can't say the same for Dennis' soybean crop and my corn crop. If we don't get some rain soon, our production's going to be so low that some bills may not get paid.

"I'd intended to talk to Mom about irrigation, but that was when Steve started yelling to me to come to the barn. That little bull calf will come in handy when he's sold. He'll make up for some of the loss in income if the crops don't yield very much."

Mrs. Weber looked over my shoulder at Janet in the dining room and said, "I can't believe Janet's right in the middle of what's going on in the dining room."

I turned and looked, and Janet was helping the doctor rewrap the gauze on Paul's arm. I wondered why she'd come out and washed her hands in the kitchen sink. Apparently, Mom had her First-Aid box with clean gauze and tape handy in the dining room somewhere. Mom was watching Janet and the doctor like we were. She glanced out at Mrs. Weber in the kitchen with an amused expression on her face. Paul wasn't noticing any of us because his arm was still very sore. I suddenly had this really sorry feeling for Paul. Nothing was interesting about Janet helping the doctor. All I could think of was getting Paul back to the hospital to take those additional tests. I felt badly that we had not listened and followed Dr. Lynn's advice at the hospital.

My thoughts were interrupted when Marianne said, "The vet may be right. Janet might have it in her to be a veterinarian or even a doctor or nurse."

Mom glanced our way again and smiled. I said a silent prayer. *Thank you, Lord for Mom, and help Paul to heal.*

I noticed Paul's face was not as pale as it had been. His cheeks were red like he had a fever. Dr. Lynn noticed it, too, and felt Paul's forehead. He shook his head *no,* and Mom felt Paul's face, too.

"Paul, are you feeling okay?"

He shook his head again, and said, "I did when I came in, but now, I don't."

I went into the dining room and asked, "Paul, would you like to go upstairs to your bed?"

I was surprised when he said, "No, I have baby chickens to take care of."

Dr. Lynn smiled, "Paul, you don't have more easles or measles, like you said at the hospital, do you?"

Paul frowned, "It isn't easles, and it isn't measles. Its weasels, and we're getting a new dog to keep them away."

Dr. Lynn looked at Mom, but said to Paul, "You're right, Paul. Its weasels, and they're a nuisance. Does your mom have a thermometer?"

I said, "Stay right there, Mom. I'll get the thermometer."

I got up to get the thermometer out of a kitchen drawer, and heard Paul say, "What for? My chickens don't get fevers."

I had to smile, but Janet giggled and looked at her mother and Marianne still sitting in the kitchen. She decided to join them. She said, "Paul doesn't look well. He looks sick. Maybe I should stay more than a week and help him with his egg business."

I handed the thermometer to Mom. She made sure it was at the starting point and put it in Paul's mouth. I went back to the kitchen. Mrs. Weber said, "Janet, you can come home as soon as you feel ready. Why don't you come Saturday and see your room, and then you can decide?"

I said, "Janet, we may need you to come out for a little while each day and help, anyway."

Dr. Lynn looked very serious, and when he took the thermometer out of Paul's mouth and read it, he shook his head and said, "Son, your body temperature is 101 degrees. Do you think you and your mom could come back to the hospital and let another doctor check you and see why your temperature isn't 98.6 degrees?"

Mom's face looked like she was going to cry, and Paul noticed, "Mom, I'm okay."

Dr. Lynn patted Mom's arm and said, "Mom, we will do what we can to find the cause of Paul's fever."

He turned to Paul. "Let me take you back to Cape Girardeau with me. Mom can come, too. We won't need to call for an ambulance or 911. Janet can take care of your hens and chicks. Will you go so your Mother and I can stop worrying about you?"

Paul looked at me. I had gotten up from my chair in the kitchen and went the few feet into the dining room. I wanted to hear exactly what was being said. Paul's face had such a pathetic fearful expression.. He said, "John, will you come, too?"

"Sure, Buddy, I wouldn't dare stay here and leave you—at Cape Girardeau."

I almost said, 'at the hospital,' but I figured Paul might have thoughts of Dad and Grandpa dying and not coming home. I glanced at Mom, and she was looking at Mrs. Weber in the kitchen.

She said, "Just a minute."

Mom went to the kitchen and asked, "Rachel," that's Mrs. Weber's first name. "Rachel, do you think you can stay here today and possibly tomorrow so we can take Paul back to St. Francis Hospital? "

Mrs. Weber had heard about the lab reports and possible leukemia when Dr. Lynn explained it earlier to me and Mom. She stood up, and hugged Mom. She said, "I'd be glad to stay. You can take Marshall back to Cape Girardeau to pick up his car at the hardware store. Marianne can go back home, if John will take her, to wait for her Dad to come home so he won't be alarmed to find me gone. I'm sure he wouldn't mind coming out this evening, also."

Mom was thinking, and I could hear her commands before she said anything.

"John, ask Steve and Robert to show Rachel where everything is in the kitchen. There's hamburger thawed for spaghetti sauce. Steve can make it. I'm sure Robert will want to help. Dennis can make a salad."

Mrs. Weber asked, "What do you want me to do?"

"Oh, John, go to the linen closet, and get clean sheets and pillow cases for Mrs. Weber. She can take Grandpa's bed. Check his bathroom and give her clean towels."

Mrs. Weber was still looking at Mom. Finally, Mom said, "Rachel, all you need to do is sit by and watch the way these boys operate. Keep all arguing down to a dull roar."

Mom laughed, but it wasn't a natural laugh. Mom was obviously worried about Paul and leaving the situation at home, too.

It was almost four o'clock, already, so I moved quickly. I ran upstairs to the linen closet and got the sheets, pillow cases, and towels and took them to Grandpa's room downstairs. Mom had left a pile of Grandpa's old clothes on the bed, so I stacked them neatly on a chair.

Mrs. Weber came in and said, "John just leave the rest to me."

I took off without even saying thank you so I could talk to the boys outside. All three of them stopped throwing the basketball and looked at me like, *What's going on?*

I looked at them and said as seriously as I was feeling, "Paul has a fever, and Dr. Lynn wants him to go back into the hospital for further tests. Mom left some orders for us to do. Steve, Mom wants you to make some spaghetti sauce, Robert your job is to cook the noodles, and Dennis, you make a salad for supper. Mrs. Weber's going to spend the night in Grandpa's room, and I'm going with Mom and Paul. We're taking Marianne home on our way. Mrs. Weber is in charge. Please show her what gentlemen and good helpers you are. Dennis, I should be back in time to milk the cows. Janet will take care of the chickens for Paul. Any questions?"

Steve threw the ball at the hoop and said, "Yeah, what time is it? I should start the spaghetti sauce now."

Robert said, "I've never cooked spaghetti noodles before. You'll have to show me what to do."

I turned to go back into the house and heard Steve say, "There's nothin' to it. Let's go in and tell Paul that we'll be prayin' for him."

I walked back toward the house and prayed. *Thank you, for that last remark Steve made, and Lord please help Paul.*

Chapter 8

Mom left for Cape Girardeau with Dr. Lynn. I took Marianne home in the truck and went back to make sure Mom's orders were carried out. Steve had already started the spaghetti sauce, and Dennis was washing lettuce. Robert was sitting at the table reading the label on a large package of spaghetti noodles while Janet and Mrs. Weber were changing the sheets on Grandpa's bed.

I thought, *I used Grandpa's bathroom a lot, so does Dennis and Steve when they come in from the barn. I wonder if I've left anything dirty in there. I better check.*

I walked past Janet and Mrs. Weber to the bathroom. I said, "Oh," and turned around. Janet grinned

"It was a mess," Janet said, "Dennis picked up all the dirty towels, and I shined it up."

She laughed and Mrs. Weber was chuckling too.

"John, I don't know what you've done to my family to make them work, but I like it."

I smiled with them, "It's all about consequences! Around here we like to see the results of our work, and we don't like the consequences when we don't work."

Janet looked at me. She said, "Yeah, no money, no fun. Mom, the Moore boys have projects that pay them, and they put money into the family account after they've given to God. If they need or want something, they go to the family account to see what deposits they've made. If they don't have enough, they can't buy what they want."

The look on Mrs. Weber was priceless. I wished I had a camera. She raised her eyebrows, smiled; like she had suddenly had a treasure placed in her hands, and was puzzled, too, about why someone would give her something. She said, "John, my daughter is collecting eggs! This I have to see."

Janet giggled and said, "Com' on, Mom, I'll take you to the hen house now. We'll see what's there."

I asked, "Has the floor been washed today?"

"Yes, Paul showed me how to put that stinky stuff in that bottle on the hose and wash it down."

I sighed and relaxed because I was afraid Paul might have tried it and gotten the solution all over him, again.

Janet said, "Don't worry, Paul told me to be very careful and not get the stuff on me."

They started out the door, and I said "Janet, let me wash the floor the next time. Did Paul give you any rubber gloves?"

"I used your Mom's gloves out of the shed."

I said, "Good, Janet," and turned away to go upstairs. I washed up, put fresh clothes on, and headed for the hospital. As I was leaving, Dennis and Steve were setting the table. The conversation was about how they set tables and wrapped napkins at the café. Robert was listening as though it was some great feat that they had done at the café. He asked, "What did you get paid for rolling napkins and setting tables?"

I thought, *that question sounded like Steve. He's always thinking about some money-making project.*

Mrs. Weber and Janet came back in the house from the hen house. Mrs. Weber said, "Janet, you've been here almost a week. Do you have a project yet?"

Janet looked at me like I was supposed to answer, but she said, "I've been helping with the henhouse, collecting eggs and cleaning them, too. Paul shared his money with me when he sold some eggs to their cousin, Stacy, for the café in town."

Dennis asked if I was staying for supper. I told him no because Mom had not eaten, and I wanted to make sure she went to the hospital cafeteria and had supper.

Steve stirred his tomato sauce and said, "Good, I don't want her fainting again. I'm not good at being a nurse for any reason."

Janet said, "John, I brought in six eggs. They're in the porch refrigerator. I'll wash them."

I said, "Thank you, Janet."

Mrs. Weber was looking around at all the activity in the kitchen. She looked at me and said, "Interesting!"

Steve found some French bread in the freezer and had Robert laying it out on a cookie sheet. They were really concentrating on what they were doing."

I said, "Well, guys, I'm out of here. I'll call if I'm going to be home after seven-thirty. You don't need to save any spaghetti for us. Mrs. Weber, you just sit down and enjoy being served."

Mrs. Weber smiled and said, "Bye"

As I walked through the back porch, Janet was already getting the eggs out of the refrigerator to wash them. I said, "Bye, Janet, and thanks."

As I walked to the car, I wondered what Janet was thinking about. Her face was still a little swollen, and her bruises were turning yellow. I'm glad we were keeping her busy. She didn't look very good, but hadn't complained.

I thought, *when I get home this evening I'm going to talk to Janet because she may be hiding what happened to her and putting it all deep inside her. It helps to keep her busy, but she still needs to sort out her feelings and not bury them.*

I prayed for Paul and Janet all the way to Cape Girardeau. I didn't know what the problem was with Paul, but it worried me. Lines in a song popped into my mind. *Don't worry, be happy.* I had to ask, *Lord, are you talking to me again?*

It was getting cloudy when I turned onto Highway 55. I wondered if it would rain. I noticed the brilliant blue sky behind the dark clouds, and I couldn't help but pray as I watched the traffic near the hospital.

Lord, you made the clouds and the beautiful blue sky. The stars will shine tonight, and they will still be there behind the clouds. So, God, I know you're still in control. Help me remember that, no matter what happens with Paul.

I parked the car in the hospital's multi-level parking garage. God seemed to be talking to me ever since I left the farm. He reminded me that He was the one that hung those stars in space, and as long as I listened to Him, I would have the wisdom I needed to handle Paul's problem, Mom's health, Janet and Robert, and all the things that go on at the farm, no rain for the crops, all of it felt like it was on Mom and my shoulders. I was talking to myself, again, when I opened the hospital door, I said, "Lord, You don't have to give it to me all at once." Or, like Steve likes to say, "sock it to me." I really felt like that was what had happened.

I stepped on into the waiting room and pharmacy area, and I heard a familiar voice, "John, are you praying again?"

I knew the face, but for a second I didn't recognize the bomb squad officer in his street clothes. He introduced himself to me and said, "I'm Tim Waine. I met you on that Sunday afternoon at the Weber's place in Chaffee. I heard you say when you lifted Mr. Weber out of the car. 'God, help this man and his family.' You, also, sat down in your car and prayed out loud before you left. We were all impressed with you. How're things going with the Weber family?"

I took me a moment to get my thoughts back to the present and why I was at the hospital.

I said, "Janet and Robert are out at the farm with us, and on the surface they seemed to be doing all right. I plan to talk to Janet alone tomorrow because she might be hiding her feelings. I don't want her to have a sudden panic attack later. Outwardly, the bruises on Robert and Janet are healing well."

Then Officer Waine asked, "How long will they be on the farm?"

"Marianne and her mother are redoing the bedrooms at the Weber house, so when Janet and Robert come home all the bad memories will be somewhat obscured."

"That was good thinking," he said.

I wondered why he was at the hospital, so I asked, "What brings you here?"

Officer Waine's face was one big smile when he said, "I'm a new father of a baby girl—seven pounds, four ounces. I've been up all night, so I'm headed home to shower and sleep, but what brings you to the hospital?"

I congratulated him on his new daughter, but looked at the door and the people coming in and said, "My youngest brother had surgery on his broken arm, and his blood tests came back with a high white count. For some reason, his hemoglobin is low. He had a fever, so Mom brought him back in for more tests. Dr. Lynn said it might be Leukemia, but we won't know until more tests are run." I glanced at my watch but went on talking. "Mom brought Paul in about an hour ago, and I'm on my way to join them. Mrs. Weber is staying at the house with the teenagers. I imagine she will need rescuing by the time I get home."

Officer Waine patted my upper arm and said, "John, I should let you go. I thought your platter was full already, but someone just handed you another dish—right?"

"Yes, but God is good. He's my strength right now."

He started to move toward the door, but said, "Are you still thinking about becoming a police officer?"

I raised my eyebrows and smiled. "God didn't tell me to think about it. He told me to go for it. In fact Robert Weber and my brothers, Dennis and Steve, have joined me. We're going to replace one bad cop with four good ones."

The officer had a surprised expression on his face.

"Well, John, you can use me as one of your reference, but now you better go see your mother and brother, and I had better go home. Hope to see you soon."

He went on out the door, and I went to the reception desk and asked if Paul was in a room. I had no idea where to go. The white-haired lady with a pink jacket called several places and finally found Paul and Mom on the pediatric ward. He had just been admitted.

"Where's that?" I asked.

I must have had a forlorn look on my face because another lady said, "I'll take you."

When she said, "take you," it reminded me of the word *forsake* and what God told Joshua in Joshua 1:5: "I will never leave you nor forsake you."

I smiled, and the lady looked at me as if she thought I was delighted that she would show me the way to the pediatric ward. I really was happy because I didn't even know what pediatric meant. I smiled more, though, because when she told me she would take me it reminded me that God was not going to forsake me. He was going to lead the way through this elderly woman.

We got on the elevator together, and she asked, "Do you have a family member here?"

"Yes, my ten year-old brother is in for tests."

I noticed hearing-aids in her ears. Then I realized why she spoke hesitantly. She probably learned to speak through therapy. I sometimes feel sorry for myself for things I can't control, but I was the one blessed by her sweetness and help that day. I could hear, walk and was not sick as most people in the hospital were that day.

I said to her, "Thank you for asking, we are hoping Paul will be okay."

She smiled again as the elevator stopped, and we stepped out. The lady pointed down the hall.

I nodded and loudly said, "Thank you."

I felt self-conscious, walking down the hall like a little boy in a great big body. I had to tell myself, *Get your act together.* I stopped at the nurse's station and asked which room Paul Moore was in. A girl looked at her computer monitor and told me, "room 2025." I looked at the signs on the corners of the halls and went in the direction the arrow pointed.

I glanced in one of the rooms, and there were nurses on two sides of a bed. I suddenly had a terrified feeling like it was Paul's room. I wanted to cry, but I couldn't. I was needed here at St. Francis Hospital for Paul and Mom. I heard a voice in my head again. The voice said, *Do not be terrified! I won't forsake you.*

I shook my head, remembering the scripture verse that I had memorized and made as my motto. God was using it just for me.

I walked in Paul's room, and Mom was watching Paul sleep. I asked her if she had eaten anything.

She frowned and said, "I'm not hungry."

I went back into the hall, intending to go back to the nurse's station and see if someone would order a sandwich or something for Mom, but Dr. Lynn was talking to another doctor down the hall. He saw me and beckoned for me to join them.

Dr. Lynn said, "Good to see you again, John. This is Dr. Sides. He's a hematologist and he's read Paul's lab tests. The most recent tests show Paul's white count at a dangerously high level, and his hemoglobin is low. We think he needs to be flown to St. Louis. Would you and your mother agree to that?"

"Have you talked to Mom about it yet?"

Dr. Sides said, "No, I was on my way to see Paul and your mother when I ran into Dr. Lynn."

All I could think to say was "Oh." I turned to Dr. Lynn and said, "This stress is going to hurt Mom. It's only been four months since her kidney transplant. She fainted Friday when Paul broke his arm because she hadn't eaten after a stressful day at work. Is there time to get her a sandwich?"

Dr. Sides took my arm and said, "Let's go see Paul and your Mom."

We walked back to Paul's room. Dr. Sides introduced himself and then walked over to Paul. He felt his pulse and looked at his chart.

"His temperature is still 101 degrees. Mrs. Moore, I've reviewed Paul's latest lab report, and his white count is at a very dangerously *high* level and his hemoglobin is low. We need to act quickly, and I suggest we fly Paul to St. Louis."

I could see Mom's emotional radar go up. She looked at Paul and then at me.

"What do you think, John?"

I shook my head and said, "We should do what the doctors think is best. Do you feel up to making a trip to St. Louis?"

Mom didn't answer my question. She just looked at Paul and reached for his hand. I thought she was going to lose it, and if she did, I would, too. Inside I was crying, but outwardly, I wasn't.

I looked at both doctors and asked what would make a white count raise and a red count drop at the same time to make a little boy sick. Dr. Lynn turned to Dr. Sides and hesitated.

Dr. Sides answered, "Leukemia, Toxoplasmosis, which is sometimes called cat fever; a toxic substance absorbed into the skin could cause the problem."

He looked at me when he said that, and my head began to reel. I looked at Mom, "That's it!"

All three of them looked at me, waiting for an answer.

I told them, "About ten days ago, Paul and I cleaned his chicken house. Paul insisted on using what Grandpa used to hose down the floor. He got a bottle from Mom's shed and poured it into the container attached to the hose. I checked the bottle, and it said 'not dangerous for poultry.' That's why Grandpa purchased it. Paul was so anxious to use the hose and sprayer that he didn't attach the container lid on tight enough. I fixed it for him, but he had already sprayed it on himself and everywhere else. I had to tell him to be careful, several times, but he thought the walls and everything in the hen house should be sprayed. I didn't think about it at the time. I figured a little boy couldn't get into much trouble with a hose, but apparently Grandpa always did the spraying. Paul was never allowed. He had gloves on, but his clothes were soaked, and he was wearing short sleeves."

Dr. Sides asked me if I had gotten any on me. I told him, perhaps a little. Dr. Lynn was talking to Mom while Dr. Sides and I were talking. Dr. Lynn was calling our house. He asked me, "Which one of your brothers should I talk to?"

"Dennis, but let me talk to him."

I took the phone, and it was still ringing. Dennis finally answered.

"Dennis, the doctors think the stuff Paul uses to disinfect the hen house is what made him sick. I need you to go out to Mom's shed and get the bottle on the shelf over the sink. It has a picture of a hen with a broom in her hand, sweeping. Take the phone with you."

I waited, and I could hear Dennis open the creaky, shed door. Steve and Robert were shooting hoops, and I heard Steve tell Robert he did a good job on the spaghetti noodles.

Robert said, "Thanks, next time I'll do the sauce."

Dennis came back on the phone, "I found it."

"Good, I'm going to let you read the ingredients to Dr. Sides."

Dr. Sides took the phone and started writing on a note pad from his shirt pocket. Dennis couldn't pronounce some of the words, so he was spelling them. As Dr. Sides said the words Dr. Lynn was writing them down, too.

I watched Mom, and her face was getting white. I hurried into the hall and found a nurse.

"I need a Coke, and I need it quick. My mother hasn't eaten, and she's on the verge of passing out."

Dr. Lynn stepped out to see where I went, and he heard what I said.

He said, "Pam, get the Coke, please."

We walked back inside the room just as Mom slumped over in her chair. I went to the bathroom, got a cold wash cloth, and wiped Mom's face. She woke up just as the nurse walked in with a Coke. Dr. Lynn took the Coke and said, "Mrs. Bonnie Moore, We can't have two patients here. Drink this Coke."

Mom apologized feebly. She looked up at me and said, "I'm sorry, John."

Paul woke up because of the commotion. He saw me wiping Mom's face and said, "I didn't break my arm again, Mom. I just don't feel good. I don't even have measles—I mean weasels."

Dr. Sides didn't know what was funny, but Dr. Lynn did. We both laughed. Paul broke the tension we were feeling.

The nurse was standing there. She asked. "Do you still need me?"

Dr. Lynn said, "Yes, go get Mrs. Moore a ham and cheese sandwich, please."

Paul said, "I'd rather have pizza."

Mom relaxed with a big sigh and smiled. Dr. Sides was on the phone calling down to the pharmacy for something to counteract the disinfectant Paul had gotten into his system. He asked for it to be brought to room 2025. For some reason, the number started going over and over in my mind. I asked, "Do you think this will solve the problem?"

Dr. Lynn said, "I don't know, but we'll see. Right now, I'm still thinking St. Louis Children's Hospital is an option. We'll wait and see what a dose of the medication does."

Dr. Sides had gotten off the phone and said, "I want to get another lab report about two hours after Paul is given the antidote."

I don't know why I asked, "Do you think giving him blood would work? I'll give him some of mine."

Dr. Sides said, "John… it is John, isn't it? I was just thinking that, too, but we need to check your blood to make sure whatever disinfectant you were exposed to hasn't affected you, also."

I assured him I had on gloves, and I made Paul turn off the hose before I tightened the bottle on the hose.

He said, "Well, let's check on it, anyway, and if it is good, we'll go ahead and take some for Paul, assuming everything else is a good match for a blood transfusion for him."

I knew the only disinfectant I got was from Paul's irrational spraying. Then I thought about Janet and Steve doing Paul's work for him.

I looked at Mom, and her color was getting better, so I went to the other side of Paul's bed and called home again. I could tell the doctors were wondering who I was calling, but I had to call before I could say another word or go down to the lab.

Steve answered. I said out loud, "Thank you. Lord."

Steve said, "I'm not God, this is Steve."

I chuckled, "You are the one I want to talk to. When you hosed down the hen house, did you use any disinfectant?"

"No, I just used the hose and water."

"What about Janet?"

He turned to her and asked her. "She said only once because you'd already cleaned it. She used gloves when she cleaned it, and she didn't use much because the smell was so bad."

I took a big sigh of relief and said, "Thank, God," again.

"John, you are talking to Steve, not God." Steve laughed and asked, "What's going on?"

I told him about the disinfectant possibly being what made Paul sick. I said, "The doctors were giving him something for it, and I was going to be checked, too."

He said, "John, you're germ free. I just know it." He chuckled again.

"Okay, Buddy, be funny, but Paul's a sick boy, and it might have been the disinfectant that did it. Call Pastor Bishop or have Mrs. Weber do it, so he can get the prayer chain at church started for Paul."

I'm sorry, John. I'll call him."

I put the phone down slowly and turned around to find a nurse giving Paul a shot. He whimpered, but closed his eyes and went back to sleep. The room seemed to be busy as a Lab Tech stepped in and asked, "Are you John?"

"Yes," I answered.

Dr. Lynn and Dr. Sides both stepped out in the hall. I sat down on the end of Paul's bed and rolled up my sleeve. The technician swabbed my arm and drew out two vials of blood from a vein on the inside of my elbow—then put a Band-Aid on it. I raised my eye-brows at Mom and said, "Easy as one-two-three."

Mom put on a faint smile. "Thanks John, you're my hero!"

I realized that Mom's sandwich had not come. "I'm going after that sandwich for you."

I didn't get very far, because the nurse Dr. Lynn had told to get the sandwich met me at the door.

She said, "Here's your mom's ham and cheese on rye, and here's one for you with chips."

She smiled at me, and I'm sure I looked like a giant to the nurse because she couldn't have been more than five feet tall. I gave the tray to Mom. She was ready to eat.

"Oh, they put fruit on here, too. I'll have to thank her for this."

Mom devoured the food as though someone might take it away from her. Maybe she thought she might not be able to eat anything if they took Paul to St. Louis. I enjoyed my sandwich, too.

The phone rang, and Mom stood up from the chair she had sat in for the past two hours and answered it. It was Marianne.

She said, "Mom called me. How are things going with Paul?"

Mom said, "We don't know just yet. In another hour or two they will take another blood test and see what Paul's white count is doing."

Mom was looking at me, and I thought it might be Pastor Bishop. She thanked her for praying for them and said, "Would you like to talk with John?"

She handed me the phone. It was good to hear Marianne's voice. I can't help myself, she has a comforting effect on me. I told her what I knew and if things didn't improve with the antidote, Paul would be flown to St. Louis Children's Hospital.

Marianne said, "If you don't mind, I'm going to call Kaitlynn and Matthew. They can start the prayer chain at their church. I know Kaitlynn will want to know. I'll call her—that's if you don't mind."

I was relieved to have someone be strong for me, so I said, "Yes, please do. She will want to know, and Marianne, thanks. You are the greatest."

I paused, and she said, "Am I supposed to fill in the last word—I am the greatest monkey, piano player, or—what?"

"Marianne, you are that and much more, and I appreciate you. Thanks for being you."

"You are welcome. I'll call Kaitlynn, right now. I'll see you later. Bye—I love you."

I just said *thanks* again. I know she understood my feelings at that moment. I'll have to tease her about being the "greatest monkey."

Two hours had passed, and we had not heard from the lab or the doctors. I was beginning to think maybe I should go home and help milk the cows. The phone rang and Mom was dozing, so I answered it. It was Dennis. "If you were about to leave to come home, you needn't come.

Robert wanted to try milking, and he did very well. The stalls are cleaned, the cats fed, and Mrs. Weber even came to the barn and did that. How is Paul?"

I told Dennis, that It had been two hours, and we were still waiting on lab reports. "If my blood is okay, I'm going to give some of mine to Paul. They said it might help. But we haven't heard on my blood tests to see if it is okay."

"Well, if they need mine, I'll come up there and donate blood, too."

"Thanks."

Doctor Sides walked in as I was talking, so I told Dennis I would call him back.

"It's been more than three hours since we administered the antidote, so now we check to see if the white count has come down."

A lab tech had come in with Dr. Sides, and the technician went right for Paul. I hated to see them stick a needle in Paul's arm again, but I knew they had to do it. Dr. Sides asked Mom how she was feeling. She told him much better, but she couldn't think about herself at the moment. Dr. Sides looked at me, "John, when you get home, destroy whatever is left in that bottle. You show some evidence of having an elevated white blood count also, although it is still in the range of normal—just a high normal. I think you can fight off the problem, however just in case we would like to give you a shot, also. I would like to give Paul a unit of blood, but not yours. Do you have other family members who could give?"

"They will be here in twenty minutes."

I waited for the lab tech to move, and I grabbed the phone and called Dennis. When he answered, I said, "Dennis, high-tail it up here. They can't use my blood."

"I'll bring Steve, too. "

I added, "You will have to have Mrs. Weber bring you as I have the truck, and Mom's car is up here, too."

He turned to Mrs. Weber and she got on the phone. "We'll all *be* there in twenty minutes, or as long as it takes for all of us to get in the car, and head to Cape Girardeau."

I said, "Okay, I'll wait for you at the door; park in the parking garage on the east side of the hospital."

I told Mom I would go down and wait for them. I did, and when I neared the coffee shop and gift shop, I smelled food and told myself to go in and look for something that Mom could eat. Sweet rolls and doughnuts caught my eye immediately. I purchased the largest sweet roll that I could find for Mom and I ate one, too, with a cup of coffee while I waited.

In just a little more than twenty minutes, Mrs. Weber, Robert, Janet, Dennis, and Steve were going into the parking garage. The parking crew men watched all of them as they came out of the lower level of the parking garage and walked toward the hospital. One of them said to the other, "There must be a teen-ager admitted to the hospital."

I heard it and said, "No, just a ten year-old boy, whom everyone loves. He may have just a reaction from something on the farm or leukemia."

One of them said, "Oh, I'm sorry to hear that."

"Two of those boys are our brothers. The others are staying with us for a while."

By then, Dennis and Steve had arrived at the door. Mrs. Weber was trailing behind them with Janet and Steve. I was glad to see them. One of the parking crew men opened the doors and said, "Hope all goes well for your loved one."

Steve's mouth went immediately open. "It will. He's gonna get my blood—or Dennis's blood."

I just smiled at the man, and went on through the doors after them. I was to take them to the lab. I stopped at the desk to get directions. The volunteer looked at Mrs. Weber like she was the one to give blood. The teen-agers with her all looked too young. He said, "I'll go with you."

Thirty minutes later, both Dennis and Steve had given a pint of blood. I was concerned about their ages, but since they both had adult body size on them—Dennis being six feet and Steve at almost fifteen and five-feet-eleven inches, I guess the technicians thought it okay. They questioned the ages, and I told technician that I would sign for them. Steve said, "Yeah, he was emancipated two years ago, so he can sign."

I could have socked Steve because I had to explain it was to carry on the responsibilities on the farm and to sign whatever needed signatures. The lady just said, "Oh."

We walked out of the lab with a smile because the technician offered the boys each a sucker. They took them and put them in their pockets. Steve said, "I might need this to bribe Paul. He'll take a sucker in a minute because he hasn't had candy in a long time."

He was chuckling to himself, but I could tell it was a nervous laugh. We went to the elevators to go up a floor to level two. We could have gone up the stairs, but I missed where they were located. When we got off the elevator, Dr. Lynn was standing in the hall by the elevators, talking to his cousin, Mrs. Weber. I thought he had gone home, but he apparently came back to check on Paul or someone else. He looked at me, and I guess he knew what I was thinking, because he said, "The house got awfully quiet and lonely, so I decided to come back and check on you and your mother. Did she ever get anything to eat—and you, too?"

I vaguely remembered Marianne saying Dr. Lynn's wife had passed away about three years ago, and his children were all grown and away in college or married.

"Thanks for asking. They brought us some sandwiches, and thanks for coming back, too."

I thought, *wouldn't it be nice if Dr. Lynn and Mom could get to be friends?* I said to myself in a whisper, "Lord, hold my thoughts on that."

Steve looked at me strangely. "John, why do you talk to yourself?"

"Because—I guess—I talk to God all the time and it sometimes comes out louder than I want."

Dr. Lynn directed us to the family waiting room across from the nurses' station. I told the guys that I would come back for them one by one, but I already sensed Robert and Steve were in some kind of mood that I didn't appreciate. They were laughing and talking about the young student nurses. I overheard a remark and promptly scolded Steve. "You are in a hospital and there are people here in a life and death situation. Your brother is one of them. Give the patients enough respect to keep your thoughts to yourself for the next thirty minutes."

Mrs. Weber said, "—and that goes for you, too, Robert."

Janet was very quiet and I feared what this visit to the hospital so soon after her release might be doing to her.

I said, "Mrs. Weber, do you think you can take Janet down to the gift shop and get something for Paul?"

I got out my wallet and handed Janet a twenty dollar bill. I winked at Mrs. Weber, and she caught my drift and said, "Sure, we can do that."

They turned to go to the elevators, and I turned around to go to Paul's room just when Pastor Bishop and Marianne stepped off the elevator. It was good to see them. I shook Pastor Bishop's hand, gave Marianne a quick hug, and said, "Would you sit down here with the boys? I'll be back to get Dennis and Steve one at a time to visit Paul.

Your Mom and Janet got on the other elevator as you got off. They went down to the gift shop."

While I was talking to the boys and Mrs. Weber, Dr. Lynn must have gone back to Paul's room because he came around the hall corner and said, "John."

He had a concerned look on his face. I started toward him, and Dennis saw his expression and said. "I'm coming, too."

We walked back to Paul's room. Paul's face had a pale look, and Mom's was as white as a sheet again.

"Mom, what is it? Are you okay?" I asked.

"I'm okay. I'm just getting tired sitting here."

I looked at Dr. Lynn, and he said, "I'm taking your mother down to the cafeteria. She needs to move around a little bit and get her mind on something else—at least for one hour."

Dennis took Mom's hand. "Mom, I'll stay with the boy. Please, go."

Dr. Lynn reached for her other hand and said, "Come." Mom responded and got up from her chair.

Dennis looked at Paul, walked over to the bedside, and said, "Paul, wake up, this is your big brother Dennis. Mom needs you, so fight, boy. Fight this infection."

Paul stirred, and said, "I'll carry the clothes in a basket the next time."

Dennis glanced at me and back at Paul with a smile. "No, Paul, I'll carry them downstairs the next time."

Paul tried to turn on his side and whimpered, but he said, "Okay."

Dennis looked like he was going to cry, so I said, "Dennis, he's going to make it!"

Dr. Sides stepped in the room, heard what I said, and said, "Yes, I believe he's going to make it. The white cells have come down, but not as much as I had hoped, we should know more in twenty-four hours. We are going to go ahead and give him a transfusion. We'll give him one from Dennis first."

He looked at Dennis and said, "Are you Dennis or Steve?"

"I'm Dennis. Steve is down in the waiting room."

Dr. Sides shook Dennis's hand and said, "You and your brother are a good match for Paul."

Dennis' face showed pleasure. The opposite of what it was a minute before. He said, "I'm glad. He's my buddy."

A nurse came in with the blood pouch and attached it to the I.V. stand beside the bed with Paul's other medication. Dennis was watching every move she made and finally asked, "Is that my blood?"

The nurse glanced at Dennis and asked, "I don't know. Did you give blood for this young man?"

"I hope that's my blood and, yes, I did give blood for this young man. He's my brother."

The nurse chuckled a little and said, "Well, we are hoping your blood does your brother some good. We'll keep your other brother's blood on reserve."

Dr. Sides beckoned for me to come out in the hall. I followed him. He turned to me and said, "John, Dr. Lynn is talking to your mother. We still want to rule out the possibility of leukemia, so we are going to watch him for a few days and run more tests. It there's not a significant change in three days, we'll want to take him to Children's Hospital in St. Louis. We're keeping that as an option."

All I could think to say was, "I appreciate what you're doing."

Then I remembered what was said about my blood, so I asked. "Dr. Sides, someone said my blood was altered, too. Was that you?"

"Yes, it was me. You're still in the range of normal, so I wouldn't worry about it. If you should start having a fever, be sure to call me."

I thought about the corn and soybeans, and how they needed rain. I shook my head and said, "Dr. Sides, in the past year my grandfather died, my mother had a kidney transplant, my sister's husband developed Hodgkin's cancer, my girlfriend's family were almost killed by some hoodlums, our henhouse had weasels, my corn and Dennis' soybeans are starting to dry up for lack of rain, and now Paul is sick. Do you think you can clone me, so I can be two people to take care of the family and farm? Dr. Sides, I can't afford to get sick."

Dr. Sides patted me on the upper arm and asked, "How old are you, John?"

"I'm eighteen, sir. No, I turned nineteen a week ago, but with so much going on, the day passed and no one noticed, not even me. I've been an emancipated young person for almost two years as I had to be the sole support of the family until Mom was able to go back to work. I've had more responsibility than young people ten years older. Sometimes I wish I could be a little boy again."

I must have sounded like a little boy, too, as Dr. Sides said, "John, hang in there. We will do what we can for you and your family. You make sure you don't skip any meals and get rest. I want to check your blood count in a week, okay?"

I sighed and said, "Thanks—thanks for being here tonight."

He smiled. "Dr. Lynn impressed me with how important this family is to him and you are to each other, John, so I decided to come back after my family dinner. You are an okay person, John. I'm going home, now, but I'll call back in later to see how Paul is doing. The transfusion should kick in pretty soon."

I walked on down the hall with Dr. Sides. Steve and Robert were giggling like two little girls. I said, "Excuse me, Doctor. I have two little boys to deal with."

Dr. Sides grinned and said, "Well—goodnight."

He walked on toward the elevators, and I said, "Okay, Steve, let's go."

He got up and punched Robert on his way out of the chair. I was about to give him a good tongue-lashing, but Marianne said, "A week's worth of tension has been spilled."

"Oh. Steve, let's go."

I didn't say any more to Steve and he turned into a gentleman as we walked down the hall. I watched Steve's face as he approached his little brother's bed. He said, "He's *not any* better?"

Dennis said, "Only a little. That's my blood they're giving him. The technician said they were putting yours on reserve for Paul. He may need it, too."

It hit Steve hard. I could tell when he asked, "He's not going to die, is he?"

Paul moved and opened his eyes. He saw Dennis still beside him. He frowned and turned toward Steve and me. He yawned and said, "Steve—only...."

Steve stepped closer to Paul and said, "Only what—Paul?"

Dennis spoke up and said, "Paul, are you awake?"

He answered, "Of course."

Steve patted his leg. "Yeah, buddy," but he hurried for the bathroom with tears in his eyes. I heard him say, "God, he's my little brother. I need him."

I knocked on the bathroom door and said, "Steve." He opened it, and I gave him a big bear hug. He just said, "Thanks, John. Tell me what is going on. Where's Mom?"

"Dr. Lynn insisted Mom go with him somewhere—possibly the cafeteria. He acted like he wanted her to get out of the room for a little while and walk or get something to eat."

Steve went back into the room and flopped in the chair Mom had been sitting on. I couldn't read his expression. I think he was still trying to get himself together—*man that he thinks he is.*

I stepped out of the room and saw Mom and Dr. Lynn approaching the room with Mrs. Weber and Janet. They stopped in the waiting room. Dr. Lynn came on down to the room.

Dr. Lynn wasn't fooled with Steve's countenance. He walked over toward Steve, looked out the window, and casually turned around, and put his hand on Steve's shoulder. I waited to see what he was going to say.

He said, "You young men in this room—all four of you came into my life a week or ten days ago. You really smashed in the door, so to speak. I was a lonely man and, all of a sudden, I find a mother and her four sons overwhelming me with feelings. I don't know what or how to handle them. Marianne and I have talked several times, and she is convinced that there is no other family like yours and that makes me want to know each of you better each day. She also told me that God has a way of slapping us in the face sometimes with reality, and meeting all of you, showed me what a recluse I've become. I have even been ignoring my own children.

"I want you to know that I have begun to care for Paul beyond being just a patient, and I'm going to see that we get to the bottom of *why* he is ill. I'll be with you, each step of the way, until he is better."

Dr. Lynn squeezed Steve's shoulder and patted it. "Is that okay with you, Steve?"

Paul answered for Steve and said, "Yes."

We all looked over at Paul swallowed up in the bigness of the bed. Dr. Lynn stepped up to the bed and took Paul's ten year-old hand. Looking down at him he asked, "Does that mean it's okay with you, too, Paul?"

Paul smiled and said, "You will make a good dad some day."

Dr. Lynn's mouth dropped open, and he paused. "Whoa, son, I think your mother would have a lot to say about that."

Paul sighed, and we thought he was drifting back to sleep. We were all looking at each other for a moment, not knowing which one of us should say something. Paul opened his eyes again and said, "Mom's a girl. She can't be a dad. She can only be a mom."

Dr. Lynn burst out laughing and broke the spell. He patted Paul's leg and said, "You guys are all thinkers, aren't you?"

Paul said, "Dennis and Paul are stinkers, but I'm not." At that, Dennis and Steve started laughing. Dennis said, "No we're not, but you are, Paul. The way we've been worrying, like we have, over you."

Dr. Lynn said, "I believe our boy is going to make it, but we'll stay on top of things. I believe some prayers are being answered."

Mom walked in the room, and Paul raised his head up and said, "Mom, where've you been? We've been waiting on you."

Mom looked at me and then the other boys with a puzzled look on her face. "Paul, you were asleep when I left you. How long have you been awake?"

He shrugged his shoulders and looked up at the I.V. He stared at it for a second and said, "What are they giving me?"

Steve quickly said, "Dennis's blood. Can't you tell?"

Paul looked at me, but said, "No, Steve, Dennis is more red-blooded, isn't he, John?'

The tension in the room was slowly being defused by our little brother. Dr. Lynn said, "Paul, your brothers, Dennis and Steve, both came to the hospital and gave some of their blood to help save your life, and it appears to be working."

Paul looked at Mom, and she shook her head *yes*. He lay there in silence, and we were all wondering what to say, so I said, "Paul, Janet, and Robert want to come in the room to see you. Is that okay?"

"Yeah," was all he answered.

Steve said, "I'll go get them."

"Wait a minute." Steve stopped in his tracks, and Paul was looking at me. He asked, "Since Dennis and Steve saved my life, does that mean I'm gonna have to pay them back sometime—like doing chores for a week or skinnin' chickens by myself?"

Dennis couldn't help himself. He just had to burst out laughing. He said, "Paul, you're my buddy, so no payback is necessary, but you sure can skin those chickens by yourself."

Steve left the room to get Janet and Robert, but a nurse walked in to check the I.V. Dr. Lynn asked, "Would you mind checking this patient's vitals?"

Paul grabbed his sheet up around his neck tight and said, "No! Mrs. Weber and Janet may walk in."

Dennis had to leave the room, he was laughing so hard.

Mom said, "Honey, Dr. Lynn means your temperature and your blood pressure. That's what he means by vitals."

The nurse was smiling, but she held her composure. She turned to Dr. Lynn and said, "Normal."

The phone rang, and the nurse was inches away from the phone, so she picked it up. She said, "Yes, he's right here." I thought she meant me, so I started to go for the phone, but she said, "Dr. Lynn."

He took the phone and said, "Yes—Yes—Yes. I believe we have experienced a miracle before our eyes. Paul's temperature is down, too. He is awake and talking. Yes, we'll keep him overnight and check that again in the morning. Thank you...bye."

Dr. Lynn was smiling from ear to ear and shaking his head. "That was Dr. Sides. He would like for Paul to stay overnight, and we'll do another test in the morning."

I spoke for Mom and said, "Yes, that would be good. I'll stay with him, and Mom can go home and get in her own bed. Dennis can drive

Mom home. If Mrs. Weber wants to go home to her own bed-that would be fine, also.

Janet, Robert, Marianne, and Mrs. Weber stopped at the door and wanted to know if it was okay to come in. I said, "Yes, but let Steve and me out so it won't be too crowded."

Dr. Lynn said, "Me, too," and walked out ahead of me. Dr. Lynn pulled Mrs. Weber aside and said quietly, "They *are* a great family."

He was smiling at Marianne. I wondered what he had said, Marianne told me later.

It was getting close to ten o'clock, and I was tired. I found a chair off to the side and sat down in the family waiting room. Visiting hours were finished long ago. Closing up the barn and chicken house for the night still had to be done, so Mrs. Weber took the boys home. Mom stayed awhile longer. She said she would let Marianne drive her car to take her home, with Janet, too. Dr. Lynn left after stopping briefly by the nurses' station. Dr. Lynn must have said something to the nurses, as they didn't chase us out of the family waiting room even though visitor hours were over.

I sat there for a while thinking about Paul and my thoughts went to the communication Janet and Paul had with each other. When Janet and Mrs. Weber went down to the gift shop earlier in the evening, Janet purchased some metal puzzles for Paul to separate. He started working on them immediately. She also got a small box of candy, and I suspected it would be gone before he fell asleep. They seem to understand each other, even though Paul is only 10 and Janet is 14 years old.

Mom came to the waiting room, with Marianne and Janet. Mom said, "We're leaving now, John. Please try to get a couple of hours of sleep." I walked them to the elevator. Mom turned and gave me a hug, and I said, "Mom, you get some sleep, too."

Janet said, "I'll make her go to bed."

I chuckled and said, "Good, Janet, you do that." I patted her arm.

Marianne said, "John, go on back to Paul's room. I'll try to be back sometime tomorrow, too." She patted my arm like I had done to Janet.

After the elevator door closed, I went back to Paul's room. I had a very lonely feeling, almost like I was a child walking down a hospital hall by myself. When I walked into Paul's room, he was trying to get out of bed. He said, "I've gotta go to the bathroom."

I helped him, and it wore him out to walk ten steps with his I.V. stand. He said, "Now I know how Mom felt when she was in the hospital."

It didn't take long before he went to sleep. He had been through an ordeal, and his little body needed all his strength to mend. I prayed that God's will would be done with Paul, and that the rest of us would trust God. I was sitting in the recliner chair beside Paul's bed, reading the Gideon Bible that was left in the room, when Dr. Lynn walked in. He said, "I brought you something."

It was a huge piece of chocolate cake. All I could think to say was, "Wow! Thanks."

I didn't ask him why he was still at the hospital. He volunteered to tell me. He said, "John, I've had a hard time going home to my empty house. It's so quiet, and no family is there. I miss them, but they all have their own lives to live now, and I wouldn't want it any other way. My youngest son is your age and is not home for the summer. He decided to swap a semester at the SEMO University for one in England. He is staying on for the summer semester. He turned nineteen back in March. I'm glad he is getting this experience. His mother would have been proud of him. She died three years ago of cancer. I haven't dated nor have I had any desire to do so. That is—until I met your family. I really would like to get to know your mother better, but she is off limits to me until you give me the go-ahead."

I raised my eyebrows and said, "Oh yeah?" I got up with my empty plate and plastic fork, went to the bathroom, and threw it in the trash. Dr. Lynn was probably wondering what my answer meant.

I was going to say something else, but a nurse came in to check Paul's vitals again. She nodded her head and said, "Dr. Lynn, everything is still normal." She turned out a light by Paul's bed, and Dr. Lynn said, "Thanks." She left the room.

Dr. Lynn was looking at me like he was waiting for an answer or to explain my, *oh, yeah,* comment. I hardly knew what to say. I chuckled and said, "That cake was good. Now, I need some milk to finish off the crumbs on my pants."

He jumped up and two minutes later came back with a carton of milk. He must have gotten into the nurses' private refrigerator. It did give me time to pray.

For some reason I said silently, *What do you think, Lord?* I got my immediate answer. God said, *Let your Mom decide. She will talk to me.* I was shaking my head in disbelief again, when Dr. Lynn walked in with the carton of milk.

He asked, "Is something wrong, John?"

"Nothing is wrong. When you walked out the door, I said to God, 'What do think, Lord?'

God answered quickly and said, 'Let your Mom decide. She will talk to me.' So—I guess you will have to talk to Mom about getting to know her better, and whatever the future holds will be fine with me."

"John, with that answer, I had better go home and get some sleep."

He started out the door and stopped. "John, you seem to have a direct connection to heaven. Am I right?"

I smiled and knew God had just dropped a wonderful opportunity right in my lap. I said, "Yes, Sir, I do. Jesus removed the barrier between God and me when he died on a cross for my sin. He did it so he could bring me into harmony with His father, God. I was born a sinner, and God provided for me a means of forgiveness for my past sins and for anytime I might fail him in the future. Jesus' death, resurrection, and His forgiveness is how He cleared the pipeline to heaven. God is my father, too, now. I was adopted into his family when I gave my life to Him. It's as simple as that."

Dr. Lynn said, "Good, John. I'll see you tomorrow."

I wondered after he left if what I said made any sense to him, at all. Well, time will tell, as they say. Perhaps he was checking to see if I was a Christian. I sat there wondering why he said, *Good, John.*

Paul slept all night long. I slept in the recliner chair that didn't want to recline all the way. A nurse gave me a pillow and a blanket, but it was the most uncomfortable night I have ever had since Dennis and I decided we were big enough to sleep on the ground outside in a sleeping bag. About four in the morning, we rolled up our sleeping bags and went in the house to our own beds. We told Dad it started to rain. I know he didn't believe us, and he shouldn't have, because our pride wouldn't admit that we couldn't stay out the whole night on the hard ground. I think we were about seven and nine years old at the time. The memory of that night has stayed with me.

It is seven-thirty in the morning, and all I've done is comb my hair with my small pocket comb. My teeth need brushing. A lab technician just came in—he took a vial of blood from Paul, again.

Paul was still asleep, and the man woke him up. Paul looked at the man like he could care less who he was. He said, 'Not again. You took all my blood already. Now you're getting Dennis's blood."

The technician laughed and asked, "Who is Dennis?"

"He's my brother."

Paul laid his head back and frowned. I felt bad for him, but it had to be done. The technician gathered his stuff together and left the room.

I sat there for a moment wondering when Mom would be coming to the hospital when she walked in the room. It was almost eight o'clock. A girl with Paul's breakfast walked in behind Mom. Paul tried to sit up with all the bracing on his arm. Mom helped him to a sitting position. She took the cover off his food and said, "Umm. That looks good—pancakes and sausage."

I gave Mom a hug. "I'm sure glad to see you and glad that you didn't sleep in that chair all night."

Dr. Sides walked in and said, "Good morning. I understand we have a miracle boy here."

Paul looked at him with a mouth full of food and said, "I could... have...told... you...I would get better."

Dr. Lynn walked in and gave Paul a raised eyebrow look and asked, "Is this the same boy who was about to take a helicopter flight to St. Louis?"

Paul looked at him and then Mom and me. "You mean you guys got to take a ride in a helicopter, and I didn't get to go?"

Dr. Sides said, "Paul, only you were going on a helicopter ride—and this one you definitely didn't want to take. The Med-Vac is to transport sick patients to a hospital in St. Louis and get them there as quickly as possible. We thought you were so sick that you needed it. But, here you are sitting up eating breakfast."

Paul swallowed a bit of pancake and said, "I didn't eat last night. This is my supper, too."

Dr. Lynn was smiling and said, "And I see you have learned to eat one handed with that arm in a sling. In a couple of days, we want to x-ray your arm again to see how it is healing on the inside."

Dr. Sides asked, "Paul, when did you break your arm?"

Paul turned and looked at me, but Dr. Lynn answered. "Last Friday. I put pins in it as he broke both bones."

Dr. Lynn described the breaks to Dr. Sides. The two doctors were talking like we weren't in the room, and I was gathering from what they were saying that the break might not have been from the fall totally, but perhaps some cancer in the bone—only they didn't say cancer.

I looked at Mom and she was shaking her head *no*. I spoke up and said, "Mom, all of Paul's test will not be complete until they can do some follow-up ones today and perhaps tomorrow. So relax for now, okay?"

Dr. Lynn looked at Mom with a concerned look and said, "Bonnie, I'm sorry. John is right. If Paul's blood counts are pretty well back to normal, we will know for sure that it was the disinfectant that was used in the henhouse. I suspect, though, that we may have had two things going on at once. We'll see if the white count normalizes in a couple of days. The blood that was given yesterday should have helped bring the red count back up. Dr. Sides and I will stay on top of things for you—and Paul."

Mom looked at Paul, back at the two doctors, and said, "Thank you."

Paul asked Mom, "Did you know I have Dennis's blood in my body? I thought he was more red-blooded. My chickens are more red-blooded than Dennis's blood is."

Dr. Sides finally laughed and said, "Well, Paul, what color was Dennis's blood?"

Paul looked at me like I should answer for him, but I shrugged my shoulders. He wasn't going to get any help from me.

He stabbed another piece of pancake with his fork and said, "W-e-l-l, it wasn't yellow, that's for sure."

I had to walk out of the room to keep from cracking up. I was having a hard time not laughing loudly. I heard Dr. Lynn say, "Paul, I believe it looked sort of maroon color, did it not?"

I stepped back in the room to hear what Paul's answer would be and tried to keep a straight face. He was looking at Dr. Lynn with his fork and a bit of pancake half-way to his mouth, when he said with a frown, "I've never heard of that color. The only *maroon* I know is when you get your boat stuck on an island."

Dr. Sides had the biggest grin on his face and he said, "Paul, you are right, but right now, I want to listen to your heart and look in your mouth and ears."

Paul laid his fork down and took a drink. Mom pushed his tray away and said, "Paul, finish your breakfast later."

Dr. Lynn patted my arm, and we both walked out to the hall. He said, "He's quite a little guy, isn't he? He started my day off right. How did you sleep last night?"

"Awful in that chair. I need to go on home, get my teeth brushed and help with the morning chores, and then take a hot shower. I hope Mom left her usual list of chores, as I'm not in a mood to tell anyone what to do today."

Mom came up behind me and said, "Yes, John, the orders are all laid out for the day. Mrs. Weber stayed on, so she would be there when I left this morning. She left to go home around seven to see her husband before he left for work. She said she would be back around nine-thirty or ten. Dennis and Steve were getting up when I left. You can go home now. I feel all right this morning and ate a good breakfast, so don't worry about me. I'll call you around eleven, okay?"

Mom handed me her car keys and told me where she'd parked. Dr. Lynn said, "It was good to see you again, John—you, too, Bonnie. I'll check back in on Paul's progress, but right now I have a patient to see prior to surgery, so I'll be on my way, too.

Chapter 9

It took me about five minutes longer to get from Cape Girardeau to Chaffee because I was so sleepy and I was afraid that I might fall asleep at the wheel, but I made it home.

Everything at the farm was going right on schedule with the chores. I looked at Mom's "to do" list and she had written down *Janet-dust the house and Dennis-vacuum or sweep all the floors. Steve and Robert-do the laundry.* She had a note beside that, saying she had already sorted the loads on the floor. Mom is very particular about the wash.

I found Dennis and told him that I was going to put some quarters in jean pockets and Mom's slacks, but for him to tell Robert to check the pockets, make sure they were empty and any money would be his or Steve's tip for whoever was doing the laundry.

Mom had also written on the list that Cousin Stacy would be out for two peach cobblers and one apple. They were in the freezer. She also wanted four dozen eggs—to make sure they were clean. She said, *please look in the freezer and see if there are enough cobblers, but if not, Steve should make the crusts and Robert help with the filling.* For me, I was to till up the garden.

I told Dennis, "I'm going to take a thirty minute nap, head for the garden, and then go to the fields to plow up any weeds that were surviving the drought."

Dennis informed me that it wouldn't do any good as it probably was too late for the crops. I told him, "Then we need to go into town and see what we can do about an irrigation system, even if we had to get several sprinklers and attach a garden hose."

I went upstairs to the shower and couldn't think about anything except losing our crops. Later when Mrs. Weber came, I was still trying to take a nap, but I couldn't go to sleep. I could hear talking and giggling, so I got up intending to scold some kids, but Marianne was there and she was teasing the boys. She and Janet were doing the dusting but talking to the boys from the dining room. She had tied two pretty aprons of Mom's on Steve and Robert and was calling them Stephanie and Roberta. I walked on through the kitchen and said, "You can joke all you want as long as you get the work done."

I know I was frowning. I had decided to go down the road to a neighbor's farm. They had an irrigation system, and I wanted to check it out. Marianne followed me out. I should have known. I hadn't bothered to tell anyone where I was going. She said, "John, you didn't say good morning, hello—or anything. What's going on? Don't you think you are being a little harsh this morning?"

I leaned back on the truck seat and sighed. "Marianne, you are right. I'm so stressed out from almost losing Paul, maybe having one good hour of sleep last night, and now Dennis is saying he thinks it is too late for an irrigation system. I don't want to lose the farm. We count on the crops to carry farm expenses. I was going down the road to check out what type of irrigation system the Jenkins farm is using. I'll go back in and talk with the kids."

I stepped out of the truck, and Marianne gave me a hug. She said, "You are forgiven. Come back in, talk with Dennis, and take him with you. He needs to be in on whatever you do. Mom may have some ideas, also."

Marianne took my hand, and we walked together back to the house.

Steve had already started rolling out dough, and Robert and Mrs. Weber were peeling apples.

The peaches were thawing. I sat at the table and said, "I'm sorry, guys, for my attitude. If you don't mind, I'm going over to Jenkins farm to see what their irrigation system is like and talk to them. We have to do something, before it is too late, or we'll lose our crops altogether."

Mrs. Weber said, "You go on, John. We'll manage in here."

Dennis walked in the back porch and yelled, "John, I need you out here. Mom's tiller is deeefunnnct!"

That was all I needed to hear. I told Dennis to forget about it because I wanted him to go with me to the Jenkins farm to talk to them about their irrigation system. He was ready to go—anything would be better than messing with Mom's tiller. He was as frustrated as I felt. I said, "Don't worry about the tiller. Mom had that job on the list for me to do. Come with me. I'm going over to the Jenkins's place and checking out their irrigation machinery."

We headed back out to the truck. The Jenkins farm was adjacent to ours, and the house was very close to our property line, but his lane came off the farm to market road, so we had to go down our lane and then turn up his lane.

Mr. Jenkins was out beside his barn when we drove up. Dennis said, "Good. He's home."

Mr. Jenkins watched us as we drove into his driveway. He walked up to my window and said, "The Moore young men—what is my pleasure for seeing you this morning?"

"Mr. Jenkins, we've come over to talk to you about your irrigation system," I said. "We need to put one in pretty soon, or we will have lost all our crops for this season. We can't afford to lose them. Paul is in the hospital right now and running up more medical expenses. Thank God for our insurance, but running back and forth to Cape Girardeau is already eating into our household expenses. I want to save our crops if I can."

Mr. Jenkins said, "Well, get out of the truck. Let's talk. Let me run into the house for just a moment and get my papers on it."

Mr. Jenkins wasn't gone more than two minutes, and Dennis doubted that we could save any of the crops. He said, "John, I hope we aren't getting into something that would cost us more than we can pay for. If we get anything from the crops, it will have to go on the mortgage. Irrigating may be expensive, and we still might lose the crop."

I was too tired to think, much less listen to negative thoughts. I told Dennis, "We had a miracle with Paul, so we'll ask God for another one. He controls the universe, but He wants us to do what we can to help preserve it, and if that means an irrigation system—that's what we will do. Pray, Dennis."

I leaned on the truck front bumper, and Dennis was four feet from me shuffling his feet in the dirt. Mr. Jenkins came out of his house with his catalog and specifications on his irrigation system. He asked, "Boys, how many acres do you have in crops?"

Dennis said, "I think thirty in corn and ten in soybeans."

"Oh—you have more that I thought you have. Okay—let's look at prices and at how much each unit costs. You know you can attach several together."

I looked off toward Mr. Jenkins's fields, and it looked like his units covered a half-acre to a full acre at a time, so I asked, "What does each section cost? I suppose we can do at least one- half acre at a time, so we don't run the well dry. I want to at least save Dennis' soybean crop, which is only ten acres."

Mr. Jenkins looked at me and very bluntly said, "You need to put in a second well to use for irrigation."

"How much will that cost?" Looking at me, Dennis asked.

Mr. Jenkins looked off at his barn thinking, "Well, let's see," he said, "It depends on how deep you have to drill—probably six or seven thousand dollars."

Dennis stepped back and said, "John, we are better off going home and praying."

Mr. Jenkins chuckled, but neither one of us was in the mood for laughing. I asked, "May I borrow your catalog for two days and go out and look at your units?"

"Sure, let's go."

He handed me the catalog and said, "I marked the page that has my unit on it. Prices are probably higher now."

We walked out to his irrigation station, and Mr. Jenkins talked like his system was the only one on the earth. He was so proud of it. He explained every detail. After listening to him, I wasn't sure we should do it or could even afford it. So, I thanked Mr. Jenkins, and we headed back to the truck and home. I was beginning to think Dennis was right. We should just pray for rain.

When we pulled in the farm yard, we ran over a hose which was running out to the field. I don't know where the kids found the hoses, but Mrs. Weber was standing with Steve, watching a sprinkler cover a twenty or thirty foot circle of Dennis' soybeans. Dennis grinned and said, "Will you look at that?"

My first thought was—*There goes our well,* but I said, "Lord, bless our well with lots of water."

Dennis asked, "Where did you find the hoses and sprinkler?"

Steve grinned. "They were coiled up under Mom's workbench. We took Paul's hose, too.

The sprinkler was under the work table, too. It doesn't cover much, but perhaps with the tilt of the land, some will run down a few more feet."

I said, "Good thinking, Steve."

Mrs. Weber was watching us and smiled. She said. "John, I grew up with a hose and hoe in my hand. We didn't know about irrigation systems, and we couldn't afford one if we had known. My folks paid off our little farm from our gardens."

I said, "Well, fortunately we only have about a year left on our mortgage. If things don't improve, I'll be headed to the bank to ask for an extension on the loan or work something out with them."

Mrs. Weber raised her eyebrows like she had a thought, She asked, "I don't mean to be nosey, but how much are your mortgage payments."

I told her, "Almost nine hundred dollars a month, but we usually pay it once or twice a year. When the crops come in, when Steve sells a heifer, or when we've saved from other incomes, all the money goes to the mortgage. Mom picks up the slack from her job at the railroad office."

Mrs. Weber didn't answer immediately. She was thinking, and said, "John, you are paying a little less than twelve thousand a year. How much are the interest payments on the loan?"

I said, "I don't know. I'll check with Mom."

I started back to the house. I was thinking *my corn should be a foot higher.* I wasn't sure how much good the sprinkler hose or the water that was going to the soybeans would help. I shouldn't have been thinking about that because Steve was right beside me. As we talked, he said,

"John, find out how much the interest payments are. We can shop for a loan and pay off the bank. Maybe we can get a lower interest rate? That would help."

"Steve, where did you learn all about interest payments and loans?"

He said, "Well, in 4-H we talked about loans on farms and how they worked. Not a whole lot, but I went home and asked Mom about our farm loan, and she explained it to me."

Then when she bought the café and sold it to Cousin Stacy, I asked her how that worked. She said Cousin Stacy gave her the amount she'd already paid on the loan. I think she said it's called equity or something like that. Then the payments were transferred to Cousin Stacy on the papers at the bank. Mom's name was taken off the mortgage loan and Cousin Stacy's name was put on the papers. Then Cousin Stacy gave mom a check to, also, pay for all the equipment and furniture."

I said, "Steve, I'm glad you're my brother, and you have an interest in business. Someday you may be a banker, and I can come to you for a loan."

He laughed and said, "John, call the bank. You know we have my new baby bull calf. In a few months, I can sell it and maybe make enough to pay off some of the loan. You know he's a dandy. I might breed that cow again."

Mrs. Weber was walking along side of us. She said, "Boys, I've about decided Robert can spend the summer with you. I've never met a finer bunch of boys, and you sure know how to assume responsibility. Just a week with you, and I can see Robert maturing.

Steve and I laughed. "Around here, if you don't work, you don't eat," Steve laughingly said. "You should see the portions Mom put on my plate when I was Paul's age because I didn't do the jobs she gave me. Mom would never let us go without eating something. She would put about three bites of each food on our plates. It was obvious we hadn't done our duties. As I got older and someone else had to do my job, everyone knew when it came to dessert. Whoever's plate had my share was the person who had done my work. Mine had three bites, and theirs was twice as much. I would try to trick Dennis into slipping me an extra bite when mine was gone, but Mom would get upset and say, "No way!"

Steve chuckled to himself and said, "Yeah, I learned a hard lesson. Maybe that's why I learned to cook. I probably thought I could get a couple of bites in my mouth as I was cooking, especially the dessert."

I told Steve, "Even if that's true, I'm glad you cook."

I thought about different ways Mom used to get us to assume responsibility without a lot of scolding. She was pretty clever, making us think we were so successful, and it was a pleasure to do a job for her. I'm sure Mrs. Weber would laugh, seeing me sorting clothes and checking to see if anyone had left change in the pockets. That would be our tip for doing the job. Dad left change in his pockets, and Mom would do the same in her slacks. When I discovered it, she told me, "Never tell your brothers until they learn how to sort clothes."

I told Dennis I liked to do laundry because I always got change from Mom and Dad's pockets. I didn't tell him Mom and Dad left the change on purpose. He's told me several times, "You keep leaving your change in your pants pockets. Steve is getting rich off you."

So when Mom put Dennis on laundry duty, I would purposely take all my change out. He thought he'd gotten through to me. I really was giving it to Mom, and telling her to put it in her dirty slacks. I told Mom that Dennis had warned me about leaving money in my pockets, so she should let him think I had learned my lesson. Mom laughed and always took my change when it was Dennis' turn to do the laundry. He started fussing at her for being forgetful, but he would say, "I got almost a dollar from the laundry today."

Mom would wink at me and say, "John, did you leave money in your jeans?"

That's a ritual that I hope I can continue with my children someday. It's a good memory, and lately all we've had are bad experiences.

Paul came home from the hospital after two days of sticking needles in his arm. His white count was still a little elevated. They want him back in two weeks, but if he starts running a low temperature again, Dr. Sides wants to see him immediately.

Dr. Lynn checked Paul's arm and took another x-ray before Paul left the hospital. It was healing, but slower than he expected. He said, "The elevated white count could have slowed down the healing."

He told Mom he was still concerned about Leukemia, but he would take Paul's recovery so far as a gift from God, and he would trust God to continue the healing process. I appreciated that.

It's now the last of June, and Mom surprised me with a birthday party. It's a week late, but that's okay. She must not have said anything because she was so concerned about Paul, and she wanted the party to be a real surprise. It was. I thought it was just a youth social. Since I had graduated to the college and careers class at our church, the youth wouldn't want me to be part of their socials, but Marianne was helping plan everything, and she wanted me to go, so I went.

Marianne had arranged everything for Mom with Pastor Bishop and his wife. The college and careers class was there with the youth, and Pastor Bishop had even arranged for the detective and policemen at the Weber's house that awful Sunday to be at the party.

There are times when this six-foot-three-or-four-inch frame body gets in my way. I'm an emotional person, and I was at such a loss for words that I hid my face like Marianne does when she cries. I know my face was red, and I really wanted to cry, but not being a little boy anymore, I couldn't. Mom made up for whatever celebration I lacked at graduation with this party. Marianne even had a video of my life put together. I don't know how Mom got the pictures for Marianne without me noticing. It was all a surprise.

One of the policemen had a application and catalog from the Southeast Missouri Law Enforcement Academy at Southeast Missouri University. I hadn't thought about it anymore. When Paul got sick, my concern was for him and the drought. I appreciated the officer taking the time to get the forms for me.

Marianne secured an aptitude test from somewhere and had copies for everyone to fill out as though they were me. She had each person read specific answers on the form they had filled out. Many commented that I like to take command of situations. I laughed, but the detective gave me a thumbs up when I looked at him.

I smiled and said, "I guess you saw me in action on that one. I hope I don't ever wimp out when someone needs me."

When he was leaving, he told me I probably wouldn't wimp out on anyone if I stayed as cool in a crisis as I did at the Weber's home.

I said, "Thank you."

We left the church with an assortment of gifts. Several had gone together and gotten gift certificates. One was for Orscheln Farm and Home Supply in Cape Girardeau. My first thought was irrigation supplies. I would check that out. I really appreciated that gift certificate.

I helped Mom and Marianne clean-up the fellowship hall at the church, and then I took Marianne on a date by herself. It was something we hadn't done in a while.

Chapter 10

Marianne and I went directly to Orscheln's Farm Supply Store. We picked up a couple of soaker hoses and a longer hose than those we were using at home. Dennis would be able to soak at least an acre each day. I checked with the folks at Orscheln's about different well companies. After our purchases at the farm supply store, we stopped at Ruby Tuesday's Restaurant for supper. I looked over the brochures I had picked up, and I thought about what Mr. Jenkins said about drilling a well. It was looking like a better idea every day. If we dug the well this year, we could invest in the irrigation system next year.

Marianne listened patiently as I talked about my tale of woe regarding the crops and the drought.

Finally, she said, "God is trying to make you exercise your faith and trust Him."

I looked at her and sighed. I had to smile because those were the exact words I told Dennis, just weeks before. I had to apologize.

I said, "You're right. Instead of worrying, I'll call Clark Well, Drilling Company and at least get an estimate of what it would cost to put in another well."

I took another bite and looked around at the people in the restaurant.

Marianne asked, "What are you thinking about now?"

I told her how Steve had encouraged me to check our mortgage payments and the amount of interest to see if I could space out the payments for two years.

Marianne smiled, "Sounds like Steve at age fifteen has a business head on his shoulders."

Another week went by, and we had about a quarter inch of rain. It wasn't much, but enough to make the corn green. I called about a well. Without looking at the terrain and not knowing if our farm was on a lot of rock, Mr. Clark said an estimate would be seven dollars per foot for the drilling and seven dollars per foot for the casing. In our area, He might have to drill as far as six hundred feet. I decided it was time for a family conference.

Paul wasn't able to stay up late. He said he felt very tired, so Mom helped him cover his arm and start his bath. He called for Dennis to help him dry off and into his pajamas. Dennis put toothpaste on his brush and came back down to the kitchen table. Mom had gotten a calculator, and Steve was already sitting with a pencil and paper waiting for Dennis to come back.

Mom already knew that I called the Clark Well Drilling Company in Cape Girardeau, and they had given me an estimate for drilling a well. I told Dennis and Steve what they said, and I told them it ought to be put some place out in our fields so we could get the irrigation going.

Electricity to the well would also have to be considered, but the major problem was money.

After I told them the price, Steve was already pushing his pencil and had taken Mom's calculator.

He said, "John, go with Mom to the bank after she gets off work on Monday. No, that won't work. The bank will be closed by then. Make an appointment for someone to talk to you during Mom's lunch hour at noon. See if the bank will loan us ten thousand dollars on top of our current mortgage loan. It may take us five more years to pay off the loan, but you, Dennis, and I will be working, so we can pay it off without a problem."

I looked at Steve, "Why did you say ten thousand? The cost of the well may be only about eight thousand. Why ten?"

The look on his face was the look he gives Paul when he loses patience with him.

"John, if the crop doesn't come through like you and Dennis are hoping, you'll need the money for seed for the next year."

"Oh, okay," I said. "We wouldn't have to use the extra money unless we have to draw on it for the mortgage some month."

Mom was sitting quietly, thinking. Finally she said, "Let's get a personal loan for fifteen thousand and pay off the mortgage. Perhaps the bank will take just the house if we can't pay the loan off."

Steve's face lit up as mom spoke. He said, "Mom, that's good thinking because the bank can't take our land if only our house is on the papers for a guarantee or a back-up for the loan. I think they'll do it."

I laughed. Steve thought I was laughing at him, but I was really thanking the Lord for the business knowledge that Mom and Steve had, and for Steve's wisdom at such a young age. Joy came over my whole being. It was like a load was gently lifted off me.

Dennis poked Steve and asked, "What kind of books and magazines are you reading upstairs?"

Steve was puzzled by the question and said, "You know. It's just my Future Business Leader Magazines. It's from the association for the FBLA club. That's what we call it at school."

Mom said, "Well, I'm thankful to have a future business leader in my home."

Dennis said, "Mom, John, go for the loan. I'll look for a job off the farm to make payments."

Mom put her hands over her face. The she said, through her tears, "I am so proud of my sons. They're each a blessing to me. This talk with you tonight has taken a big load off my shoulders. You are ready to do what you can for this home and family. Thank you."

She got up and hugged each of us—Steve first and then Dennis. I was last.

She said, "Thanks, boys, I'm going to bed, and I'll be reading for a while."

Steve said, "I'll clean up the kitchen *again,* Dennis and John. I'll get the coffee ready for breakfast, too."

Dennis started to say something to Steve, but instead he took his glass and my glass to the kitchen sink. He just said, "Goodnight, Mom."

I added, "Well, I'm going out to the barn for a last-minute check, and then I'm heading to bed, too. These concerns are taxing my brain, and I'm tired."

Dennis got up from his chair, "I think I'll go out with you, John."

I thought it a bit strange Dennis was offering to help do any last minute chore. He ran upstairs for something. He was folding a brochure and putting it in his pocket when he came through the kitchen again. He went out the door in front of me.

"What's up, Dennis? We don't lock the shed, and we hadn't planned to turn off the water hoses tonight."

Dennis didn't say anything until we were half-way to the barn. Then he pulled the brochure from his pocket.

"I want to show this brochure to you when we get in the barn under some light. Tonight when I was helping Paul with his pajamas, I noticed he had several little bruises on him. I asked him how he got them, and he said, 'I don't know. They were there yesterday.' I just told him to be careful and not bump into anything, but look, John, bruises are a symptom of leukemia. I didn't want to say anything to Mom—especially since it's bedtime."

I took the brochure from Dennis, read some of it, and looked at the pictures. "Did you notice if Paul had a fever?"

"No. His body was hot from his bath. Mom's going to be stressed out for sure. She'll quit her job, and Paul will have no insurance. I'm going in town tomorrow to apply at several stores, including the café. I think I can work from six to ten three nights each week and all day Saturday. That means you'll have to handle the milking and other chores with Steve, and I'll have to use the truck. I'll see what I can find for the rest of the summer. I know I'll make enough for one month's mortgage payment or one month's household expenses."

Dennis's mouth was rambling on, and I could tell he'd been worried about Paul and Mom.

My mind went back to what Marianne said to me, *It looks like God is testing our faith, and trust in Him.*

"Dennis, we need to pray for our whole family and trust God to lead us."

He folded the brochure and put it back in his pocket. He said, "Yeah."

He walked down the row of stalls and looked in at each one. A cow had knocked over her water, so he refilled it.

"I'm finished, John," he said.

I turned out all the barn lights, except for the one we leave on, inside the barn. I went out to the outdoor faucet outside the barn and turned it off. Dennis followed me. "Believe it or not, Dennis, those are clouds up in the sky. Maybe we're going to get some rain, yet. It's a great picture of our lives right now. We have a lot of clouds hovering over us, but when the rain comes, there will be a blessing in it. Let's trust God that Paul is okay, but if he isn't, let's look for God's blessing in the situation. Okay."

I was beginning to sound like a counselor again, and I don't think Dennis felt any better, but he said, "Yeah" again and began walking toward the house. I dragged myself over to the chicken house. I really felt tired. I said, *I'm here God, what are you going to put on my plate now.* The hen house door was locked, so I went to the house. Dennis and Steve were still in the kitchen. Dennis was showing the brochure to Steve. I said, "Goodnight," and went on upstairs. I was ready to get some good sleep.

I said, "Goodnight, Mom," but there was no answer. She stepped out of Paul's room and said, "Come in here, John."

My heart skipped a couple beats. She had just felt Paul's head, and he was burning up. I felt his head and said, "Mom, he has a high fever." Mom knew that.

I asked, "Do you want me to call Dr. Sides or Dr. Lynn?"

I looked at the clock and said, "It's almost 10 o'clock."

Mom said, "Let me take his temperature before you call. They'll ask what his temperature is."

I went to get the thermometer in the upstairs bathroom and shook it down when I came back.

Mom said, "Call Marshall, and he can decide if we should call Dr. Sides."

"Marshall?" I should have remembered who that was, but at that moment, I was only thinking about Paul and his temperature.

"Yes, Dr. Lynn. Call him first," Mom said.

It had only been three weeks since Paul broke his arm. Maybe not that long. Sometime during those weeks, Mom and Dr. Lynn had become friends on a first-name basis.

Mom woke Paul to get the thermometer under his tongue. He whimpered a little and said, "Mom, I don't feel well."

Dennis and Steve apparently heard something and stood behind us waiting. The dim light in the room revealed a look on Dennis' face that said, *I thought you were going to wait until morning.*

"Mom was checking on Paul when I came upstairs," I said. Mom pulled the thermometer out of Paul's mouth. She read 102 degrees. Steve looked at me, then Dennis, and said, "I guess he gets my blood this time, and maybe he'll stay well."

He was serious when he said it, and he didn't mean to be flippant. I think he was hoping Paul would stay well after two pints of blood.

We had a quick family conference. Dennis said, "John, why don't you let me drive Mom and Paul up to the hospital this time. I'll be careful. You can come up after the morning chores. Someone needs to check on the well and irrigation system."

I agreed, wrapped Paul's blanket around him, picked him up, and handed him over to Dennis.

Mom had gone to get her glasses. She stuffed her comb, brush, and toothbrush into a tote bag along with a sweater. She came out of her room and said, "We're off. I'll stay with Paul tonight.

Tomorrow is Saturday, and I can sleep then."

Steve and I looked at each other, then at Paul and Mom. I kissed Mom and said, "Mom, relax. After chores, I'll be at the hospital to relieve you. Please remind Dennis to drive carefully."

"I will, but he's a good driver."

I watched them turn around in the driveway and head out the lane. My heart said to go with them, but someone needed to stay with Steve and do the morning chores. I turned out the kitchen light and left the back porch light on. Steve was sitting in the living room looking forlorn.

I said, "Steve, it's bedtime. Let's go to our rooms and pray for Paul."

The last time I looked at the clock, it was 10:20 p.m. I asked God to give me guidance and direction with the family and the farm. I asked God to heal Paul, to give Mom strength, and wisdom in her decision, and to help her not worry.

I realized Mom hadn't called Dr. Lynn, and I needed to call Kaitlynn again. I wondered if they were still up. I called Dr. Lynn first. He said, "I live almost next door to the hospital. How long ago did they leave?"

"Around 10 o'clock. They should be there in twenty minutes."

"I wasn't asleep yet. I'm going right over to the hospital."

"Thanks, Dr. Lynn. I'd appreciate that."

I called my sister, Kaitlynn, and Matthew answered. He was still up studying for his summer class. "John, what's going on? You wouldn't be calling us at this hour just to talk."

"It's Paul. He started running a temperature, and Dennis noticed little bruises on him. We were hoping his white count would return to normal, but it hasn't. Dr. Sides said to bring him back to the hospital if he started having a fever. Dennis drove Mom and Paul to St. Francis Hospital less than an hour ago."

Matthew said, "Tomorrow is Saturday, and we have plans since Kaitlynn isn't working, but I think we'll change them and come down for the day."

Kaitlynn came in the room where Matthew was studying. I heard her say, "Who called?"

When Matthew told her what was going on, I heard her say, "Yes, Matthew, we have to go home for the day."

I told Matthew to be sure to call before leaving because it's still an option to put Paul in the St. Louis Children's Hospital. Kaitlynn took the phone and said, "We're coming down. Period."

"Kaitlynn, I just told Matthew to call before you come. I'll call you in the morning or you can call me."

Kaitlynn settled down and said, "Please call me as soon as you know something."

"I will, Kaitlynn, try to get a good night's sleep. We may need you to relieve Mom, and stay with Paul one of these days. Please pray for us—especially for Paul."

I went back to bed and felt like my summer was moving too quickly. I fell asleep sometime after eleven-thirty and woke up at six. I figured I'd had enough sleep, so I got up. I wanted to get the chores done and check in with Mom by 7:30 A.M.

My first thoughts were about when Dennis came home last night from the hospital. It was while I was talking to Kaitlynn. He said, "Dr. Lynn was waiting at the door for them. He came out with a gurney and a warm blanket. He took Paul from the car. The orderly stood back wondering what use he could be, but did wheel the gurney back into the hospital. Dr. Lynn told me not to park. He said it was getting late and he would check Paul into the hospital." Dennis chuckled, "He sounded like Dad."

I said, "Ok, I can't stay awake any longer. I'm going to bed."

We both went to bed, and all three of us woke up about the same time.

I put on my dirty clothes to go to the barn. The timer had already started the coffee pot downstairs, and I could smell the coffee. I grabbed a cup on the way through the kitchen. I milked both cows, fed the cats, and let the cows out to the pasture. Steve and Dennis came out about thirty minutes later. Steve had to check his heifers and the baby bull calf. He's so proud of him. I heard him talking to the calf.

"One of these days, I may just keep you and start a herd of cattle just like you."

I let it go. It was one more thing I didn't want to think about. Dennis strained the milk, carried it to the house, and started breakfast. I let Paul's chickens out of the hen house and gave them some chicken feed and clean water. Steve was still cleaning out the stalls and putting fresh straw down when I went back to the barn. I helped him finish, and we were back in the house by 7:35 a.m. It's surprising how fast the chores can get done when there's a crisis in the family.

Mom called and told Dennis Paul's white count had risen, and Dr. Lynn and Dr. Sides want Paul to go on to St. Louis, but they won't move him until this afternoon. She had asked for her twin sister's telephone number and asked for one of us to call Kaitlynn. We sat down and ate Dennis' breakfast of cereal, juice, and coffee. That's about the extent of his cooking, but I was happy he had fixed it. I told the boys, "Eat up. We may have to miss a meal today."

I went in Grandpa's room and called Kaitlynn. They were ready to come on down. I told her the hospital's phone number and Paul's room number, so she could talk directly to Mom. She also said she would call Mom's sister and brother, Aunt Barbara and Uncle Al.

I called Marianne next to ask her to start the church prayer chain for Paul. Mr. Weber, Marianne's dad, answered and he said, "Oh, just the man I was going to call this morning." He started talking to me about our mortgage and going to the bank. He would co-sign a note for us. I wasn't ready to start thinking about that, so I agreed to go to the bank with him, and asked to speak to Marianne. I told her about Paul."

She said, "Pastor Bishop would want to go up to the hospital and pray with Paul before he leaves the hospital. I'll call him.

"That would be nice," I said, "I'll keep you posted on what's going on."

As I hung up the phone and sat back down in my chair, Dennis was saying no about something and Steve was saying yes. I told them, "This is not the time for arguing."

Dennis said, "John, let me take the car to town for gas and a wash job. Mom doesn't need to drive a dirty car to St. Louis."

Steve said, "But, John, we need the car to go to the bank sometime. We can clean the car later."

I felt like clobbering them. "All of us are going to town at nine o'clock. Dennis can drop us off at the bank and then get the car cleaned. Mr. Weber's going to meet us there. He's already arranged for a loan. All we need to do is go in and sign the papers."

Steve had a surprised look on his face. "Well, when did this all take place? We just had the family conference last night!"

"Just now, when I called Marianne, Mr. Weber answered. He said Mrs. Weber told him we needed an irrigation system and our mother had confided in her about drilling for a well. He said he wanted to let us know that he called his friend, Jason, at the bank. He wants us to come to the bank. Mr. Weber wants to co-sign for us on a loan. He said, 'I know you guys would be good for it.'

"I told Mr. Weber, we'd meet him at the bank, so we don't have time to worry about the dirt on the car or fuss about anything else this morning. I know we have a crisis with Paul, but let's get this taken care of while Mom's in St. Louis. There's going to be a day when we have to do things on our own, anyway. Mom's health is okay at the moment, but we have to make sure she's as least stressed as possible."

It was already eight o'clock in the morning, but we hadn't taken a shower yet when Mom called. She said Paul's condition was about the same. He wasn't too happy about waking up again in the hospital. I told Mom we would be up to see Paul around ten o'clock and asked if she wanted us to bring her anything.

She said, "Make sure my black slacks are washed, and find my small over-night suitcase. I'm going to come home and pack while you boys are at the hospital."

We hurried to do the household chores. We had forty minutes. I did the laundry, Dennis cleaned up the kitchen, and Steve made our beds and brought more dirty clothes down to the laundry.

Cousin Stacy called, and I told her what had happened and that Paul would be transferred to St. Louis Children's Hospital. I assured her we'd get her eggs to her this afternoon. She had called because she needed more eggs at the café.

I was having a hard time getting to the shower because the phone kept ringing. Aunt Barbara, mom's twin sister, called from St. Louis. She had just talked to Mom. She wanted us to know we were welcome to stay with her, if we should decide to drive up Sunday. I told her I hadn't found anyone to do the farm chores yet, but I would let her know later if we decided to drive to St. Louis.

I hurried to Grandpa's bathroom shower before the phone could ring again. I stripped off my clothes and stepped in the shower. *Lord, here I am just as you made me—stripped of everything.* I started laughing and then had an overwhelming urge to cry again. I prayed, *Lord, sometimes I'm just a wimp. Please, make me strong.* He answered me quickly again. *What do you think I am doing by taking you through these rough waters?*

Those verses from Joshua hit me again. I had finally memorized them. *Have I not commanded you? Be strong and courageous. Do not be terrified: do not be discouraged: for the Lord your God will be with you, wherever you go.*

I washed, shaved, and put my clothes on in record time. I had to find a Bible, read the verses, and make sure Dennis and Steve read them before we left the house. It was eight-thirty-five. Both boys had their clean clothes on and were sitting at the kitchen table buttoning, their shirt or tying a shoe. I said, "You were quick!"

Steve chuckled and said, "I thought you'd be getting after us if we weren't ready by eight-thirty."

I shook my head and reached for Mom's Bible on the little table under the wall phone. I said, "Guys, I can't fuss at you this morning. God just spoke to me because I complained to him about not being strong. Sometimes I really feel like a wimp. I want you to read the scripture he gave me as reassurance.

"It's Joshua 1: 9. Dennis, read it out loud while I put a load of clothes and Mom's slacks in the dryer."

When Dennis finished reading, Steve said, "Man! Mom needs to read Kaitlynn's motto from Isaiah 43:1-3 and these verses in Joshua."

"I'll leave her Bible here, on the table, with a note. Hand me a piece of paper." I said.

I wrote the note and said, "Let's go!"

It only took five minutes to get into town from the farm. Mr. Weber was already there waiting for us. He was standing outside the First National Bank of Chaffee. We went in the lobby with him, and a man came to greet us. Steve was scoping the bank's interior and everyone in it. After the morning is over, he'll have memorized everything about getting a loan.

The loan officer, named Mr. Angle, directed us to the bank's conference room. A lady watched us as we filed past her desk. For 15, 17, and 19 year old boys walking to the conference room with the loan officer was probably a bit unusual to her, but then she spoke, "Boys, I'm sorry to hear about your brother. We prayed for him this morning and will continue to pray. If there is anything we can do to help you while your mother is with Paul, please call us."

It was Pastor Bishop's wife, Kathy. She was smiling and I said, "Thank you. I didn't know you worked here at the bank." As I started to walk away, she chuckled and said, "Yeah, a long time."

I couldn't think of anything to say, so I said, "Thanks for praying," and followed Dennis into the conference room.

We sat down in the plush chairs around a long table. Steve sat down first and I could tell he was thinking about the chairs. The conference room had a long table with eight plush chairs that tilted, swiveled, and rolled. Steve was rubbing his hands on the arms. He was probably thinking, *these chairs are great.* But Mr. Angle said, "Yes, we are all sorry to hear about your brother. I do hope his treatment makes him well."

Then he said, "I understand you need a loan."

Before I could answer, Steve spoke up and said, "Yes, Sir. We're going to expend our mortgage for another few years, so we can put in a well and an irrigation system."

I corrected Steve's word for expend to extend, and he never even heard me. He just went right on talking and said, "Mom decided the best thing to do would be to get a personal loan, pay off the mortgage, and get enough for the irrigation system and the medical expenses Paul will have."

Mr. Weber looked at me as I shook my head. I couldn't believe Steve. His business head must have thought about this since we had our family conference. Mr. Angle tried to be serious. He looked at me and said, "I've looked over our mortgage papers, and you have only about a year and a half on the farm note."

Steve interrupted again and asked, "Is a note the same as a mortgage?"

I said, "Steve, I'll explain later. We have to get up to the hospital."

Mr. Angle answered Steve, anyway. "Yes, it is. So your mother wants to get a personal loan and put only the house up for collateral?"

I said, "Yes, Sir," before Steve had a chance to say any more.

Mr. Angle said, "Well, let's see here." He flipped through our file. "Your house was worth $80,000 twenty five years ago. Do you think it's still worth that much?"

Mr. Weber said, "My wife thinks it is."

Mr. Angle said, It's surely worth more than twenty thousand, isn't it?"

I said, "Yes, but we're only thinking about ten or fifteen thousand dollars—enough to pay off the mortgage and put in a well and an irrigation system."

Mr. Angle asked, "How long do you want to make the note? Ten years?"

Steve asked, "What do you mean?"

I answered, "Yes, we should be able to pay it off in ten years. I should be drawing a salary as well as farming."

I heard Steve say quietly, "Oh." I knew Steve's "Oh" meant he had learned something.

He was feeling the arms of the leather chairs as though his mind was far away, but it wasn't. He said, "I'll be selling off a heifer or two, also, and will pay on the loan. I mean note."

Mr. Weber and Mr. Angle looked at each other. Mr. Weber said, "The boys will be good for it."

I looked at my watch and wondered if Mom was waiting. I said, "Mr. Angle, I'm able to sign any papers. I'm also planning on going to Southeast Missouri University Law Enforcement Academy this fall. As soon as I'm done, I hope to be making a steady salary. Dennis will follow in another year. In the meantime, we'll still be farming, and Mom hopes to continue working."

Mr. Weber said, "These boys have managed to make the mortgage payments even when their mother was having her kidney transplant. They have a good credit history. I will be happy to put my name as a back-up on the loan."

Dennis walked into the conference room. He was done getting the car cleaned and a tank of gas. I asked him what he thought about getting twenty thousand and paying it off in ten years.

He looked at his watch, and I knew he was worried about the time and getting up to the hospital. He said, "Right now Mom has Paul on her mind and nothing else. If we can take the money and mortgage worry from her—let's do it."

Mr. Angle got up and said, "Excuse me. I'll be right back."

When Mr. Angle came back, he had papers for us to sign. I signed, and then Mr. Weber signed them, too, and then he handed us each a copy. He handed me a check for twenty-thousand dollars. I know my eyebrows went up as I had never seen a check that large. Mr. Angle said, "Sign the check and I will apply it to the present farm mortgage. Do you want to put what money is left into your or the family account?"

Steve was crowding me to look at the check. He said, "It's a personal loan. Better put it in the family account."

Mr. Angle looked at Steve, "Son, how old are you?"

Steve looked embarrassed. He said, "I'm fifteen, Sir."

Mr. Angle glanced at Mr. Weber and said, "Steve, when you graduate from high school, come see us for a job."

Steve said, "Thank you, but I'm going to the police academy, too, and I'm going to have a business, too, someday."

Mr. Angle just said, "Oh… good."

We walked out of the bank at ten o'clock and headed for Mom's car. I'm sure Mom was wondering where we were. Our twenty minute trip to Cape Girardeau was rather quiet. We were all thinking about what we had just done at the bank. Finally, Steve asked, "Do you think Dad would have done what we did today?"

Dennis adjusted his seat belt and said, "What made you think of that?"

There was silence again. Then Steve said, "Because Dad had bad weather some of his farming years and he didn't make a whole lot of money from his crops."

I still didn't say anything, until Dennis asked, "What are you thinking, John."

"Just a minute," I said. We were just turning onto Highway 55 from Highway 74, and the traffic was backed up a little. I needed to pay attention to my driving.

I finally said, "I was thinking about what Steve said. Dad did have some bad weather, but he had his back-up job on the railroad to pay the bills. That's another reason why I want to become a policeman. It will give me a paycheck every month."

I handed Dennis my cell phone and said, "Call Mom and tell her where we are."

He dialed her and said, "Mom, we're almost there. About five minutes…. Okay, will do…. Bye."

"Mom said 'don't park the car. She would meet us at the door near the parking garage.'"

We pulled in at the hospital's east side door, and Mom was waiting just like she said. She said, Paul's asleep, and Dr. Lynn is sitting with him. This is Marshall's day off, so he came back to visit Paul."

"Marshall? Who's Marshall?" Steve asked.

Mom realized what she'd said, "I'm sorry. Dr. Lynn asked me to call him Marshall."

She took the keys I handed to her. She gave us hugs and said, "I'd better go. I'll be back as soon as I can."

I told Mom her slacks were in the dryer. We didn't wait for them to dry. She patted my arm and said, "Thanks, boys. I'll be back in an hour."

Mom left, and we looked at each other like *which way do we go?* I went through the double set of doors with Dennis and Steve following me. Steve hurried on ahead of me to the receptionist desk and asked, "Do you have Paul Moore in your computer?"

The lady in the pink jacket said, "Yes, in pediatrics, room 2001."

We said, "Thanks," and headed toward the elevators.

Dennis couldn't help himself. "Steve, how did you know to ask if Paul was in the computer?"

"John told me that's what he did. I watched people stop at the reception counter one day while we were waiting for John to park the car. Someone else was asking for a room number, and a lady looked it up on the computer."

My mind went back to Steve's comment about Dad perhaps having bad crops some years when there was a drought or some bug infestation. I suppose he was able to keep up the mortgage payments because he worked on the railroad.

Mom always put in a huge garden, so we never were short on food—at least not fruit, vegetables, milk, eggs, beef, or chicken.

We got off the elevator on the second floor and went to Paul's room. Paul's face was flushed, and Dr. Lynn was standing beside his bed holding his hand. He turned around and saw us. He pointed toward the door, wanting us to go out in the hall. On the way out, I noticed another bag of blood on the I.V. stand. I assumed it was Steve's blood, but Steve hadn't noticed or would have had a comment. Dr. Lynn started telling us in hushed tones Paul was in serious condition—not critical yet, but serious. "We're going to take Paul to St. Louis as soon as your mother comes back," he said. He asked if any of us had any thought about going with Mom.

We all said, "Yes."

He looked at us with such a serious look. I thought he was going to cry. He's just Paul's doctor. Doctors don't get emotionally involved with patients. It made me uneasy, and I wanted to cry, but I couldn't. There were too many people counting on me.

Dr. Lynn put his hand on my shoulder, "John, I'd like to go with your mother to St. Louis, too. My partner is covering for me. I lost a son to Leukemia. He was nine years old. I grieved for him for years, thinking I should've been a better father and not worked so many long hours. I wasn't there for him and his mother like I should have been. I vowed it would never happen again. Then my wife got sick with a different kind of cancer. I took a year off my practice, and stayed with her. She died three years ago."

He took his hand off my shoulder. It was as if he needed my shoulder for strength while he was talking about *his* family, or the gesture was so I would pay attention to what he was saying. He went on talking, "When Paul came into the emergency room, I was suddenly overtaken by feelings for all of you. I told myself over and over again not to get emotionally involved with your family. Then I would see your mother's face and your faces. You *are special,* as Marianne says. I have no idea what God is doing to me, but I feel His presence every time I see or talk to your family.

"Rachel… I mean Mrs. Weber. She's my cousin. She told me what happened to her family and how your family helped them. I'm so drawn to all of you, I can't think about anything else."

Steve's mouth, always being open, bluntly said, "That's because we don't have a Dad or a Grandpa."

I was surprised that Steve would say that, and felt I should say something. "Well, yeah, we do have a void in our family without Dad and Grandpa. I know Mom has missed our Dad, and then she lost Grandpa, her Dad."

"Maybe God is telling me I should fill that void." Dr. Lynn said.

He shook his head slowly like he was thinking, "Your Mom told me essentially the same thing, but she said I was trying to fill the void in *my* life. Whatever it is, I've lain awake at night and thought about Paul. I feel like he's become my child, my Paul. I hope you understand when I tell you I feel compelled to go with your mother to St. Louis."

Dennis was standing beside us quietly thinking. He looked at Dr. Lynn like he wanted to say something. When he noticed me looking at him he said, "Dr. Lynn, with your medical knowledge of Paul's situation, you can help Mom through this situation better than any of us. She has a lot of confidence in our ability to run the farm and do other things, but we don't know what you know about medicine. Besides, our sister, Kaitlynn, is in St. Louis, and Mom's twin sister lives there, too." Dennis chuckled even though everyone had been so serious. He said, "Perhaps you need to meet the rest of our family up there. You may not want to get involved with us after all."

Dennis giggled again after saying that. I stepped back into Paul's room and heard Dr. Lynn say, "I've never met young men as mature and articulate as you guys, but what about you, John?"

"Just a minute," I said. "Paul's awake," so I quickly added, "I agree—I ditto what Dennis said."

Paul said, "Tell him... John, tell him, I'm gonna be okay. Don't worry about me."

He had been listening to everything we said. Dr. Lynn hurried the few steps back to Paul's bedside and took his hand again. He looked down at him with a serious look on his face.

"Paul, I want to go to St. Louis with your mother, too. Is it okay if I go?"

Paul turned his body the best he could with all the metal bracing he had on his broken arm. He said, "Why? Haven't you ever ridden in a helicopter? Am I going to St. Louis, this time, in the helicopter?"

Dennis and Steve were grinning from ear to ear, but Dr. Lynn wasn't. We waited for him to answer Paul for what seemed like a whole minute. Finally, he said, "Yes, Paul, I've ridden in a helicopter. I was in the military for few years after medical school, and I got to ride many times in helicopters during the war, but right now there's a war going on in your body, and I want you to fight the enemy. Okay?"

Suddenly I had the nerve to say something, and it came out like I, also, had experience in the military. I said, "Paul, let's allow this doctor on board, okay?"

Paul quietly closed his eyes while saying, "Yes, Sir."

Dr. Lynn chuckled, but he looked at me and said, "Thanks, John."

A tear rolled down Dr. Lynn's cheek, and it made me want to cry, again. I knew I had to quit being so nervous for Mom and my brothers. My stress level was high, too.

A nurse came in to check Paul's temperature. It had come down to one-hundred degrees.

Steve said, "See my blood's as good as yours, Dennis."

Paul raised his head up and said, "Now, we're really blood brothers."

He smiled and closed his eyes again, but Dr. Lynn chuckled and said, "He's quite a boy, quite a boy."

Pastor Bishop came in, and it made a full room, so I suggested to Steve that we tell Paul we'll see him in St. Louis. Dr. Lynn went to a chair and asked Pastor Bishop to sit down. My brothers and I walked out, and I stepped back in to see if Dr. Lynn had met Pastor Bishop. He said, "Yes, but let me pray with you before you leave."

I looked back out at Dennis and Steve, and they were too far down the hall to call them back, so I said, "Okay," to Pastor Bishop. He prayed for Paul to be healed and for the entire family to have strength, patience, and wisdom. When he said, "Amen," I said it, too, and walked out of the room. I felt emotional again and wished Grandpa or Dad were here with me.

We checked out the old magazines in the waiting room. They were old issues of some ladies magazines and a few farming or *Popular Mechanics* magazines. I couldn't think to read. Dennis couldn't either.

He was just looking around at the room. He finally said, "John, what do you think about Dr. Lynn.?"

"Dennis, I don't know. I can only guess. Dr. Lynn seems to be an okay guy."

I laid the magazine I was trying to read, back onto the table beside my chair. Dad's been gone so long, and I've always thought us four boys were all Mom needed. Now that I've discovered the comfort and companionship Marianne gives me, I think there's a whole area of Mom's life that's not being fulfilled without Dad. We won't be living at home forever. It's possible all three of us will be living elsewhere within five years. Where will that leave Mom? We'll still be farming the land, but I imagine she'll get pretty lonely. I think Dr. Lynn might be lonely, too. We should all pray for Dr. Lynn until we can be sure he knows the Lord like we do.

"This may be one of those rivers we're crossing through, and we need to trust God because He said He'd be with us. Other than that, I don't know. I just need to have a talk with God."

Mom got off the elevator with her large tote bag. It was loaded. She wasn't carrying her small over-night case. She saw us and looked down the hall toward Paul's room. She immediately thought something might be wrong or Paul might have already gone to St. Louis. She walked toward us with a questioning look on her face. I said, "Dr. Lynn and Pastor Bishop are in Paul's room, Mom. There were too many people in the room, especially when the nurse came to check Paul's vitals. "Mom, Paul's temperature is coming down,"

Mom smiled. She said, "People are praying, and I've prayed. I prayed all the way up here from Chaffee… Are you all okay? You look like you have something on your mind."

"Yes, Mom, I guess we do. We're wondering about you and Dr. Lynn."

Mom smiled radiantly, and I knew something was going on between the two of them. She shook her head and said, "Not to worry, not to worry."

"What do you mean?" I asked.

"Dr. Lynn has express an interest in me. He's really fallen for Paul, and he's very impressed with you guys. I asked Rachel Weber everything I could about his past, and she finally told me everything she could think of. She said if I wanted to know anything else, I would have to ask him.

"I needed to know about his relationship with our Lord, so I asked him. He said his wife was a very devoted Christian woman and played the organ and piano in their church for years. He said they both accepted Christ as their personal Savior when they met some kids involved in Campus Crusade and Inter-Varsity Bible Organization in college. He told me medical school, and Orthopedic Residency, and family took so much of his time that he only went to church with his family when he could. He told me it was a good habit that he'd broken, and he felt Satan's was keeping him busy on purpose."

I noticed Mom had picked up her tote bag and put it back down a couple of times as she was talking. I said, "Mom, I'll carry it."

Mom said, "Oh," and put it back down. She glanced at Dennis and Steve. They were looking up at her from their chairs and listening intently. Mom went on to say, "After he lost his wife and his four children were gone from home, he realized all the extra hours at the hospital were not worth the loss of fellowship. His children have seemed to follow his pattern of being too busy for what really counts. Somehow he's latched onto our family like we're God's second chance for him. But, boys, remember God often covers many bases at the same time in his work.

He may be using Satan's work with Paul's sickness to bring our family and his family together.

"Think about it. God did allow for Dr. Lynn's wife and your Dad to be taken from us for a reason."

I said, "But, Mom, what are your feelings for him?"

Steve said, "Yeah, Mom, he seems nice, but we don't know him yet, either."

Mom looked at all three of us and then down the hall as though she really needed to go down to Paul's room, but she said, "As far as my feelings for him, I'm not sure. I promise you, boys, that I will continue to pray about this, and I ask you to pray, too. I don't want to make a mistake with my feelings for him. I am drawn to him as a person.

Time will tell, and God will tell all of us if Dr. Lynn is right for our family."

Mom picked up her tote bag and turned toward Paul's room. Dennis said, "We'll pray, Mom."

Steve just said, "Yeah," but I asked, "Mom, how do you want us to pray?"

She took a couple of steps away from us, but stopped and looked at me. "Pray that God will receive the glory in all we do and that we obey his directions."

I said, "Okay." Mom turned and went on to Paul's room.

Dennis said, "John, why'd you ask a question like that? You know that's how we should pray."

I reached for a magazine off the table beside me. "I know, Dennis. I just thought she might say we should pray that we can all be together, or something like that, but you're right. Mom is right, too."

Steve sat quietly for a moment, and his business-oriented mind was considering all the angles again. "Hey, wouldn't it be something if Mom married Dr. Lynn, and he paid off the loan we made this morning?"

"Nice, yes, but his name and your name aren't on the loan papers. Mine Is!" I reminded him.

Dennis chimed in saying, "Yeah, John, but we aren't going to let you pay it off by yourself."

Steve laughed and said, "I might."

Dennis pretended to hit him. "Yeah, and that pretty little bull calf might be gone some morning when you go out to check on it."

Steve laughed again and said, "Just kidding, just kidding."

"Don't forget you are in a hospital," I said. "Pipe down."

Dennis, Steve, and I sat in the waiting room until Pastor Bishop came out and said, "I'm leaving. Your mother wants you in Paul's room right away."

All three of us bumped into each other trying to get up in such a hurry. I said, "Thanks," to Pastor Bishop and we rushed to Paul's room. Mom looked concerned. She said, "They're coming for Paul, and they'll be here in a few minutes. I thought you boys would want to be here."

Pastor Bishop followed us back to the room and said, "Let's join hands and pray."

Mom reached for Paul's hand and Dr. Lynn's hand. I took his other hand and Pastor Bishop's hand. Steve and Dennis were on the other side of Pastor Bishop. We circled the bed. Our Pastor prayed for a safe flight to St. Louis and for the doctors at the Children's Hospital to have the knowledge and wisdom to diagnose and treat Paul. He said, "Lord, we give You the Moore family—each of them individually—that they'll be encouraged by You. I pray that they'll feel You by their side through this experience. I pray that Paul will be able to endure whatever lies in his path, and He'll do it for Your glory. I lift up Dr. Lynn, also, Lord. Strengthen him in his relationship with You. I pray in Your Holy name, Amen.

Paul said, "Thanks" and smiled.

I could tell he was feeling better. The Med-Vac pilot and paramedic men were standing at the door in their blue jump-suits and had a gurney with them. I quickly said, "Mom, how're you going up to St. Louis?"

Dr. Lynn looked at Mom, waiting for her to answer. "Boys, I'll have a huge load off my mind, if you can stay here and mind the farm. Get everything caught up and ahead of schedule, and then come up to St. Louis for the day—maybe the day after tomorrow. Kaitlynn and Matthew will be waiting at Children's Hospital when Paul gets there. Bonnie and Uncle Al will probably be there, too, a little later. Dr. Lynn's going to drive me. He knows where the hospital is, and he knows the area around it, so I feel confident letting him take me. Besides, you boys may need my car here, and you can use it to make your trip to the city."

Pastor Bishop and Dr. Lynn stepped out of the room. Dennis and Steve followed, so a nurse and one of the Med-Vac men could push the gurney into the room. They wrapped a warm blanket around Paul and put him on the gurney. I thought, *It's July. He won't need that.* Then I thought, *Yeah, he will. When they get up high in the sky, it will be cool.*

We each said, "Bye, Paul. See you in a few days," or something similar as they pushed the gurney out of the room and into the hall where Dennis and Steve were standing.

I picked up Mom's tote bag. It was heavier than I thought it would be. She smiled and said, "Four changes of clothes and an outfit for Paul to come home in."

I said, "Oh," but Dr. Lynn took the bag from me and ushered Mom on down the hall following the gurney. I had a jealous feeling like I should be right beside Mom. Then I realized, someday Mom wouldn't be beside me, but Marianne would be. I prayed, "Go with them, Lord."

Steve grinned and said, "Prayin' out loud again, John?"

Chapter 11

Paul was taken to the St. Louis Children's Hospital. He's been there five days, and the diagnosis was definitely Leukemia. He was moved to the oncology unit where he started treatments. The doctors are closely watching the healing of his arm. Mom has been very encouraged with the statistics on the success rate with Leukemia.

My sister, Kaitlynn, is taking turns with Mom staying with Paul. She is working at Dillard's Department Store, and Matthew is still not very strong yet, so he is taking classes this summer and keeping busy at their church. Mom said Kaitlynn is happy being a wife, even though she isn't quite twenty-one yet. She likes her part-time job, and she has a servant's attitude. She must have the gift of hospitality like Mom. Mom can think of more ways to help others. That makes me happy.

Mom said she spent one night with her twin sister, Aunt Barbara, while Kaitlynn stayed with Paul. Kaitlynn has also been keeping Mom and Paul's clothes washed and ironed. Aunt Nancy and Uncle Al brought some books and more hand puzzles for Paul to read or work on when his fever is down.

Mom reads to him, or he reads to himself, but he gets very tired and wants to rest or sleep again.

Matthew decided Paul needed some sporty pajamas instead of the hospital tux, as he calls them. Matthew and his sister, Julie, went shopping one evening when Kaitlynn was at the hospital. They bought Paul some slippers and two pair of pajamas—one pair had race cars all over them, and the other had basketballs in a sports print.

Paul liked them but he said, "What I really need is underwear. I feel naked half the time."

He complained of that before he left the hospital in Cape Girardeau. When Dr. Lynn called last night, he told me, "Be sure to get Paul's underwear, and bring it when you come up." He chuckled again, and said, "He's quite a boy."

Dennis, Steve, and I planned to go up to St. Louis to visit Paul on Saturday, after the morning chores were done, and come back later the same day. Dr. Lynn said he was planning to go back up on Saturday, too. He said we could ride with him. Dennis was a little uneasy about all three of us boys leaving the farm and, uneasy about riding with him, too. I assured him that it might be a good time for us to be obnoxious kids and see what Dr. Lynn is made of. He laughed and said, "Yeah, we could ride with him and put Steve up to something."

Steve nixed it and said, "No way. We may be going against God's plans for Mom and Dr. Lynn, and I'm not going to help you out."

I laughed and gave him a knuckle on his upper arm, "Did you really think we'd do something obnoxious?"

Steve shrugged his shoulders, "No, I didn't. You were expecting me to do something."

Dennis and I laughed. I said, "Sorry, Steve," and ran my fingers through his hair. "You're a good kid."

"Thanks, John."

Dennis just had to say, "Only when you are around, John."

Steve went after Dennis, had him on the floor in a flash, and put him in a wrestling hold

"Uncle! I give. I'm sorry Steve. Let me up."

I walked out of the laundry into the kitchen, laughing, and before I could get outside, they both were on me, but they didn't get a good hold. Dennis stumbled and fell. I stepped over him as he was getting up and had him clenched between my legs at his waist. I grabbed Steve at the same time that I stepped over Dennis and had him in a head lock.

All three of us were laughing when Dr. Lynn's car came up the drive. "Uh-oh, we have company," I said.

Both boys relaxed under my hold, and I let them go. I said, "Steve, clear the table. Dennis, straighten up the dining room. Pronto!"

Dr. Lynn had a minute walk from where he parked his car, so I closed the door to the laundry and pantry. Steve was wiping off the table, and he let me go to the back door.

I was slightly amused seeing Dr. Lynn standing there in blue jeans, old brown loafers, and a faded blue-green shirt. The first thing he said was, "I came to help you guys with your chores."

I looked back at Steve and saw him drying off the table. He said, "Good. Do you know how to make cobblers and wash off eggs?"

Dr. Lynn walked on in the kitchen, and I followed. Dennis came from the dining room and said, "No, he can muck out the stalls for me."

We started laughing again, and he said, "Why don't I finish washing the dishes for you?"

I said, "Good Idea. Good Idea." I helped. The dishes were done and put away in five or six minutes.

I slipped into the laundry room while I was waiting for a few more dishes to be put on the rack. I transferred clothes from the washer to the dryer and reloaded the last load Mom left. Steve came into the kitchen from the back porch, having washed all the eggs. He saw me coming from the laundry room. "How much change did you find in my pockets this morning, John?"

Dennis was still working on straightening up the living room and cackling like Paul's chickens. I said, "Okay, Dennis, what's so funny?"

He came to the kitchen looking at Steve. "Steve how old are you?"

"...about as old as you act sometimes," Steve flippantly answered.

I said, "Steve, that was uncalled for!" I sounded like Mom.

"Well, I have a lot on my mind this morning, and he laughed at my question to you. What's he think is so funny?" Steve gave Dennis a look like, *what is so funny?*

I said, "Never mind, Steve. Dennis thinks he knows a secret and has one over on you."

Dennis flopped down on a kitchen chair and said, "I do have a secret that our businessman, here, hasn't caught on to yet."

I knew what he was talking about, but I said, "Neither do you, Dennis."

Dr. Lynn was looking at all three of us and said, "Well, I *do* know the secret, and I think your mother has the greatest imagination in coming up with the secret." He was smiling. Mom apparently told him how she got us to do the laundry.

Dennis couldn't help himself, he just had to tell Steve the secret. "Steve, Mom always leaves change in her pockets, and Dad did the same, because whoever did the laundry got to keep the change in anyone's pockets. That's why I warned John I was getting rich off his pocket change, so he stopped doing it. That's why you never find change in his pockets."

Steve looked at both of us, "You're lying. I always found change in John's pockets."

Dr. Lynn started laughing with us and said, "And I know the rest of the secret."

I looked at him and said "Shhh!"

Dennis started to reach for me, and I moved. "Okay, you're going to muck out my stall and milk my cow for two days if you don't tell us.'

I chuckled again. "Well, the truth of the matter is I *didn't* leave any change in my pockets for you. I always gave Mom a quarter or dime and a couple of pennies and had her put it in her slacks or Steve's jeans when it was your turn to do the laundry. Then I had her put it in your jeans when it was Steve's turn to do the laundry. One day I didn't have any change, so I left a dollar bill in my shirt pocket."

Steve's face brightened. "That was my laundry day. Thanks. I guess Mom was a little ornery for doing that, and you were, too, but now we know how to do laundry and don't mind doing it. Let's not tell Mom we know the full secret."

Dennis headed back to the living room, but turned back and said, "Steve, now that the secret is out, should we let Mom and John do the laundry?"

"No way! Let's not tell Mom we know, and she'll keep paying us with her change for doing the wash."

Dr. Lynn moved from the sink and said, "Now, is it Steve who wants to be a businessman?"

Dennis added, "Yes, and he thinks of more ways to make money. You should have heard him at the bank the morning Paul went to the Children's Hospital in St. Louis. We negotiated a loan, and Steve tried to do all the talking."

"I did not… John wouldn't let me."

Dr. Lynn's voice took on a serious tone, and he asked, "Is your mother aware of this?"

I said, "Yes, we had a family conference. Mom agreed that we should extend our mortgage payments another year or two, and get a new well dug in a field somewhere, so we could put in an irrigation system. Dad and Grandpa had really paid down the mortgage, and that was fortunate for us. Mom suggested that we take out a personal loan and use the house for collateral to pay off the mortgage, but we needed to get enough to dig the well. Her reasoning was that if something should happen, and we weren't able to pay off the note, at least we would still keep the land. That night, Paul began having a fever. Dennis took Mom and Paul to the hospital, and I called you."

"Mr. Weber arranged for us to go to the bank the next morning. He co-signed for us. We figured that to pay off the rest of the mortgage and to put in the well, we'd need at least ten or twelve thousand dollars. Mr. Weber talked us into taking twenty thousand because there might be medical expenses that were not covered with insurance with Paul. As it is, Mom has had to use all her vacation and sick-leave time to be with Paul, and she may even have to quit her job, but we hope not. Then Paul would have no insurance. Dennis and I are willing to take part-time jobs in addition to farming to keep Mom from getting overly concerned about indebtedness and crop failure. I planned to enter the Southeast Law Enforcement Academy this fall, but if I have to, I'll delay it a year. Paul's and Mom's health are our top priority right now. I may have to go back to the Farmer's Co-op for insurance if Mom loses her job."

Dr. Lynn asked, "When's your first payment due?"

Steve said, "Not until the tenth of August, and we should've sold enough eggs and cobblers to pay for some of the bills. The payments are less than two-hundred a month. I have a heifer that I'll be selling, so I can use the money to keep the payments going for the rest of the year."

Dennis added, "I'm hoping to get enough from my ten acres of soybeans to cover, at least, some of the household expenses. The crop is in dire need of water, and that reminds me, I need to go out and change the sprinklers."

Dr. Lynn looked at me. I told him, "My corn crop is getting to the point that it'll have to be plowed back into the ground if we don't get some rain or dig that well.

"I have fifty acres of corn this year. I'm leasing twenty acres from the farmer next door. And it would really hurt if there was nothing left for taxes or seed for the next year. That's another reason we raised the loan up to twenty-thousand, so we'd have enough to start again next year.

I don't like Mom worrying about finances, about her job, about us, about Paul, and about Kaitlynn's husband, Matthew, who is not well yet with his Hodgkin's cancer. It seems like every time there is a crisis and our concerns are great, God allows something else to be thrown at us, and then He assures us that we'll get through it, too."

Dr. Lynn was leaning against the kitchen counter listening to us. He said, "You guys are younger than my children, and I'm amazed at the concern and love you have for your mother and each other. I appreciate that."

Steve's face took on an impish look, and I knew he was going to say something. He did. He said, "You wouldn't if you had come five minutes earlier. John had Dennis in a head-lock and me down at the same time."

"Aw, I could have gotten out of it," Dennis said. "But he had you tucked between his knees, and I was afraid you'd get hurt."

We all laughed a little. I said, "It was play, and we needed it."

Dr. Lynn said, "As long as your play doesn't break any more bones."

Steve said, "We'd never do that if Mom were here. She'd make us go to the Weeping Willow tree and get our own switch."

Dennis gasped, "Steve, you know Mom's never done that. Why'd you say that? She'd have given us extra chores like washing the windows or shining the woodwork."

I was just kidding. One of my friends said that was what his grandmother used to do. I thought it was a good idea. I'm sure his mother dropped the punishment because he needed a different kind of punishment."

I thought, *Yeah, he probably got too big for her to spank.* I went back to the laundry room, unloaded the washer, and transferred the wet clothes to the dryer, and then went back to the kitchen. Dr. Lynn said, "Let's go out and see where you want to put that well."

Steve said, "You go on. I have to make some cobblers for Cousin Stacy. She said she's coming out this afternoon. She said she wants to make sure we're behaving, too."

He walked back to the eggs on the sink on the back porch, laughing, and saying, "Yeah, I'm tellin' on Dennis and John." A car was coming down the lane, and it looked like the Weber's car. It was their car. Mrs. Weber brought Robert and Janet out to help us do whatever chores needed to be done. I was glad because I found more apples that were canned in the pantry, and we still had peaches in the freezer. Steve and Robert could whip the cobblers out quickly. I will have to tell the boys to go check the apple trees because they should be getting close to picking.

Janet knew about Paul's egg business, and she could wash eggs on the back porch as gently as Paul and Mom. There were already at least three dozen in the back porch refrigerator. Janet loved the baby chicks, and she could coax some of the hens off the nests as well as Paul could.

I sent Robert in the house to work with Steve on the cobblers, and I told Janet to go collect the eggs, and then make the beds.

Mrs. Weber walked out to the fields with Dr. Lynn and me. As we walked, Mrs. Weber said, "Marshall, do you remember the summer job we had taking tassels off corn?"

I know I must have shown some surprise that Dr. Lynn knew something about farming,

He said, "Yes, I remember. Dad was upset that we would go to the neighbors, and work in the fields but wouldn't help at home in his fields. I really did help some, but Mom was intent on me not being a farmer, so she would make excuses for me *not* to work in the fields. I had to help a lot, but dad was always financially strapped for some reason. Working for pay that summer gave me a taste of earning money. Knowing what I do now, I regret not helping Dad more. He lost the farm when my brothers and I went off to college because he had no help. Mom didn't help matters because she wanted us to use our brains and do something more financially rewarding. Dad died disappointed in all of us. I regret that.

"We all could have taken a spring semester off to help Dad get a good crop in the ground and then help him harvest the crops in the summer, but Mom wouldn't hear of it, and she encouraged us to stay in school. She didn't realize her life would have been much better if she'd been more supportive of Dad and worked alongside him."

I took it all in—what they were saying—but I didn't say anything to them. If Dr. Lynn and his siblings were my brothers or sisters, I would have kicked butt. There was no excuse for not helping cheerfully. I had a greater appreciation for Mom and Dad as we walked.

I stopped about half-way down the edge of Dennis's soybean field and said, "Dr. Lynn, how did you get into a profession that was caring for people 24/7, and yet you grew up not caring for your Dad's desires for your family?"

I wasn't meaning to be disrespectful, and I'm glad he didn't take it that way. He looked at Mrs. Weber, then at me, and said, "John, I met my wife, and then I met the Lord face-to-face. It took some real grooming on the part of my Christian friends to show me what a self-centered, egotistical person I was. I hope I'm never that way again.

"It's interesting. I see in you, John, the very attributes I lacked as a young person. You and your brothers have it right. Don't ever change. When Dad got sick, I did stop my schooling for a whole year and took care of him. My brothers thought I was crazy or something, but then they didn't step back and take a long look at themselves like I did. I apologized to Dad over and over for not being the son he deserved.

Dad purchased an acre of ground and built Mom a small house on it. She was never satisfied, and she let him know. I prayed earnestly for my mother to come to know the Lord. I spent hours helping Dad make a nice garden on the back part of his acre. He loved the soil, and it flourished under his care, but Mom didn't seem to notice.

"A lady at our church was an influential person in the community, and Mom admired her."

Mrs. Weber asked, "Was that Mrs. Kerchoff?"

"Yes, she befriended Mom, and gradually won her over, and helped her see her need for God in her life. Mom was in her upper sixties then, but she made a dramatic turn around when she accepted Christ as her Lord and Savior.

"I came home one day from town, and Mom was helping Dad in the garden. It was then that Dad could begin to see the change in Mom's life. Dad accepted the Lord into his life not long after, but his blood pressure caused massive damage to his heart. He died at seventy-two, holding my hand and Mom's hand. Mom grieved over the years of unhappiness she brought him. When she died three years later, we were all together for her funeral, and I was asked to speak."

Mrs. Weber said, "I remember that. Your sisters and I were fairly close growing up, but we seemed to go our separate ways after high school and college. It was good to see them again, but they weren't too happy when you gave your testimony of being a selfish young person with no thought of caring for your parents. They knew you were indicting them, too."

"Well, that's okay. Dad and Mom left me every earthly thing they had, and that didn't make matters any easier for me. I'm still an outcast to them, but I am praying for them. The little bit of assets that Dad and Mom left me, I invested for my siblings. When they give their lives to the Lord and admit they should've been better sons and daughters, I'll share it with them. Earthly goods stay here on earth, and in heaven we'll have all we need. If they refuse to heed the witness I've given them, then all of it will be left to missions."

I finally interrupted their memories and said, "Dr. Lynn, why did you choose medicine?"

He smiled and said, "The father of my girlfriend was a doctor, and he talked me into going on a two-week mission trip as a helper. My eyes were open to the tremendous needs in other countries. Somehow during those two weeks, God impressed upon me that I should go back and finish my degree. I changed from education to pre-med. It took me another year and a half to pick up more science subjects. My dear girlfriend stayed with me, and her dad encouraged me. We married, and I went on to medical school. Why I took an orthopedic residency, I don't know. It probably was because there were openings at that time, and I needed the money the orthopedic residency offered. Plus, I didn't have to move."

Mrs. Weber smiled, "My family was always proud of you. It was an honor to have a physician in the family. My folks were Christian people, but they were not committed to the Lord, or the local church. Dad used to say, 'God has a hand on that boy.'"

Dr. Lynn laughed heartily, and said "Really?"

I just stood listening. There was a ten-foot wide area of grass between Dennis' soybeans and my corn. We used it as a road for the pick-up truck or tractors. I crossed over it and lifted the leaves of a plant to see how much Dennis' soybeans were affected by the drought. I took a few steps farther, went to the other side, and pulled back the sheaves of a corn cob. It was way underdeveloped. I tried another one, and it wasn't too bad, but in another week its growth would be stunted unless it got water.

I sighed and shook my head in disgust. Dennis walked up behind me. He walked right past Dr. Lynn and Mrs. Weber.

"John, would you come here and look?"

We walked to where Dennis was using the sprinkler from the hose. There was a definite difference just a few feet away where the water had not reached.

Dennis shook his head and said, "John, we have to do something and soon."

"Okay, the money is in place. Let's go back to the house and call Clark's Well Drilling Company. They've already given us the estimate per foot that they would drill down to find water. It's probably higher now, so we better give them a call and get something on paper."

Dr. Lynn and Mrs. Weber were trailing behind us, but Dr. Lynn said, "Have you decided where you want the well?"

I glanced at Dennis, and he said, "Probably right in the middle of these fields, but we'll see what Mr. Clark says, he has had experience, and we don't."

We walked to the house, but as we approached the barn, Dennis said, "Dr. Lynn, would you like to see our cattle stock? Steve has a couple of heifers and one young bull calf."

"Sure," he said.

Mrs. Weber added, "I want to take a peek at the newest one and then head to the house to check on the boys and the cobblers they're making."

I said, "Would you send the boys out to the apple trees to see if any apples are ready? I think we need another week, but this drought, I expect the apple trees are suffering, too."

"Dennis, Steve, and I planted two apple trees and two peach trees a couple years ago, and this is the first year they are really producing."

Dennis got a worried look on his face and said, "I think I'll take the hose from the garden and give the trees a good soaking. Steve can't lose the cobbler money, too."

I sighed and said, "Good thinking, Dennis. That'd be one more thing thrown our way to worry about, huh?"

When we stepped into the barn, three cats welcomed us. I picked up their water bowls and started toward the barn faucet, but Dennis still had the garden hose attached to it. He'd be looking for it. I unscrewed the hose, filled the two cat bowls, turned the water off, laid the hose down, and walked away. Dennis reattached the hose, but he didn't say anything. He turned the water back on.

Dr. Lynn said, "You guys work together like two surgeons doing an operation. You anticipate each other's moves and just do whatever the next step is."

I wasn't sure what he meant because I hadn't noticed that I had left the hose off and the water off.

Dennis chuckled, "I guess we do. I couldn't leave the water off from the barn because it's watering my soybeans."

We walked through the barn. The little bull calf was prancing around his mother. Dr. Lynn was impressed. "That's a dandy," he said, "Is that the one Steve said he'd sell to make payments on your loan?"

I started thinking about the loan again, but said, "Yes, but he's thought about building a herd with this one before selling him. But if he sells him, it should make one payment on the loan—maybe two. He has those two young heifers by the north fence. They are coming along nicely, and biologically they have no relation to the bull calf, so Steve might start a small herd before he graduates high school. We'll need to sell off the calf's mother some day. Between Steve's FBLA club and his 4-H club, he sees himself as a rich man by the time he graduates. He'll only be a sophomore this year, so who knows, maybe he'll have a sizeable bank account by then. Steve's not afraid of work. I know he doesn't see himself making apple and peach cobblers for Cousin Stacy all his life."

Mrs. Weber said, "Oh, I should go in the house and see how those boys are doing with the cobblers." She turned and left us, walking back through the barn.

I heard Janet yelling, "Mom, come quick! There's some kind of animal in the hen house, and it has a chicken by the neck!"

I shot through the barn like something had stung me, leaving Dr. Lynn staring at me like he'd done it. I was about to say what Paul said when he was under the influence of his anesthetic: "Those dumb weasels!" Only he used a stronger word.

I reached the hen house with Janet and Mrs. Weber close behind me. I was so angry that I forgot to duck my head far enough for my six-foot-three-inch body, and I hit my head on the top of the door frame. I was stunned for a second, but there—just like Janet said—was a weasel with a hen in its mouth. It dropped the hen and ran through the little door hatch, that we let the chickens in and out of each day.

I picked up the hen and said to Janet, "Steve and Dennis are going to be furious. They said they'd scalded and cleaned their *last* chicken, and I don't blame them. Let's not tell Paul. He doesn't need to hear about this."

Dr. Lynn came to the door of the chicken house and said, "John, what happened?"

Mrs. Weber and Janet stepped out, and I followed them. They were looking at me peculiarly. I was standing there with a hen dripping blood from its neck. I had blood running down my forehead. Dennis had gone back out to move the sprinkler hoses, and he saw us running into the henhouse. He was just walking toward us to see what had happened. He took one look at me and asked, "John? Looks like you forgot to duck."

"Funny, Dennis."

You might think that weasel was popular. Steve and Robert came out of the house to see what was going on. There were five people looking at me standing there with a dead chicken in my hand.

Steve said, "Oh, Paul's going to be upset about losing another hen. John, what did you do to your head?"

"I hit it on the top of the door frame. Are you guys going to just stand there looking at me or are you going to take this chicken and get it cleaned up for supper?"

Dennis seems to always have a wise-crack at the most inappropriate time. He said, "I've sworn off chicken strips and chicken nuggets. Steve can do it."

I finally reached up with my free dirty hand and wiped my forehead. Dr. Lynn reached for my hand and pulled it away, replacing it with his handkerchief. He wiped the blood off the area just inside my hair-line and said, "John, I need to take you in town and get some stitches in your head. You have a nasty cut there, and there's no telling what kind of bacteria is lurking in the wood of the henhouse."

Mrs. Weber took control. "Janet, take the chicken up to the house. Dennis and Steve can tell us what to do with it."

Robert was looking at his mother and said, "Not in the kitchen. I have one more cobbler to make."

Steve laughed. "John, can I get my camera and take a picture of you with your bleeding head and bleeding chicken? I'll label it: *No Winner!*"

I was about to knock his fifteen year old head off his shoulders, but I said, "Just go get the large canning pot and put water on to boil. Mrs. Weber, Dennis and Steve know what to do with the hen."

I started walking toward the house, and Janet reached down and took the dead hen from me.

"I'll lay it in by the dirty eggs, okay."

"Thanks, Janet."

I went on to the house following Janet. Everyone else followed Janet and me in silence. You would have thought it was a funeral procession for the chicken. I went to Grandpa's bathroom and washed my hands. Then I reached for a clean wash cloth from a shelf and cleaned my face and head. I did have a big gash in my head. Dr. Lynn was standing in the bathroom doorway. He said, "Sit down on the edge of the tub and let me look at it again."

I did, and he immediately said, "John this really needs to be cleaned with an antiseptic. It needs about five stitches in it. How does your neck feel? You must have a good whiplash to hit your head like this."

My neck hurt a little, but all I could think was, *Mom doesn't need to hear about this.*

"Please don't tell Mom about this. I'll cover it with my hair or something, so she won't have to worry about another medical bill."

Dr. Lynn patted my shoulder and said, "Let's go. I'll take you in my car, and don't worry about a bill. I'll take you to my office. Your mother won't ever have to know—at least not now."

When I walked back to the kitchen, Steve said, "I'm sorry, John."

Dennis had that Cheshire cat grin on his face again. "Me too, John. Janet and Robert are going to learn where chicken meat comes from."

Mrs. Weber just smiled and said, "I'll see you two later."

The phone was ringing, and I stopped in my tracks, thinking it might be Mom, but it was Marianne. Mrs. Weber answered, and she was telling Marianne that I was on my way to Cape Girardeau to get stiches in my head.

I said, "Let me talk to her."

"Hello, Marianne, please don't worry about a little gash on my head. My brains are intact." I chuckled when I said it.

She didn't let me say another word. "I'm going to meet you in Cape, so Dr. Lynn doesn't have to come all the way back to Chaffee."

All I could think to say was, "Whatever you want to do. I'll see you later."

I looked at everyone standing in the kitchen, looking at me, except for Robert; he was covering the apple cobblers with aluminum foil. I couldn't help myself. I said, "Janet, will you sweep the back porch? Dennis, call Clark's Well Company, and water those fruit trees. Steve and Robert, take care of that chicken."

I looked at Mrs. Weber, and she said, laughing, "I'll take care of the laundry. Have the sheets been washed this week?"

Dennis had to say something. "No, we don't believe in washing our sheets, but Mom made us do it last week anyway."

As I stepped out on the porch, I heard Robert say, "He's like a sergeant, isn't he?" I chuckled to myself and walked to Dr. Lynn's car. He was already in it, and he had the motor running. I climbed in holding a washcloth on my head and said, "Typical day around here."

He smiled as he backed the car up and said, "Keeps life interesting, doesn't it? There's never a dull moment."

"I'd welcome a boring day."

Dr. Lynn changed the subject and said, About that well, John."

We discussed the pros and cons of it, and I think I convinced him it may be too late for this year, but at least it would be in place if we needed it next year. I told him I didn't know how old the well near the house was. We use it for the barn, garden, and house. We use a lot of water for the animals, too. If it goes out, we'd have the new well to tap into.

We had a nice conversation on the way to Dr. Lynn's office in Cape Girardeau. I didn't feel like I was talking to some professor or doctor, but just another man. He was very encouraging. I know Mom has good instincts, so I'm going to trust her if she develops a closer relationship with Dr. Lynn.

We walked into Dr. Lynn's office through the back door. The office girls heard us and said to Dr. Lynn as he was getting his white coat on, "We thought you weren't coming in today."

He said, "I'm here, but I'm not seeing patients, okay?"

One of them said, "We understand," but they were looking at me.

Dr. Lynn said, "This is a friend of mine, and he needs stitches in his head."

One of the girls in a nurse's uniform jumped up and said to me, "Come this way, Please."

When Dr. Lynn was about done working on me, he said, "This should heal up nicely. I had to shave a little hair away from the cut, but it should grow back, and you won't notice the scar."

I heard Marianne's voice talking to the girls at the front office. It was comforting, and I was ready to go to her. "She timed it just right for lunch, didn't she? Would you like to go with us, Dr. Lynn?"

"I'd love too, but we can't go far. Let's just hit the hospital cafeteria next door. I want to catch up on some paperwork over there this afternoon."

One of the office girls directed Marianne back to the minor surgery room. She took one look at me and said, "I'd like to brand you as mine, but not up there. You really hit yourself good, didn't you?"

Dr. Lynn said, "It would be good to take the stitches out in about a week. That'll be a good excuse to come back to the farm for a visit. I'll bring some sterile scissors."

"I suspect Dennis or Steve will be offering before you ever get out there."

"Don't you let them *touch* my work!"

We laughed and walked out the back door to go to the hospital cafeteria. Dr. Lynn hung his short white coat on a hanger where he had taken it from on the way into the office. I was so hungry I didn't care what I looked like, but Dr. Lynn had taken a sport coat from the place he hung his white coat. He chuckled and said, "I've got to preserve my image." It did cover his faded shirt and jeans a little.

At the cafeteria, when we got our food, we sat at a table near the door. Marianne said, "John, do you realize this is the third week in July? Summer is half over."

I sat there for a moment. "Marianne, if the rest of the summer is like the first half, I'm not sure I want to live it."

Dr. Lynn and Marianne looked at each other and then at me, seriously. Dr. Lynn said, "John you've had more than your share of responsibility and concerns. Do you feel depressed, sort of like you have reached a point in life where you just can't go on?"

I took another bite of my hamburger and said, "I could very easily become that way. There have been times when I've felt that I've had too many people and too many things to deal with, but I have God by my side. I've said many times, 'God, I'm only eighteen,' and each time I say it, I've gotten a quick answer: '…and I am God, Trust me.'

"I try not to complain because God has the bigger picture in mind, and my part is just a tiny part of what God's doing. I didn't mean for my remark to sound so dismal. The Lord gave me a whole year of maturing—rough times yes—but I'm okay."

Marianne leaned back in her chair and said, "Good. I was worried for a moment."

Dr. Lynn was looking at me again with a serious expression. "John, don't hesitate to come to me, sit in my office, and have a good cry. I know how you feel, and if it's any consolation, I've been there. I've come through some bleak times, but through the trials and testing, God perfects us."

"I must be pretty close to perfect then."

Marianne said, "I think you are."

Dr. Lynn looked at us with a fatherly smile and said, "Well, you young folks enjoy your lunch. I have to get upstairs and check those records or they'll kick me off the hospital staff. I'm going to call your mother and see if I can talk to your Uncle Al. He said he'd keep me up on the medical status of Paul's treatment. I know you'll want all the details, too."

I shook my head *yes,* but I had some really quick thoughts go through my head about God sending us help just when we needed it. I said, "Thanks for coming out to the farm. You know it was just another one of those times when God sent help knowing we were going to need it on the farm."

Marianne added, "It wasn't just a chance or coincidence that Mom went out to the farm either".

"No," I said, "It wasn't. All the talk between your mother and you, Dr. Lynn, gave me some idea about your life as a boy and your family. I really felt better about the friendship that has developed between Mom and you."

I was a little embarrassed after saying that, but went on talking, anyway. "I learned that farming is something you know about. It made me feel good to know that you could have pursued your own goals, but you chose to follow the Lord's leading. Mom talks to us often about that, and at my age, I think about that a lot. Mom puts the question before us all the time, 'What does the Lord want for you to do with your life?'"

I chuckled, "Mom would have fainted if she saw all the blood on my head and the gash, so God put you right there to do something about it."

Dr. Lynn was standing beside the table, rapped his knuckles on the table, and said, "I've got to go, John, but I want you to know that you and your brothers have developed a real understanding of life, and you… well, your wisdom surpasses many adults. I want you to know that. I'll see you two later."

I wasn't sure what he meant by his compliment, but I said, "Thanks. If you hear anything from Uncle Al, Let me know."

He walked away while saying, "I will."

Marianne said, "I'm done. Are you ready to go to Chaffee?"

I put my napkin beside my plate, "Yes, I need to get back to the farm."

We both got up from the table at the same time. She said, "Which way?"

I said, "Well, I think we came in the door that Dr. Lynn went out, so let's go that way." A nurse at the next table asked, "Where do you need to go?"

Marianne said, "My car is parked close to Dr. Lynn's office. We walked over here."

She told us to take the elevator up one floor and go to the front of the hospital and when we went out of the hospital to turn right."

We both said, "Thanks," left the hospital cafeteria, and found our way to the parking lot at the front of the hospital nearest Dr. Lynn's office. I told her it wasn't a mistake that she had called when she did. Dennis would have had to drive to Cape Girardeau to pick me up, or Dr. Lynn would have had to drive all the way back to Chaffee. God's timing is perfect."

Marianne smiled when she looked up at me. She said, "I know. I'm glad I thought of that after Mom told me what happened.

We left the parking lot, and I noticed that Marianne was a little reserved. She was a little quiet during lunch, too, so I asked her if there was anything bothering her.

"Sort of. I was just thinking about how fast summer's gone, and I'll be going back to school in St. Louis in three weeks. I'm wondering how the children's musical is going to do without Paul. I had Paul playing his trumpet, but that's out of the question now. I'm counting on Steve to sing. He's older than the children, so he's been my helper."

I could see why she might be a little worried. I said, "Let's see what happens. Paul loves to play, and he may surprise us all. That's still two weeks away. He'll be disappointed if he isn't well enough to play. God's still the God of miracles where Paul is concerned."

When we arrived home at the farm, the house was quiet. I wondered what was going on. Mrs. Weber was sitting at the table with Cousin Stacy, and they were talking like they'd known each other for years.

I asked, "Where's the boys and Janet?"

They both laughed. "If you go out and look at the apple trees, you'll see."

Marianne and I went out the front door where the apple trees were located east of the house. Janet and Steve were in a tree throwing apples down at Robert and Dennis. I shook my head. I thought about the documentary on monkeys and chimps that I had seen recently, how they jump from limb to limb and even sleep in the trees away from the danger below. I shook my head. The boys and Janet were acting like a bunch of monkeys. I asked them what they were doing. Dennis said, "Cousin Stacy said we ought to go ahead and get as many of the apples as we could, green or not. She looked at what was on the trees, and they were rotting prematurely because of the lack of rain. She said not to take the apples if they didn't snap off easily. A lot of the stems to the apples are dried up, even the small ones."

They had already gotten a bushel off each tree. Dennis placed a hose under the trees, and it was pure mud where the boys had been tromping around picking up apples. I picked up a full basket and said, "I'll take these in. I guess we'll have to make a place for these in the cool basement."

Cousin Stacy and Mrs. Weber came out of the house. Mrs. Weber said, "That's a lot of apples."

Cousin Stacy said, "I'll take some to the Café if you don't mind. Perhaps someone will want them by the pound. I'll have one of my employees make pies from those that are culls. Anything else the boys bring in, they can put in the freezer or we will can them."

Cousin Stacy picked up a basket, so I carried mine farther away from the tree and all the mud, set it down and then took her basket from her.

I thought about Mom and my sister, Kaitlynn, always doing the cutting and paring apples for canning. I looked at Mrs. Weber and said, "Paring and cutting up apples is something I've never done. Mom, Kaitlynn, and Steve always did it."

She chuckled, "Me either, so I think we will make it a project for everyone after chores tonight," she said. "We're going to make apple dumplings, apple fritters, apple jelly, apple bread, and maybe even bake an apple cake."

Cousin Stacy walked past me, "Maybe I'll be able to come back tonight and help."

She picked up one of the big bushel baskets again. Marianne nudged me and whispered, "Take the basket from her."

"What—Oh! Cousin Stacy, give me that basket. Let me carry it to your car."

"Thanks, John, I really wasn't thinking. I just had a million recipes running through my mind from what Mrs. Weber said. Apple fritters and apple dumplings sound like a good addition to our café menu."

I carried the apples to Cousin Stacy's car, wondering if they'd been picked too early. I'll just have to trust God on that, too.

Dennis brought another basket to the back porch and said, "We left quite a few on the trees. We'll see what a good watering tonight will do for the rest of them."

Mrs. Weber looked at her watch, then at the kitchen clock, and said, "John, all the beds have been stripped and washed. I'm going to leave. All the laundry is stacked in baskets. Where is Robert? We need to leave."

I walked past her to the laundry and said, "Thanks, Mrs. Weber. We've really needed your help—Janet and Robert's, too."

Janet and Steve were talking with Cousin Stacy, but they heard Mrs. Weber ask where Robert was. Both of them were laughing with a touch of ornery excitement in their voices.

"We left him in the apple tree, Steve said, "He said he was stuck and couldn't get down. We thought he'd figure it out if we left him."

Cousin Stacy was walking out the door to go back to the café, but she was stern. "Go get a ladder."

Steve didn't move an inch. He said, "Robert is not dumb. I told him sitting in the tree is like life. Sometimes, you have to sit and think. Then come up with a solution before you act. I'm hiding when he comes down because he is *mad*."

I looked down at the floor. Both Janet and Steve had tracked mud in the house with their shoes. "Now I'm angry! Go out to the back porch and take off your shoes. Look at the floor."

Mrs. Weber shook her head and said, "Oh, my! John, I really need to be going."

I put on my sergeant's cap and said, "Mrs. Weber you've done enough already. Thank you for doing the laundry and thank you, Janet, for cleaning the eggs and helping with the hen house, but you, Steve, go get the mop. I'm going out to see about Robert."

I rounded the corner of the house just in time to see Robert make a leap to the ground and slide in the wet rotten apple mess under the tree. His mouth was open and muttering all sorts of revenge on Steve and Janet. If only I had a camera at the moment Robert sat down on the ground and looked at his fingers. A seventeen year old didn't make it any less a picture than a small child who first discovered mud would slide through toes and fingers. It took all I could do to keep from laughing, but I said, "Oh, Robert, I was coming to help you down, but… I think your Mom would prefer you leave those clothes here and ride home." I started to say naked and laugh, but held it in and said, "Take your shoes and socks off and leave them on the step. Then go in and take a shower in Grandpa's bathroom. I'll get you some clean clothes."

When Robert came around the corner of the house, Steve was just hanging the mop on Mom's clothes line. He didn't see Robert, but Robert saw him, and before Steve could turn to go back to the house, he got a wet sock on the side of his face, and a shoe flew over the top of his head.

Robert said, "Where's Janet?"

Mrs. Weber laughed as Janet rounded the car and jumped in from the other side.

Robert yelled at her. "Just you wait, Janet. I'll get you."

Mrs. Weber said, "Robert, go take a shower. I'll come back this evening to get you."

I had to laugh with Mrs. Weber. It did me good to laugh. I told Mrs. Weber she needn't come back. Robert could drive back to town with Marianne, or Dennis could take him home.

I asked what size clothes Robert wore, and he was Steve's size, so I told her goodbye and decided to go for Steve's favorite shirt for Robert to wear home.

Steve had gotten in the shower upstairs, so I had to hurry and get the shirt. I did a quick check to see if he had taken it to the upstairs bathroom with him—sure enough the shirt was on a hanger on the back of the door. Clean pants, underwear, and socks were on a stool in the bathroom. I grabbed all of them and took them down to Robert in Grandpa's bathroom. I told him to hurry as these are the clothes Steve had planned to put on. Robert asked, "Where is Steve?"

"He's upstairs in the shower singing, at the top of his lungs. He didn't hear me open the bathroom door."

I said, "Hurry. I want you standing outside the upstairs bathroom fully dressed when Steve opens the door and starts yelling for some clothes.

"I want you to say, 'Sorry, Steve, John brought these to me. Revenge is sweet, sometimes.'"

Dennis was sitting at the kitchen table oblivious, to what was going on. He was thinking about something deeply. Finally, he surfaced from his thoughts and said, "John, what's going on?" I told him Robert was getting harmless revenge on Steve for not helping him out of the apple tree. Robert fell when he jumped down and got mud and apple slime all over him.

I was telling Dennis, when Robert came running through the kitchen from Grandpa's bathroom. That was the quickest shower any seventeen year-old ever took. Dennis and I followed Robert. Just about the time we reached the bottom of the stairs, we heard Steve yell.

"John, where are my clo…." Then Robert said, "This is my revenge. I *love* these pants, and this shirt is just my color, as Marianne would say. John thinks so, too."

Steve yelled, "John!"

I went on upstairs, laughing, and said, "Dennis will take you home, Robert. He's ready if you are."

I handed him a pair of socks and a pair of shoes I thought would fit. He looked at them, and said, "These will do." He grabbed the shoes and hurried back downstairs. Steve was standing in the bathroom doorway with a towel around him.

Dennis said, "Hurry, Robert, we need to get you out of here before Steve comes back downstairs."

I told Robert we'd pick up Steve's things tomorrow, and his dirty clothes would be clean. Dennis and Robert were gone by the time Steve found more clothes to wear and came downstairs. He was really mad at me, but I told him Robert's revenge wasn't nearly as bad as what he and Janet did. Leaving Robert without a ladder or anything could have resulted in a serious injury. If he jumped and landed wrong on the wet ground or slid on a rotten apple, he could've sprained an ankle or broken a bone. Even though the lowest branch wasn't very high, what he had to jump onto—or over—was a little dangerous.

I asked Steve, "How did Janet get down?"

"I helped her."

Steve sat at the kitchen table for a moment and said, "I'll call Robert tonight and apologize."

I said, "Good thinking, Steve."

"What do you say we call Dennis on his cell phone and tell him to stop somewhere and bring us some hamburgers and fries? I'm not in the mood for cooking, especially with a bushel of apples staring at us. I wish Kaitlynn was here. She's good at peeling and paring apples."

Steve said, "Yeah, a couple of hamburgers sounds good to me. Where's Marianne? Does she want one, too?"

I looked back in the living room. She was sound asleep on the couch, missing all the fun. I called Dennis. He was just leaving the Weber's house. I said, "Dennis, if you have any money, would you bring us some hamburgers and fries? Marianne is still here, too."

"Three dollars is all I have with me. Call the café and ask Cousin Stacy if she'll have the cook fix us up some hamburgers, and I'll stop by and pick them up. Tell her I only have three dollars with me and I'll pay for them the next time I'm in town."

I told Dennis I would, but I hated to do that because I knew Cousin Stacy would include a dessert and whatever else she could think of.

Dennis came home forty-five minutes after I called. He said, "Cousin Stacy sent two hamburgers a piece, fries, and she wants our opinion on her fresh apple cake made with apples she got this afternoon from our trees."

I knew she would send something extra along. The hamburgers hit the spot, and the cake was really good. It was still warm because it had just come out of her oven. I called her, and told her maybe Steve and Robert could bake a couple of apple cakes instead of cobblers for the next week. She said, "I've been thinking on that already."

I cleaned up the kitchen and let Dennis and Steve relax before we did evening chores and started working on the apples. Mom called, and we all talked to Paul. He was feeling lousy from his chemo therapy, but he was anxious to get home.

Mrs. Weber called to ask about Marianne. Marianne took the phone and said, "I'm on my way, Mom." She walked out the door as soon as she hung up the phone.

I walked her out to her car and she said, "I should have gone on home, when Mom and Cousin Stacy left. I've always told other girls, they should never put themselves in a place where they might be tempted to do something they shouldn't or that others might be tempted with them. Here, I went to sleep on your couch with a house full of boys, not that all of you aren't to be trusted, but I need to walk the talk. Right?"

I said, "I think God knows it was innocence on your part, and he'll protect your reputation."

I chuckled and said, "Don't worry about it. I might have been tempted, but I had too many other things on my mind. Besides, your brother was here. He would have protected you from me."

Marianne just smiled and said, "Yeah. I've got to go on home."

I reached in the car, patted her shoulder, and said, "I'll call you tomorrow."

I watched her drive around our circle drive between the barn and house thinking, *Cape Girardeau talks about putting in a round-about on some streets, and we've had one on the farm for years.*

I went in the house, and Dennis said, "Mom called again. She said she has to get back to work next week. Kaitlynn's going to take a week off and say with Paul. After next week, Paul might be able to leave the hospital and go home with Kaitlynn. Matthew will care for him in the daytime when Kaitlynn's at work. She said, 'Paul won't be very happy, but that's the best we can do for now. I can't lose my job and insurance.'"

I said, "I'll call her back. She can tell Kaitlynn to take two days off, not a week. I'll go up and stay two or three days with him. At least on the days Matthew has summer classes. Maybe Paul will be able to go to Kaitlynn's before the week is up, and Uncle Al, or Aunt Nancy, or even Trevor or Aunt Barbara won't mind spending one day with Paul."

I asked Dennis if he could manage the farm if I went up to St. Louis for a couple days. He said, "For the normal chores, yes."

I called Mom back. Mom agreed, "We'll work it out. I'll tell Kaitlynn to only take two days off. I think it'll be better for her."

I told Mom that we were going to try to peel apples before it was barn chore time. She reminded me to put some lemon juice in the bowl of water that we put our peeled apples in. I always wondered what kept the apples Mom peeled from turning brown. I chuckled to myself because I learned something new. Dennis and Steve talked with Mom again. I think we all felt better after hearing her voice.

After putting our peeled apples in the freezer and cleaning up the kitchen, we all went to the barn. We had the milking done and the cows put up for the night in record time. I walked to the hen house to lock it up for the night, and I caught that weasel in the hen house *again*. It was just sniffing around, and I was glad. I scared it off, checked all the drainage holes, and pushed the little hatch door down. It seemed easy to slide up and down, so I opened the door to go to the shed and saw Dennis walking toward the house. I yelled at him to bring me a nail and hammer. If I had to nail the hatch down every night, I'd do it.

I told Dennis, "We just have to get another dog, and it has to be a dog that has instincts for catching rats. I think they call them ratters. In the meantime, we need some kind of latch on the little door."

Dennis said, "Yeah, I wish I'd thought about that when we were talking to Paul earlier. He wasn't very alert and cheerful. Matthew said that was because of the cancer treatments. It makes people sick. Let's pray that we find a puppy or a younger dog—one that we can train to not bother the chickens and yet go after the weasels."

I nailed the little door shut and went on to the house with Dennis. It was hard to relax. Steve noticed it first. It was getting close to ten o'clock, and he was sitting at the table with a piece of paper in front of him and a pencil in his hand. He was staring off into space. I asked him if he had called Robert and apologized to him, even though I agreed with Steve's opinion of thinking before acting. Robert could have gotten down if he had done some good thinking, which he finally did. The danger was all the rotten apples, and the wet ground under the tree, not to mentioned all the bees that were all over the rotten apples.

I had to speak twice before Steve realized I was taking to him. He finally said, "Yeah?"

I asked him what he was thinking about.

He said, "Mom and Paul, Kaitlynn and Matthew, Dr. Lynn's visit this morning, Mrs. Weber, Robert, and Janet coming out to help us, and Cousin Stacy showing up, too. Then I thought about Robert slipping when he jumped out of the apple tree, and you busting your head on the chicken house door, and a weasel killing another chicken, Then Marianne calling just in time to go get you from Dr. Lynn's office.

I wonder if tomorrow will be more relaxed. I'm almost afraid to go to bed tonight. The slats under my mattress might fall out one by one."

Steve laughed nervously. What he said made me think I'm not the only one who feels pressure from all the crises in our family. I made a quick decision to talk to him about how much he trusted God.

I said, "Steve, would you fix me a cup of hot chocolate and one for Dennis, too?"

I can't always read a face, but this time it was obvious. He was disturbed that I could only think of my stomach when he was so burdened. I should have gotten up and said, "Steve, let me fix *you* a cup of hot chocolate, and let's have a brother-to-brother talk,' but I didn't. The kitchen seemed to always be where Steve enjoyed working and fixing things to eat or drink.

I shared with him my feelings about all the stuff that goes on in our family and how I've had to pray and ask God to give me wisdom and patience with everything and everyone. He agreed.

We both left our cups on the counter by the sink and went on to bed. It had been a long day. I felt like I was already walking in my sleep and almost lay down on the living room couch where Marianne had been sleeping. It looked so inviting, but Mom has instilled the ritual of brushing our teeth before going to bed, and I knew that I was going to have to climb the stairs to do it.

All three of us went to bed and crashed. Our day was over.

Chapter 12

It's been two weeks since Mom left Chaffee, and Paul was air-lifted to Children's Hospital in St. Louis. It's been almost two weeks since Steve and I had our late night talk, too. Dennis came down that night for a snack, but he only said one thing. I was glad because what he said summed up all that I had been saying to Steve.

Dennis said, "I heard you talking and decided to let you two alone, but I know what you were talking about. I'm not blind to everyone's feelings around here. I just want you to know that there's only one way we're going to survive this family's ups and downs, and that's for each of us to learn which things are beyond our control and which things we can do something about. You both need to go to bed. Now, I'm going to be Mom. Brush your teeth!"

Dennis flicked Steve on the head with his fingers that night, like there was a bug on it and left the kitchen laughing. Steve jumped up and said, "I'm going to get you sooner or later, Dennis. You better watch out."

Steve picked up his cup and said to me, "Tell me, John. You helped Robert give me some harmless revenge. I need to do something to Dennis."

I just laughed and said, "I'll sleep on it. Let's go to bed, and don't forget to brush your teeth."

After locking all the doors, I went upstairs and thought. *That's it. Steve can do something with Dennis's toothbrush—something harmless.*

I went back down to the kitchen and found Mom's brown gravy paste. I think its dehydrated beef stock or something she uses to make gravy. I took it up to Steve. He thought it was hilarious. He put a little gob of it on Dennis' toothbrush and ran back downstairs to put it back in the kitchen.

Dennis came out of our room and said, "I wish you two would hurry up and get in bed. I can't relax with those stairs creaking every time you go up or down them."

Steve came back upstairs with the stairs creaking with every step. He walked past Dennis and said, "I'm not going back downstairs for anything, so good night." He was grinning.

Dennis went back in our room. I said, "Goodnight, guys" and went to the bathroom to brush my teeth. I heard Steve in his room laughing. He put the gravy paste on *my* tooth brush, too. I used Steve's toothbrush to clean mine off, and then I went to bed laughing.

Dennis wanted to know what was funny. I said, "Oh, just something between Steve and me. He thinks he put something over on me. Goodnight, Dennis. Don't forget the Well Company will be out early in the morning."

The verse, *laughter does good like a medicine*, came to my mind. I said, "Thank you, Lord, for leaving your written word with us."

I must have gone to sleep as soon as my head hit the pillow. I woke up with the sun shining in the window and Dennis yelling, "*What* is on *my* toothbrush?"

I sat up on the side of the bed, ran my fingers through my hair, and looked at the clock. I had overslept. It was twenty till seven. I walked to the bathroom and said, "It's called harmless revenge. Oh, taste and see—the Bible says."

Dennis sniffed his toothbrush and said, "It smells like roast beef."

I laughed, and Dennis said, "So that's what you were laughing about last night."

Steve heard us laughing, and I smelled coffee. I knew Steve was waiting for Dennis to find his toothbrush. He came to the bathroom door fully dressed and said, "John told me revenge doesn't have to be mean. But it can be harmless and sweet, or did he say *tasty?*"

Dennis rinsed off the toothbrush with a smirk on his face. I knew he had something in mind for me or Steve. I'll keep my eyes and ears open.

I grabbed my jeans and went back to the bedroom. I heard Steve telling Dennis, "It's Mom's gravy paste."

Steve walked past my door laughing, and I heard the stairs creak as he went down. He yelled, "John, would you and Gravy Breath hurry up and get down here. I made pancakes, and they're getting cold."

Dennis started down the steps just as I came out of my room. I couldn't help saying, "Dennis, isn't this a much better way to start a day than some gloom and doom on our minds?"

"Yeah, but since you put Steve up to that stunt, you'd better watch your back."

I laughed again, but I knew he would do something.

The phone was ringing, and I grabbed it as I sat down for breakfast. It was the Well Company. They said they were running late and would be out in an hour. I hung up the phone and said, "Thank you, Lord."

Both boys were looking at me waiting to hear who called. I said, "That was Clark's Well Company. The man said they were running late and wouldn't make it out here for an hour, or maybe a little more. We can relax."

Mom came home last week and worked at the railroad office. Kaitlynn took two days off work to stay with Paul. I stayed two days with him, and Dr. Lynn went up one day during the week so Mom could work, but Uncle Al was there, too, so he left early. Paul is going to be released from the hospital this weekend when Mom goes back to St. Louis. He will stay with Kaitlynn and Matthew for another two weeks. Aunt Barbara looks so much like Mom that Paul has bonded with her. She has volunteered to stay with Paul while Kaitlynn works and Matthew can't be there. The whole family has worked out a schedule. I know Paul's humor has kept all of us from being emotionally distraught over his leukemia, especially since it came so soon after Mom's kidney transplant and Grandpa's death.

I have had so much on my mind: my responsibilities on the farm, getting another well dug, checking out the irrigation systems, Paul's health, Mom's health, and keeping Dennis and Steve from arguing. I haven't had time to see Marianne, but that is going to change. Tonight we are going on a date. I talked to her yesterday, and she was all smiles. I will really miss her when she goes back to St. Louis.

Her church musical, with the children, is next week, and then she leaves to go back to the Missouri Baptist University. I hope she can come home on weekends at least once a month. Otherwise, I'm going to have a big phone bill.

To add to all the things that I need to think about, I got my acceptance letter from the Southeast Missouri University months ago. That means I'll be back in school soon,, too.

I need to put my pen down. The well company just drove into our driveway.

Chapter 13

Another chapter of my life began this week when I started school at the University in Cape Girardeau and the Police Academy. Not only did I start a new chapter in my life, but I started a new journal last night. I closed out my old journal. It was full. Mom insisted we keep journals of our lives. She said, "It doesn't matter what you write, but make it truthful. Write about things that happened during the day, or how you feel about something. It makes for interesting reading years later when your memory fails you for the details on some experience. Record when you had a doctor's visit for some disease. Even people who come to visit make for interesting reading."

When Mom asked me if I was keeping a journal, she added, "John, your journal needs to keep the facts about when you called the vet and what it was for. Be sure to keep the dates. Even doctor's appointments are important to remember. You may have had a tetanus shot, and that is important out here on the farm."

Then when Dennis was old enough to have his first journal, she said, "If you don't know the words to spell, draw a picture."

I remember looking at Dennis's journal, and he had drawn a picture of himself and me. It said, "John hit me." I don't remember that, but apparently I hurt his feelings, too. Dennis laughs about his picture now because he doesn't remember the incident either.

Three weeks have gone by and the men came out and drilled for water and put in our well for irrigation. They had to drill about 30 feet farther then they thought they would have to drill. It was interesting to watch the process. I hope they weren't annoyed with my brother, Steve, Dennis and me for watching. Steve's mouth was open and he asked so many questions. I had to chuckle to myself, because every time he asked a question, I was wondering about the same thing. It was good for us to watch. I know Paul would have been out there watching with us, but hadn't come home from St. Louis.

Two days after we got everything set up with the well and the irrigation system, we had rain. It wasn't much, but the weather forecast just said it would be cloudy. I was thanking God the moment I felt the sprinkles. We got just enough rain to wet the top of the ground, but it helped some. The leaves on Dennis Soybeans seemed to perk up. But we need enough rain to soak down in the soil several inches. We harvested the corn last week and our yield was small, but the soybeans should be better. We'll harvest them in a few weeks.

Paul is home now. Mom hired a person to stay with him and do some home-schooling, too, while she is at work. I almost decided to delay starting school, but after my surprise birthday party that Mom and Marianne gave me, and since the police officers came, who had asked me to consider law enforcement, I thought I would go on to school. If necessary, I would drop out or arrange my classes to be off some of each day to help with Paul.

My first week of classes at the Southeast Missouri Police Academy were interesting. I thought I wouldn't know anyone on campus, but somehow they knew me. I walked into a class on the first day, and the professor proceeded to call everyone's name to get an idea of who was there. He called my name twice. I answered the first time but he called it a second time, so I raised my hand when I said, "Here!"

The professor said, "John, I was looking forward to meeting you."

Then he proceeded to tell the whole class that I was instrumental in catching a criminal policeman, and I'd decided to replace that bad cop by becoming one.

The class laughed. He chuckled and said, "I mean, he decided the bad cop needed to be replaced by a moral, hardworking, young man. He convinced his two brothers and a friend to become policemen, too. Two of them will, hopefully, be students here next year."

I gave the professor a thumbs-up motion. The professor said, "Welcome, John. We're glad to have you here."

Then he began telling the class about the goons who were hired by the crooked cop to give a family in Chaffee a hard time, but they went beyond being legal about it. He told them about Mr. and Mrs. Weber being locked in the trunk of an old car, with sticks of dynamite attached to the trunk closure and key mechanism, and they had beat up the two teen-aged children in the family. As he was telling that experience, I relived it and then had a hard time getting my mind back to the present. I just shook my head and tried to concentrate on what the professor was saying. He went on and talked to them about being upstanding, moral, people if you expect to be in the leadership of a community.

He then started talking about me, again. I wished he wouldn't do that. I became a little uncomfortable. He said, "John, here is an example of a hard-working responsible young person. If you need a friend, John is one you can lean on and help you through life's problems.

He lost his Dad, in a farm accident, his Grandpa died, and his mother had a kidney transplant, and here he is in college with his youngest brother home with leukemia.

I felt like everyone had glanced in my direction or were looking at me. I felt like I needed to say something, so I did. I said, "Professor," I had a lapse of memory for a moment. I couldn't remember the professor's name. I said, "Yes, things are tough around our house and farm, but I've learned some valuable lessons through it all. I will add to what you said, "One of the things that was cemented in my mind was the difference in character and personality. I'm 19 years old now, but because I've had to be reliable and responsible, I've thought a lot about character and personality."

The professor sat down in his chair behind his desk, and I realized that this was his class and not mine, so I said, "I'm sorry."

He said, "John, go ahead, but let me call off these last three names. Then I want to hear what you have to say about character and personality."

He called the three names and asked, "Who would like to help John out and give us a good answer for what it means to be a man of character.

A girl on the front row raised her hand and the professor nodded to her and said, "Okay." She looked back at several in the class and said, "Santa Claus comes across as a jolly child-loving person... that's personality. It's what people see or hear from a person, but the same Santa Claus may be a rotten man on the inside that molests children, lies about it, and destroys a child's life in private—that's character and a bad one."

The professor looked at me and asked, "Is that right, John."

I said, "She's right. A good example of that was that crooked cop. He was always kind to me. He even stopped me once because my tail light was out on my Grandpa's truck. I asked him if he could show me how to take the cover off the back light and he did it. Then he told me what stores would carry the same light bulbs.

"When I was taking my little brother to the hospital with a broken arm, he stopped me for going too fast. Instead of giving me a ticket, he called his dispatcher about where he was and what he was going to do. He told me to park the truck; *he* was going to take me to Cape Girardeau. He didn't give me a ticket either time. I thought the man was a good man. That's how he came across to me. But, when it came to a girl that he wanted, he became a stalker and he hired someone to break the law for him. There had to be some personal ethics or sense of what was appropriate or not appropriate behavior that didn't match up with the badge that he wore."

I was so nervous, that I found myself fiddling with the zipper tab on my notebook. I wondered what I had really said. I think I sounded like I did when I'm talking to my younger brothers.

The professor asked, "Do you agree with John? Raise your hand if you do. Any disagree?"

He then added. "I agree with both of you. It's a shame that we have people with shoddy characters walking the street today, but have great personalities. As young people, you need to be able to discern which it is. You can do that by asking some simple questions about what they think about news items, or what they might do in certain situations. Sooner or later they will reveal their dark side, so be aware.

I looked on my schedule to see what the professor's name was. I was in Professor Harrison's class. I wondered how he was going to go with his subject for the first day. Maybe he was just wanted to see what the mind-set was of the young people in his class, about laws or morality, and all that. He asked the question. "If the founders of our great nation knew that morality had to be based upon something that could be applied to every individual, do you think they spent time thinking about what might be relative or 'true for you, but not for me,' or do you think somewhere in their minds they had to design some laws which could be applied in any given situation? We pay a lot of attention to what we call 'situational ethics.' But, should a policeman or a police woman stop and examine every situation or must he always adhere to a hard and fast rule?"

One guy said, "Sometimes?"

The teacher asked, "Would you care to explain our answer?"

The boy in the class looked like he was Steve's age. He must have graduated when he was still 15 years-old. He looked too young to be enrolled in college, but he gave a good answer. He said, "Well. It would seem to me that sometimes there might be a real good reason why a law was or is broken—like John's brother's broken arm. It seems like a police officer should be able to think fast before he slaps a ticket on someone. To just give a warning, might come under situation ethics. Don't you think?"

Some of the students shook their head yes, and waited for the professor to answer, but my mind went straight to my little brother, Paul. He would attach "don't you think?" on the end of his sentences, too. Paul seemed to process a lot of information in his brain, and when

I would answer him, his 'Oh' word would follow or he would say again, 'Do you think?' as though he wasn't sure he agreed with my answer.

Anyway, the professor asked the class if we agree with the boy's answer. Another girl said, "I agree. My brother-in-law was speeding, really speeding, but his wife was in the back seat of the car having my little nephew. The police stopped him. Her husband pulled over and jumped out of the car and the policeman drew his gun and was yelling, 'Stay in the car!' He was glaring at my brother-in-law like he had already thought, 'this man is going to be trouble.' My brother-in-law yelled again, 'my wife's having a baby… my wife's having a baby.' Fortunately, the officer was a daddy and remembered his training and my nephew came into this world right on the highway."

The professor asked. "Well, let's see now. I need to get your names correct here. He pointed to the young kid. "Your name is?"

He said, "Martin Turner, Sir."

Then he pointed to the girl and said, "And your name?"

"Patty Lucas."

The professor smiled and said, "Congratulations on the nephew."

She said, "Thank you."

He went on talking, "I accept your answers. I know John did, and your brother-in-law, also, stopped their vehicles. But wouldn't that cause us all, in any critical situation, to ignore a law when *we* think it is an emergency or just convenient. It hit the news big time about the man taking his father to the hospital because he was having a heart attack. The man didn't stop his car, but went straight to the emergency room door, with the police siren going, and they both were traveling at a high rate of speed. When the man ran into the hospital to get help, the police officers were right after him on foot. They arrested him.

The father was admitted to the hospital, but died, anyway. Should the man have stopped? Another boy, who was sitting next to me, raised his hand and said, "Yes, the man should have stopped, but when you get into a frightful situation like that, it's hard to make a rational decision. I'd like to ask a question, will we be trained to give aid to a person right in the middle of a heart attack? If so, the word should go out that policeman have in their car, something to give a person like that."

The professor moved to the other side of his desk and looked out the window for a second, and then turned toward the class again and asked, "Would anyone like to answer that question?"

No one said anything. The professor looked at me. I shrugged my shoulders like *don't look at me for that answer,* but it didn't matter, he asked me, anyway. "John, what do you think?"

I shrugged my shoulders but said, "Well, I don't know. It would seem that police officers could carry aspirin or nitro-glycerin with them in case they needed it. I suspect though, that the very act of *out*-speeding the cop to get your father to the hospital would have made, even me tense. It would contribute to the father's heart-attack getting worse. I know my younger brothers tell me, 'Your driving is going to *give* me a heart attack!' I think the man should have obeyed the law, stopped and run back to the police officer and said, "My father's having a chest pains and may be having a heart-attack,' And then hurried to his father's side of the car. If the police officer had a level head, he would have sized up the situation quickly and called for help or put the man in his own car and headed for the emergency room, while calling ahead, so someone would be at the door with a gurney or wheelchair."

"Do you agree with that, class?" The professor asked.

One kid asked, "What would aspirin and whatever the other stuff do?"

The teacher answered the kid. "Well, aspirin thins the blood to help prevent a stroke and the nitro-glycerin, well... I'm not sure what the medicine does, but it is given for chest pains. To answer John's statement about why policeman don't carry that kind of medicine, aspirin is an over-the counter medicine. That's known as an OTC medicine. Anyone can buy it without a prescription. But the nitro-glycerin is a *prescription* medicine and can only be given by a doctor who knows what the medicine is and has made the diagnosis that it is needed.

The class was the criminal law class, so the professor gave us an overview of the subject we would be studying. His mind went from covering medical emergencies to crime situations that we might find ourselves in when we aren't in uniform. I took notes. He almost made me want to get paramedic training, too.

His mind went from crime situations, back to emergency medicine. He said "Police officers have only a very limited amount of training in medicine or emergency medicine, so for liability reasons leave the medical emergencies to paramedics, doctors, and nurses. Lawsuits are making society greedy and unforgiving. That's my opinion but, let's get back to the subject. He must have had some incident on his mind that he was very familiar with as he kept talking. "If you should one day find yourself alone with a real medical emergency, use common sense. Immediately call for back-up and an ambulance, and…" He chuckled and added, "say a prayer."

The professor smiled when he said that, but I suspected he meant it. He went on, "When it comes to medicine, you must remember you suddenly become a lay person with no medical training—unless, you have added training as a nurse or a paramedic before becoming a police officer. Make a person comfortable, reassure them that help is on the way, and wait with them. You can carry bandages or something to stop excessive bleeding, but even that is limited. I always carry some clean towels and baby wipes in the trunk of my car for that sort of thing, but that's all."

I thought about the towels Dennis and I took out to Dad when he lost his arm in our old combine. The towels didn't do much good. He bled out too much and died anyway. I glanced out the window a couple of times. The professor glanced at me and said, "Let's see now, we've gotten side-tracked from obeying laws, and class time is getting away from us."

I had to get my mind back to the present, too. The professor continued, "We are a land of laws that are well-thought out, and they apply to everyone regardless of the circumstances or situations. There isn't any place for individuals to change a law at a moment's notice because they find themselves in an emergency.

"Always be aware of where you are, your surroundings, and what might be going on around you. I cannot enforce that awareness often enough. Things can happen right in front of us, and our minds can't go in many directions at once.

"Then if you are off-duty and come upon a scene where a man is holding a gun on someone, or you walk into the midst of a robbery, use the same common sense that you would as if you were anyone else. Since you will be trained as a cop, you are much more able to size up a situation and take control of it quickly. Often the culprit will not fear you, because you aren't in uniform. Don't give him reason to turn on you. You will be trained in martial arts, so stay calm and get the upper hand, and I would suggest you always carry your badge in a pocket or somewhere, so you can pull it out and let others know you are a policeman, and especially the culprit.

"Well, students, this is the first day of class, but I'm going to give you an assignment. Read the first two chapters of your book, and as a side thought, I would like for you to think about the word morality and why there are laws. And I would like for you to do some research and write what you find. I want the most current information that is out there. Get out your paper and pen. Question #1. The availability of illegal drugs has it increased or decreased. How many users are minors and what ages have increased? Look for last year's report if you don't find anything for this current year.

"Include in your report the answer to this second question. What do the illegal drug cost our country annually?

"Then I want you to do a survey among students on campus? I only want one or two paragraphs. Ask your friends and others, if they give themselves a high mark for their own personal ethics and character or are they satisfied with what they believe to be right and wrong.

You may get into some heated discussions, but don't allow that to happen. Just ask on a scale of 1 to 10 how they would grade themselves.

If you have trouble finding source material on drugs, I will help you on that, but I would like for you to find sources on your own first?"

Professor Harrison was smiling when the bell rang. I suspected that he thought he might even create more of awareness on campus about morality and that would be okay with me. I thought, too, that this class is going to take a lot of my time. When I passed him at the door, I asked, "Professor, how do you know so much about what goes on in my life or what happened in Chaffee?"

He chuckled as students passed behind us. He said, "I read every students profile that they give of themselves and any references given and I have a personal source. I know Pastor Jack Bishop and he told me about the incident, if I can call it that, at the Weber's home. He, also, told me about the many losses you have had in your life."

I know I must have raised my eye-brows a little, but I said, "I guess my reputation has preceded me to the campus. That's okay. I just don't want to disappoint those who are depending upon me.

I left my Criminal Law class and went to my Criminal Justice class. I felt like the next professor was continuing the lecture from the previous class. Only, he took a different approach and was essentially answering the question that the Criminal Law professor had asked us to think about, and that was morality and why there are laws.

Both professor said things that led me to believe they were Christian men. This professor asked, "Do we have any Muslims or Islamic students in here?"

I wondered where he was going to go with that question. He went on, "Remember what happened on 9/11/2001? America and its democracy is based on *Christian* principles. I don't mean a particular church group like Methodist, Catholic, Baptist etc., but principles that all church groups adhere to."

I think the professor, whose name was Dr. Stone, thought against pursuing his thoughts, because he paused, glanced down at his desk, and said, "There are people in all religions who do not agree with the principle of loving your enemies or doing good, to those who hate you. It is in the heart of some people to do harm to others, if they don't agree with you, or if there's some reason they just don't like a person or a group of people. Remember Hitler?"

He said, "Even though we base our democracy on Judeo-Christian principles, an individual has to use some degree of reasoning to maintain a sense of morality. We all learn, as children, to *lie* is wrong, or to *steal* something is wrong. Children learn by conditioning for why they shouldn't do something. Most often it's because they have learned the consequences, but as children grew older, what gave them the thoughts that some behavior is wrong? Was it just the consequences? I don't think so. It is because the parent or other care-giver has a set rules and the child must adhere to that standard and it's, also, my belief that we were created with a conscience and a desire to know—a curiousness for and about something that is good and bad. I would really like to get on a soap-box here because we have a break-down in our culture in America, and in many other places in the world, too. Sound or good principles and guidelines have been lost. Relevance has taken the place of truth and absolute truth at that."

The professor looked at me a couple of times, and I wondered if he knew me, too. I almost felt a little paranoid. He repeated the statement he had previously made. "Relevance has taken the place of truth and absolute truth, too. Class, what does that mean?"

One girl, sitting near the front, answered. "My Dad is always telling me that I needed to be more relevant. He said, 'You need to try to be more appropriate in what you wear for where you are going, and that includes what you do or say should be appropriate for the occasion.' It took me awhile to learn that our culture has *hidden* rules for behavior."

The professor looked at her for a second and then asked, "Can you give us an example of that?"

She said, "Sure… I might wear a bikini swim suit to the pool or to the beach, but I would never wear it to church."

She laughed, and the whole class did a little chuckle with her, but the professor said, "You are right. That does answer the question of relevance, but…"

He was looking straight at me, "Moore, What is meant by truth or absolute truth?"

I was nervous and didn't mean to be arrogant, but what I said came out that way. I said, "I think I could teach your class on that one, Sir."

He quickly sat down at his desk, before I could follow with an answer. Dad and Grandpa would have chided me for acting like Steve. My younger brother, Steve, seemed to always want to give an opinion on everything. Some in the class giggled, and I decided I could either allow myself to be embarrassed or come up with the answer. When I stood up and moved one row toward the front, I heard someone say, "Wow, he's tall. I guess my height does carry a little bit of authority with it, but the class waited to see what I was going to say. I paused a moment and wondered if should really say what I was thinking but I went ahead and said what I thought. "As future policemen and women, we must stand up for what is right and not excuse it away because it *doesn't* or *won't* take into account the man or woman's background, race, or education.

"I remember my Grandpa saying that, after something came out in the paper about a man getting a lesser punishment for a crime he had committed." He said, "John, I want you to read this article and remember this. If the laws depended solely upon relevance, all of us would find some excuse for why we did or didn't do something. Laws must have Truth as their basis or the foundation to build upon will get weak. We may accept what is *true* in life, but what is *true* may change, but what is *Truth* will not change."

I started to sit down, but the professor said, "That was good, Moore. Can you give us an example of that?"

I had to think for a second, and decided the kids in the class didn't look any older than my brothers, so I might as well get into the role of big brother. I said, "Well, my dad and grandpa were important people in my life. My dad died in a farm accident, and my grandfather died less than a year ago. Both men influenced my life toward what is true and what is truth. To explain the difference, I can use my blue shirt as an example. It is *true* that I have worn this blue shirt today. Today is August 30. Tomorrow, I may wear something different. So, what is *true* is subject to change. But, it will become a *truth,* that I wore this particular blue shirt on August 30. That truth will *never* change. In my mind, that is the reason why laws must be based on what is true, but also, truth. Dad used to say, 'John, if you want to grasp what truth really means, you must study truth for truth's sake.' That statement didn't really make sense to me until I understood the value of truth. Truth has to be something more than just a theory. Sometimes it is easier to understand if you think about all the erroneous or mistaken beliefs. They become the cause of all sin, disaster, misfortune, sickness, and failure in the world. When our professor mentioned absolute truth, he was talking about what is forever…. eternal. God is eternal. Whether or not you believe that God exists doesn't change the fact that God is eternal. Whether or not you believe that on August 30 this blue shirt was worn in Professor Harrison's class is up to you to believe, but the fact will always be and will never change."

I wondered if I should say any more and looked at the professor. He leaned back in his chair and smiled. He said, "This all goes back to what I said at the beginning of the class time, America and its laws were originally established upon Christian principles. Right, John?"

I started to go back to my seat, but he said, "Class, is John right in what he said about what is true and truth?"

The girl on the front row, said, "My mother said, 'all ideas start in the mind.' But don't we all have different opinions on things and wouldn't that make us all subject to failure? Wouldn't that make the foundation for our laws weak?"

I started to go back to my chair. One smart-aleck boy on the far side of the room from where I was sitting said, "Let John answer that one, too." He thought he had embarrassed me, but I knew immediately his motivation behind his statement, because he laughed when he said it, and his voice tone said, "Let's see if Professor Harrison's and Dr. Stone's boy is all that swift." I thought, *I'll bet he just heard what the Criminal Law Professor said about me in the last class.*

I looked at him, as I took a step toward my seat, and then looked back at Dr. Stone. I said, "I'll answer."

I looked at the girl and said, "Your mind is like the fields that I cultivate. It is like my mother's garden. *we* or *you and me* allow or purposefully plant seeds in it. That's why we go to school and it will produce something from it that's much larger than the seed. Or, our minds are like a telephone station in a large building that takes in messages and then clears them out to different extensions. It should keep a person fully occupied to store up worthwhile truths in your memory and then send those good thoughts out to others. All ideas and ideals, plans and purposes, aims and aspirations all begin in your mind. Where did I learn that? I was fortunate to have a mother that would quote such things to each of us, so I heard her admonitions over and over. My grandpa would add to what she said, by saying, 'Remember that good thoughts need constant attention because they carry with them health, harmony, and happiness.' It's like an irrigation system on the farm. It showers water over a defined or definite area of soil, but the water will wet the soil beyond where the irrigation system is reaching. We are like that. Professor Stones teaching will reach our ears, but what we learn will go beyond just our own minds.

My Dad would say, 'All of God's laws are laws of love, truth, and justice.' Then Mom would add, 'Let those laws rule your mind and life.' I was a big kid before I realized the full meaning of those words."

I chuckled as I probably was the tallest and biggest person in the room. "Well, I mean… I mean *old* enough to understand what the older people in my life were saying. Our family is into keeping journals, and with five kids in the family and hearing those words over and over…I finally had them fixed in my mind enough to write them down. One of the last things my grandfather said to me, was 'Son, nothing will ever give you so much satisfaction and permanent benefit as a profound study of truth.' When I started studying the Bible, I realized that when God said, 'I am the Way, the *truth* and the Life,' it made things clear. That's why our laws must be based on Truth or Christian principles, as our professors said.

I looked at Professor Stone. I really wanted to get back to my seat. He said, "Thanks, John," and I walked back to my seat. He said, "We knew you would be an asset to our program here at Southeast Missouri University. Every one of you who applied for this Criminal Justice program were scrutinized carefully for character, habits, talents, and your motivation for getting into this kind of profession. I am quite sure that John will find 99.9 percent of this class will agree with what he said.

"It is my belief that all men—meaning all people— are *created* with the ability to distinguish between what is good or bad. Even in primitive cultures, places where they can't read or write, the children are taught to respect age, and *position,* and the rules given them. I have my reasons for that opinion. There is a strong desire to do evil in the life of a child. We don't have to teach a child to be bad, but we must teach him or her, to be and to do what is good. Regardless of where you live, or if a child is yours or one not your own, as responsible people, we must show or demonstrate to them through our actions what is good. Every policeman or policewoman must have the skills in his own life to demonstrate discipline when it comes to morality. We can't have every pretty woman who gets stopped for a traffic offence flirting with an officer or not giving tickets just because *she* appeals to *him*. That's an area where discipline must take place. "Our culture in the United States expects its police force to enforce laws, so as a policeman or woman, you must have impeccable morality, integrity, and a character that is exemplary. That's what we look for in the students who come to the Police Academy and our Criminal Justice program. Of course, it helps to have a pleasant personality, too."

Professor Stone chuckled about that, and several students laughed. He said, "Tomorrow we will begin the subject to be taught in this class. I hope you are all in the right class. This is Criminal Justice 101.

"I would like to throw out a few more questions for you to think about. And, if you can come up with the latest statistics on these questions, bring me a report. It's a good way to boost your grade point average. I also, want to know what your sources are for the report." He passed out a sheet of paper with the questions on them. I looked at my watch. I knew I needed to get back home. Paul was home from St. Louis and was having a home-school teacher start today, too. Mom wants to go back to work, if one of us boys can be home, also.

My last class ended at 11:40 a.m. and I hurried to the parking lot. It was a fifteen minute drive back to the farm. I thought about Grandpa's old truck that I was driving and wondered how much longer the truck was going to last for me to use to drive back and forth to the Southeast Missouri University Campus, and the Police Academy. I also thought about my classes and wondered if the smart-aleck kid in my second class could have some issue with me. I prayed out loud, "Lord, I need your wisdom to deal with him."

By the time I reached home, I had forgotten everything about the morning that had just passed. I was hungry and tired. There was a car in the drive. I didn't recognize the car, but I knew I would soon find out who was visiting. I parked the truck near the barn and went on in the house.

It was Paul's home-school teacher's car, and she was ready to leave. She said, "Hello. I'm Deanna Webster. I'm ready to leave. I gave Paul some homework. He has two days to learn about President Washington."

I said, "Okay," and she went on out to her car. I went to Paul's bedroom. He said, "Hi, I'm glad you are home." He said it as though he was very tired. He yawned, and I asked, "Did you eat anything when you were up?"

Paul turned on his side and balled himself up like he did when he was a baby, with his knees bent and his hands tucked under his chin. He said, "Yeah, I ate one of Mom's sandwiches and drank some milk."

He yawned again and hesitantly said, "You can leave me alone, too."

I chuckled and asked, "What about your homework?"

"She gave me that giant book on the end of the bed. She wants me to learn about a President each week starting with George Washington. John, that book is for grown-up kids, not me."

He didn't raise his head up and look at me. It made me worry about how well he was, and if the medicine he was taking was a bit too much for him.

I said, "Paul let me take the book and make it simple and interesting on George Washington for you."

I picked up the book from the end of his bed. It was a bit heavy. More like a college level book. I thought, *I had better reduce the facts on several presidents.*

Paul yawned again, and I looked at the clock. My stomach told me to get something to eat. Mom left sandwiches in the refrigerator with a note. "John, these are for you and Paul. Make sure he eats one at noon. Dennis and Steve have already eaten."

I ate one, drank some milk, and found the cake Steve had baked yesterday. I ate a piece and decided, I had better get a brief rest before Steve and Dennis came home from school and then review what I had learned in my classes this morning, too. I cleared the kitchen table and went back to check on Paul. He wasn't asleep yet. I said, "Paul, I'm going upstairs. Mom should be home soon."

He sleepily said again, "Okay, you can leave me alone."

I wrote a note and taped it to the dishwasher. "Dennis, empty the dishwasher. Steve, check with Mom and see if she wants anything started for supper."

I went upstairs, and Dennis was on his bed sleeping just like I had left Paul. I wondered why he was home. I thought Chaffee started school yesterday. I looked in at Steve, and it looked like he hit the bed and just sprawled across it sideways. Both boys were sound asleep. I went back to Dennis's and my bedroom, laid down as quietly as I could, and opened Paul's history book to the index. George Washington was listed on several pages. So I opened the book to the first page listed. I didn't remember all the facts on George Washington and found it interesting.

I got up and got a pencil and some notebook paper, climbed back in bed, and wrote down the important information about George Washington's life: Where Washington was born and raised, the date he became President and some facts about his family. I thought that was what the teacher wanted Paul to learn, but as I read, I saw what Washington said in his farewell address in 1776. It could be applied to our culture and society today, even though it was well over 200 years ago.

It was interesting because we had talked about morality in Dr. Harrison's class this morning, and the need for morality in Washington's day was just as true then as it is now. Maybe morality is needed more today, with television, the internet, or other technology bringing evil to our eyes and ears. I got up and went to the computer in our bedroom that Dennis and I shared. I typed what Washington said and printed it out. I laid back down and read it again.

Washington said, "Of all the dispositions and habits which lead to political prosperity, religion and morality are indispensable supports. Reason and experience both forbid us to expect that national morality can prevail in exclusion of religious principle. Virtue or morality is a necessary spring of popular government." "Wow! That's good!" I said. Dennis sat up. "What's good? What are you eating?"

"Nothing, Dennis. I just read something."

Dennis flopped back on the bed and said, "Oh, well, read quietly, please."

I wondered if people in our government agreed, that we must have some sense of morality in the United States to make democracy work. I came to Abraham Lincoln, and he thought the Bible a perfect example to ensure morality.

Lincoln said, "Nothing short of infinite wisdom could by any possibility have devised and given to man this excellent and perfect moral code. It is suited to men in all the conditions of life and inculcates all the duties they owe to their Creator, to themselves, and to their fellow men."

I wondered if Dr. Harrison, my professor, had ever read that. When I read what Jefferson said, it didn't impress me as much as what Lincoln said. Jefferson was the third President. He said, "Injustice in government undermines the foundations of a society. A nation, therefore, must take measures to encourage its members along the paths of justice and morality."

That could mean anything. What measures? More laws and more ways to punish people, is that what he meant by encouraging people by justice? As far as I'm concerned, there is only one "just" being, and that is God. In the early days of our country, the men who drew up our constitution, had a strong belief in God and the Bible. Hopefully, I can get Paul to understand, that God knew what could be and what should be in forming the United States government.

I was reading and yawning, and finally shut my eyes. The book fell on my chest and hit my chin. Dennis was getting up and saw the book fall. He started laughing. I opened my eyes and lifted the book from my chin.

Dennis said, "You need to put your feet on the floor big brother. I heard Mom downstairs."

"What time it is? I tried to see the clock on my desk.

"It's time to get up. It's time to get your shoes back on, It's time to think about chores. It's time to help Mom with the house work and get ready for tomorrow. It's time…. Well, let me see what time the clock says."

I put my shoes back on, looked at the clock, and said, "Funny, Dennis. It's 4:12 p.m. Is Steve still asleep?"

I felt really tired, even after resting, I felt like I needed to get an hour of sleep. The first three days of school are the hardest, and I thought going to school half a day wouldn't affect me like this, but driving the twelve or fifteen miles each way in Grandpa's old truck has taken its toll on my body, too. "Dennis, we had better go downstairs. Someone, besides Paul, must be downstairs with Mom."

I yawned, picked up the papers I had written for Paul, grabbed the history book, and headed for the stairs. Dennis followed me.

When we got to the kitchen, we found Mrs. Weber and Janet sitting at the table with Steve, not Mom, Paul was awake and watching T.V. in his bed. Mrs. Weber said, "Janet was worried about the chickens and Paul's jobs getting behind, so we came out to see if we could help you."

Janet said, "The house was quiet, so we figured you guys had gone to sleep as soon as you came home."

Paul got out of his bed and came to the door. I ruffled the hair on Paul's head and said, "I'm sorry, Paul, you were sound asleep when I went upstairs. I figured I had time to reduce your history to a more interesting level before you were awake."

Paul smiled and said to Janet. "That lady who came today to be my teacher must think I'm really, really, really, re-al-ly smart, to use her history book."

Janet looked at Paul as he sat down at the kitchen table beside her. She tapped his arm and said, "Paul, I think you *are* really, really, re-al-ly smart, too. No one in the Chaffee schools knows about chickens and makes money from them like you. I think you're smart."

Paul's face lit up like a Christmas tree. He giggled and said, "Thanks."

Mom walked in the back door and looked at the crowd at the kitchen table. She said, "To what or whom do I owe this visit from these lovely ladies?"

Paul said, "They came out to see if I needed help with the chickens and eggs."

Paul paused and added, "Yeah, Mom, we need to do something nice for them."

I noticed Janet and Dennis smile at each other. But Janet said, "Paul, my room needs cleaning. When will you be available?"

Paul's expression looked serious, but Janet started laughing.

Paul said, "I don't want to clean a girl's room. They have more stuff in their rooms than boy's rooms. I'll clean my little hen girl's dirt and beds out in the chicken house." He giggled after saying that, and we all laughed. Paul laughed with us, and it felt good to laugh. It had been a hard day for everyone.

I asked Steve and Dennis, "How come you only had a half-day of school today?"

Janet answered for them. She said, "We just had sort of a trial run on all our classes today. They allowed 20 minutes in each class room, but first we had about a 45 minute time in the auditorium. The principle gave us a pep talk on how we should dress, what tardy meant, and all that stuff. Then each first period teacher called out the names that were in her first period class."

Steve added, "She had a hand-held microphone, and each teacher repeated the same thing, 'you have only eight minutes to join me outside that far door, so listen for your name carefully. Eight minutes is all the time you will have between classes to get to one class and the next. So move quickly."

Dennis said, "We all wondered, how we would know what our next class would be, but the principle went up to the micro phone on the stage and said, "Each first period teacher will have your schedules and will answer any questions you have."

I was sitting there thinking, *that must have taken some time on the secretary's part to get each students schedule in the right teacher's classroom. That's different than last year.*

Mom said, "I guess that was a more orderly way of doing it. Mailing the schedules would cost too much and having students line up behind a table with the alphabet could get a little disorderly."

Mom looked at the kitchen clock and said, "Well, folks, I need to head upstairs for my twenty minute rest. Can you stay for supper, Rachel? Boys, have you thought about what you want for supper?"

We all said, "No."

Mrs. Weber looked at her watch. "We really can't stay. Robert needs to be picked up at the café. He conned me into letting him meet a couple of girls and guys there after school for an hour. It was sort of a birthday celebration for one of them. He's going to be tired, too, so I guess we had better be on our way."

Janet said, "I have some reading and geometry problems to do. So, Paul, I'll come out when I can. Okay?"

Mom answered for Paul. "Sure, Janet, that would be good. I'm headed upstairs. Boys, surprise me with some idea for supper. I'm fresh out of thinking power at the moment."

Mom got up from her chair and said, "If I hear another train whistle today, I'll shut out the world and sleep until the morning."

Mom chuckled, but we were all looking at her. I said, "Mom, are you okay?"

"Yes, boys, not to worry—not to worry. I think having Paul home and the routine getting back to normal has made my anxious feelings go away. I'm recouping and regrouping my thoughts and feelings, if that makes sense."

Paul said, "It makes sense to me. I'm glad to be home, and I can sleep without some lady or man coming in the room and poking me with needles, making me drink something yucky, or wondering whose gonna stay with me the next day. Here at home, I have all of you and my own bed. Even though it's in a different room. My bed's more compsoble. I mean it's not so hard."

Paul knew he had mispronounced the word. His almost 10 year-old face showed he had said it wrong. He said, "It's not so high either. My bed is just more, a-a, how do you say it? Com-for-ta-ble?"

I said, "Paul, you are so right. Those sleeping chairs in the hospital rooms are hard, too,"

Steve was laughing at Paul, but he said, "Paul, you're still my buddy, and you're so compso... I mean *great* to be around. I'm glad you are home. I missed you at night when you weren't in your bed across the room."

Paul chuckled, too, and said, "Why don't you sleep down here with me, tonight? Mom can sleep in her own bed. She'll like it."

Mrs. Weber said, "Guys, I've enjoyed the conversation. Janet, we need to go."

Mom walked out of the kitchen saying, "Thanks for coming over, Rachel and Janet. I'm going upstairs and take a little nap."

Today is Saturday. We all made it through our first week of school. I took Professor Harrison the things I had written down from Paul's teacher's history book. I made a copy for myself. I still think about what the Presidents said every once in a while.

Dr. Harrison stopped me after class this morning. He asked if I could help him in a crime prevention program after school for at-risk kids. He explained some of what the kids do at the youth center, starting with getting snack and doing homework. The kids don't leave the place until someone picks them up or the parent or guardian calls to have them come home. The police department sponsors the program, and the men put in volunteer time with help from select college students.

He explained, "The kids are roaming the streets after school. No one's at home, and many of them don't have a pleasant home to go to. There's no food in the house, abuse goes on, and eventually, the kids are on the streets all the time, getting into trouble. We have three groups going on. One for girls and two for boys ages 9 to 12 and 13 through 15 years old. Usually by 15, the boys have matured enough and developed good study habits that they go on to do okay and don't get into trouble, but there are always exceptions."

I said, "It sound like a good program, but I'm not sure I have enough time."

Dr. Harrison said, "You've had experience with your younger brothers, and I'm looking for several students to work at least one or two hours in the afternoon once or twice a week."

I must have been frowning because Dr. Harrison said, "John, go home and think about it. I know you're a busy young man, but we feel you're well suited for our project."

I nodded my head affirmatively and said, "Okay, I'll let you know tomorrow."

On the way home, I thought about it, but I thought about everything at home and at the farm. All the responsibility kept creeping into my mind. *What about this? Who would see about that? Is Paul well enough for me to gone extra hours? What would Mom say? Will I have enough time?*

I thought about it all afternoon and worried all evening, too. Dennis finally asked, "Why are you walking around with a frown like you're having negative thoughts?"

"I didn't know I was," I said.

It was time for us to call it a day, for me to shut-off my thinking and rest. I told Dennis about Dr. Harrison's request and about the crime prevention program for at-risk kids. We were about to climb into our beds, and Dennis was smiling. He closed all his books, went to the bathroom, and came back, still smiling. He turned his covers back, smiling.

I said, "You told me I had negative thoughts, but what on earth are you thinking about with that silly smirk on your face?"

Dennis chuckled and said, "You know, John, we decided we'd become policemen. That program sounds great to me. Wouldn't a program like that make our job easier some day? There wouldn't be so many criminals on the street. I think you can and should do it."

I felt like saying, "Well, you do it then. I don't have much time around here as it is."

Dennis went on talking. "John, do you realize you're gone, Mom's gone, I'm gone, and Steve's gone from the farm every day, and somehow we get done what needs doing? Our morning chores are done. Our evening chores get done, and somehow the house work gets done, too. I can do more things around here. Loading and unloading the washer only takes five minutes. Unloading and loading the *dish*washer only takes five minutes. Making our beds only takes two minutes. Besides, all the extra stuff can be done in less amount of time if we try. You can do it. Besides, you're forgetting that God might be asking you to help. I'd go for it, if I were you."

I almost said, "Well, you go for it, then," but the scripture verse, *I can do all things through Christ who strengthens me* came into my mind. Dennis was over on his bed with his Bible open. He was reading out loud to me Isaiah 40: 29-31: *He gives power to the faint; and to them that have no might he increases strength. Even the youth shall faint and be weary, and the young men shall utterly fall: But they that wait upon the Lord shall renew their strength; they shall mount up with wings as eagles; they shall run, and not be weary: and not faint.* (NKJV)

Dennis went on talking. I thought, *He sounds like Dad and Grandpa.* Dennis said, "John, I'm a senior this year, and I've tried to memorize those verses. Sometimes my mind gets muddled wondering if Steve and I made the right decision to go into law enforcement, too. Maybe God has something else for me instead of following in your footsteps. I'm going through the decision- making process you and Kaitlynn did. It's hard to decide for the next year of my life when I focus on Mom, Paul, and the farm work. I get tired just thinking about it, and yet I'm faced with decision-making, anyway. Should I be the one kid that will stay on the farm and help Mom? I know God will show me like he showed you. Besides, if it isn't clear to me, I'll do what I think is best for *me*, and then maybe God will show me. But like you, I don't have the energy or the time wasting my feelings on stuff like this. I need to decide one way or the other and go with it. Don't you think? You need to make up your mind before you go to sleep on it and let your professor know in the morning, one way or the other, if you will work with the kids in the crime prevention program."

Dennis laid his Bible on the night stand by his bed. "My sermon is over." He chuckled as he looked at me for a response.

I said, "Dennis, you're right. This afternoon, I wasted a lot of time worrying about this. I'll tell Dr. Harrison. I'll try it for a week or two and see how things work out. Mom always said, 'It is better to try and fail, than *not* to try at all.' Also, if it is really God telling me that this is a job I can help do, I won't have any guilt feelings if I obey. God doesn't bless disobedience with emotional and mental peace. He's given me enough conviction to last a life time… with all that I should have, I wish I had, or I wish I didn't thoughts. I know He has forgiven me, but sometimes it's hard to make decisions."

"Yeah, I know, but it's Satan that reminds us just to keep us disturbed, don't you think?" Dennis adjusted his pillow as he said that.

It suddenly struck me that Dennis had finished his sentence with "Don't you think?" I chuckled to myself. I felt like God was saying to me. *"Don't think anymore, tonight."*

I woke up the next morning rested and ready for the day.

Chapter 14

I recorded my first week of classes at the university in my journal, and also wrote about my feelings for Marianne. I can't seem to get her off my mind. She went back to the Missouri Baptist University in St. Louis. I think she is missing her family, and is worried about them. I hope she is thinking about me, too. Maybe I can convince her to transfer to the Southeast Missouri University down here in Cape Girardeau. Right now, I don't think she wants to do that. She has so many opportunities to serve and learn where she is. Not just with her music, but with student groups that go on mission trips in the city of St. Louis, and in foreign countries, too.

I just pray God will lead us both in the direction, He wants for us go, and that my youngest brother will continue to heal. I pray also for Mom's health and whatever happens between Dr. Lynn and Mom will be for the best for all of us. The more I think about it, I believe Mom would be happy married again, and Dr. Lynn *is* a nice guy.

Well, I need to study again, so I think I will turn these pages over to Dennis. He says, "Our lives would make an interesting book."

I started this journal book months ago. I hope Dennis has enough written in his book to make a sequel to mine. I suspect he will because he's always telling me, "Mom says one of us might become a political figure some day, and our history will be an interesting reading." Dennis laughs about that and says, "Steve might, but not me. Steve has a mouth on him to try to win people over to his opinion. I don't. I wonder what reason Mom gives him for keeping his journal."

I did start working with the afternoon program for crime prevention for at risk kids. I recorded in my journal the hours I spent with Dr. Harrison at the Youth Center. Whenever I share with Dennis about the boys, he gets fascinated and wants to work, too. Perhaps God has something in store for his life working with kids that really need stability in their lives. Well, I think I will sign off on this journal page and let Dennis tell whatever he wants about me in his journal. I'm thinking about asking him to help at the Youth Center, too. So, you will hear more later, from him.

I signed the last page...*John Moore—September.* I decided not to put a year on my last page in case I decide to write more.

CPSIA information can be obtained at www.ICGtesting.com
Printed in the USA
LVOW050723210513

334746LV00003B/11/P

9 781449 753887